chance of precipitation

chance of precipitation

SCOTT MILLER

ARPress
45 Dan Road Suite 5
Canton MA 02021

Hotline: 1(800) 220-7660
Fax: 1(855) 752-6001

Ordering Information:
Quantity sales. Special discounts are available on quantity purchases by corporations, associations, and others. For details, contact the publisher at the address above.

Printed in the United States of America.

ISBN-13:   Paperback   979-8-89676-236-2
           Hardcover   979-8-89676-238-6
           eBook   979-8-89676-237-9

Library of Congress Control Number: 2024925134

To Todd

Contents

Chapter 1

JANUARY

It was a typical hotel room, nice but plain. There were two double beds and a TV that was on but with its volume muted. A tired but slightly agitated man stared out the window at another crisp winter night in the Midwest. He watched the snowflakes float down upon the glistening ground and silently fumed at his current plight. He was a college hockey coach and tonight he had seen another victory slip away. He slowly turned away from the snowy scene and sat wearily in the chair next to the window with his feet resting on the bed. Hands clasped behind his head, he grimaced as the final seconds of the game replayed in his head.

Randy Albertson had spent all of his adult life at Saint Paul University. He had played there, gotten his degree, been an assistant and for the last 22 years was the Wildcat hockey boss. He finally stood and stared at the snow as the warm air of the heater blew against his cheeks and quietly wondered why he was still involved in this kid's game. Behind him talking quietly were his two assistant coaches reminiscing about the game they had just returned from. Finally, the worn-down coach turned toward his assistants and gestured for them to sit down.

"They're coming along," Bob Jackson said quietly.

Randy glared at his longtime assistant. Bob was short and overweight. He had a buzz cut and wore wire rimmed glasses from the

1970's that always seemed to be at the tip of his pug nose. He had been with Randy for the past 22 years and though he was 12 years older, the age difference had never been an issue.

"Coming along hell," growled Randy. "I've been part of the game for 35 years and I still don't understand why it's so hard for some of our guys to play their zone!"

"C'mon Randy, you're being too hard on them. This is another young team. They're listening, just haven't figured it out yet," replied Bob.

"I know, I know...," Randy replied quietly as he watched the flakes glisten past the street lamp. "We needed 2 points though. A tie doesn't help our cause."

Kevin Banks, Randy's younger assistant stood up from the bed and stretched, his long angular arms reaching the ceiling.

"Coach," he said as he turned toward the door, "get some sleep. It's going to be all right."

"Yeah," Bob piped in, "they'll come together before the playoffs, just like always."

Randy stared out the window for a few more moments before finally glancing back at the two men who were making their way out of the room.

"I hope so," he said. "I'm not as sure as you two seem to be though. Ah hell, I'm tired and emotional. Little sleep will do me good. I'll get you guys up at six tomorrow morning, we'll get some coffee before heading back home."

The assistants nodded and Kevin opened the heavy metal door that creaked as it moved on its hinges. Randy was spent, physically and emotionally worn down. The older he got, the tougher these seasons were becoming. He lay on the bed closest to the window and turned out the light. Kicking off his shoes, he turned the volume up on the television. Figures flickered on the screen and sound came from the speakers but Randy's mind had wandered to another place.

He thought about Brenda and the kids. He missed them and wondered what they were doing. Slowly, though he fought it, his mind wandered back to the game, and he grimace as he remembered the puck zipping into the net behind his goalie with 4.2 seconds left in regulation.

The night wasn't a total loss he tried to reason to himself, the team had managed to hang on to the tie in overtime but they were now into the meat of the schedule. Simply put, a loss and a tie to a team had been behind him in the standings did not bode well.

His eyes were becoming heavy at last and mercifully all thoughts of the game emptied from his brain and he slowly faded to sleep. Outside the flakes continued to float past the lamp post to the ground.

❧

John Bart had gotten the job he had dreamed about since graduating from college eleven years before. Long a sports fan, he had tried out for every sport imaginable. Unfortunately, he had not been blessed with an athletic body but instead had pudgy legs and extra pounds. He was deficient in speed and strength and athletic ability had completely eluded him. Still, if he couldn't play in the games, he had always found ways to be in the arena.

His start had been as a team manager, putting up with the insults hurled on him by those who were gifted to compete. He had simply smiled through the hurt for he knew what he wanted and what he had to do to get there. If that meant taking abuse along the way, well, he would be tougher than the prima donnas he picked up after.

As a senior in college, he had been awarded a small scholarship because of his work ethic. He made ends meet by working in the athletic department, doing any odd jobs no one else wanted. He lined fields and took tickets, cleaned towels and sold concessions. He sometimes felt sorry for himself because he craved for the adulation of the crowds that the players received, but this only drove him to keep the dream in front of him.

John earned a masters degree in a year and then got an assistant athletic director's job at a small NAIA school. It wasn't much money, but it gave him valuable experience in all facets of his chosen profession. He showed brilliance in fundraising and streamlining budgets and soon he was moving up the food chain to larger schools and more responsibility.

This past July all the work had finally paid off when President Willard Benson of Saint Paul University had chosen him to be the new athletic director for the Wildcats. At the introductory press conference, he laid out his vision for the department and his plan to get there. After his speech, excited alumni and athletic boosters gave him an enthusiastic standing ovation. He was going to take this department up a notch, light a fire under a group of coaches that had become stagnant. His chance had arrived and he knew that he was prepared for any challenge.

John had studied his new department and had quickly determined that his coaches were comfortable in mediocrity. This needed to be fixed quickly and he knew exactly how he would do it. He picked his target carefully, wanting to make a statement. He knew he had to slay the giant and a once proud hockey program, a program that had been to Final Fives and finished national runner-up twice was that giant. Hockey had to start winning again or the great Randy Albertson would have to be forced out. The rest of the coaches would then get the message that winning mattered. Staleness must be broken and John Bart was not afraid of taking on the king.

The weather hovered around zero and the sky remained gray as Randy pulled up to his parking spot at the SPU athletic center. He got out of his warm truck and immediately his nostrils start to freeze as the bitterness from the wind bit at him. He hurriedly walked toward the entrance and entered the comfort of the 72-degree building. He made a quick stop at the main office to grab his mail and then headed to the hockey office.

At his desk he sat down and turned on his computer and began thumbing through the mail that had built up while he was on the road. There were letters from recruits, stats that had been faxed by the conference office and the usual assortment of junk mail and catalogs. He tossed them down on the desk and leaned back in his chair and was waiting for the internet to pop up when John Bart knocked on the open door.

"Coach Albertson, do you have a moment?"

"Hi John," replied Randy with a smile that had no feeling behind it. "Come on in, what's up?"

"Would have been nice to get two points last weekend," replied John as he closed the door and sat down in a chair directly across from Randy.

"Yeah," murmured Randy, knowing that something serious was up since the door was now closed. "Hated like hell to see that goal go in the last five seconds."

"Think we can get home ice for the playoffs?"

"We have a chance," responded the coach. "We need some wins though and probably some help along the way."

John sat back in the chair and nodded silently, enjoying the nervous anticipation Randy was feeling. Guys like Randy had always thought they were superior because they had been lucky enough to play and it felt good to the athletic director to see his coach trying to cloak his concern.

"Listen," John said finally. "I just want you to know that I got copied another letter to the President from a disgruntled booster."

"I see."

"Coach, there is a faction of vocal alumni and boosters voicing their concerns. They're not happy with where we're at."

Randy sat back in his chair and rubbed his forehead and he felt a tension knot growing in the small of his back. John sat quietly, enjoying the scene in front of him. He had hoped that his hockey coach would be on board but old habits and a slipped work ethic developed over years of success had ruined him. John knew that eventually Randy would have to go.

"We still have a month to go," Randy stammered. "The guys are working hard and coming around. We just have to eliminate the lapses."

"Look coach, you've had a great career here and been good for the University," said John. "But times are getting hard and we have to keep getting donations from our boosters. Winning brings in money, and hockey is the engine that drives this ship. If you're not winning, it's a problem for everyone here."

Randy looked at him stonily.

"President Benson and I both want to see you continue being successful, but we also have an obligation to listen to our constituency who help us pay our bills."

"John, are you still backing me?" Randy asked pointedly.

"Of course I am," John lied, "but I need some help from you, and that is wins, not ties or losses."

"We'll keep plugging away…"

"We need wins coach; I can't emphasize that enough."

"I know John," conceded Randy. "We'll be alright come playoff time, hang in there with me."

"Alright coach. You have a good day and let me know what I can do to help," said John, trying his best to sound sincere.

"Thanks boss."

The athletic director got up and opened the door. He turned around and took a final look at his coach and gave him a thumb's up. Randy smiled and returned the signal as John headed down the hallway toward his office.

"Asshole," Randy said quietly as he opened his email.

He scanned the messages and began deleting the ones he wasn't interested in, but then one caught his eye. He opened it and saw it was from his fan club. His 'fan' told him in no uncertain terms that he couldn't coach anymore and to find a new job. Randy hit the delete button and sat back. He was bone tired.

He looked at the computer clock. It was 8:42 am.

Randy drove through the snow toward Hayward Elementary School. In the passenger seat was his eight-year-old daughter, Tisha, who was explaining the nuances of making snowflakes. Randy would be leaving for another road game in two hours, but right now he had the important duty of getting Tish to school before the bell rang. He stared straight ahead but his mind was on events that would be happening later in the day. Tisha continued her explanation of the snowflake and Randy smiled. Suddenly her little face turned serious.

"Daddy, you know it's my birthday on Saturday."

"I do sweetie. I'll be thinking of you and I'm going to bring you back a surprise from my trip."

The daughter smiled, but quickly grew serious again.

"Daddy, how come you're never here for my birthday?"

Randy's heart leapt to his throat. Each of the last four years he had always been unable to attend his little girl's birthday party but he hadn't known that it bothered her.

"I know baby, I'm sorry," he stammered. "I promise to make it up to you next week. How about you and me go to Riley's for breakfast before school?"

She nodded sullenly and looked out the window.

"I just want you to be here when I blow out my candles," she said sadly.

"I know sweetie, I'm sorry."

The vehicle pulled up into the school line and dad and daughter sat quietly. They slowly moved forward until it was her turn to get out.

"I'll make it up to you sweetie," he said as she opened the door.

She nodded and climbed down and soon was gone into the building. He felt as if he had a hole in his heart and realized that she was growing up without him. He put the SUV into drive and headed to the college. In an hour he would be on a charter heading to Southern Iowa University. He tried to put her face out of his mind and concentrate on the upcoming opponent, but she was stubborn like him and kept coming back into his thoughts. It was going to be a long bus ride.

From his hotel room Randy looked at his watch nervously. In 45 minutes, the team would be back on the charter and heading to SIU for tonight's game. The ride from Saint Paul had seemed bumpy and the players unusually quiet though they livened up once at the hotel. Randy had managed to get about an hour's cat nap and, though anxious, was looking forward to heading to the rink. Suddenly, his cell phone rang. He looked at the number and immediately recognized it as his athletic director's.

"Hi John," Randy said as he answered it. He had a bad feeling.

"Coach, I'm sorry to bother you, but I felt you needed to know something," replied John Bart.

"What's up?" though Randy wasn't sure he really did want to know.

"I've been told that some boosters are circulating a petition for your removal."

Randy immediately went numb. It was one thing to have some disgruntled alums and boosters sending those stupid letters, but a petition raised the stakes significantly and for the first time he realized his job was truly in peril.

"Are you there, coach?"

"You're kidding," stammered Randy into the receiver.

"I wish I were," replied John, and he sounded as though he meant it. "I've apprised the President."

"What'd he say?" asked Randy.

"Coach, it's coming to a head. We can't continue to ignore this."

"Really John, I wasn't aware that you and the president had been ignoring this. I'm damn sure that I haven't been," snapped Randy.

"Calm down coach, that came out wrong," replied the athletic director. "But like I said, they're kind of calling our hand."

"So, what are you saying to me?" demanded Randy. "After 22 years and over 400 wins do I need to be concerned about my job?"

"Well, the President isn't going to do anything until after the season is over. Then I'm instructed to do a thorough review of the program."

"Jesus John," replied Randy, clearly agitated. "What exactly don't you know about our program?"

"Easy coach," replied the AD, "I'm just telling you what I've been instructed to do. I don't want you to have any unnecessary surprises. I want you to know that I think you run a very good program that has had a little bad luck the last few years."

"Well, let's see John. In 22 years, we've won 11 regular season conference championships, played in eight conference championship games, winning five. We've been to 14 NCAA tournaments, five Final Fives and been runner-up twice. Our kids graduate and don't get in trouble. I'm curious on just who you have in mind that is better than me."

"Coach, I've been given a job by the President and I'll do as asked. I'm not looking to make a change but I do need to give him all necessary information. Of course, we'll take what you just said into consideration, strong consideration. I just called to let you know of the situation."

"I see," replied Randy. "Fine, you've done that. Now I need to get the team ready for tonight."

"Good luck coach."

"Thanks John," said Randy as he clicked shut his cell phone.

"Asshole," he said softly. "Both of them."

The locker room was deathly silent. A game that should have been won had been lost. Again, a lead going into the final seconds had evaporated as SIU had pulled their goalie and gotten the game tying goal with less than 10 seconds remaining in regulation. To compound matters, it had only taken the home team 17 seconds in overtime to get the winning goal, and the Wildcat players sat at their stalls in stunned silence.

Randy walked into the locker-room and quietly spoke about the breakdowns that had led to the tying and losing goals. Most of the players kept their eyes downcast but suddenly Rick Jenson, the first-line center stood up and walked out of the meeting and into the restroom.

"Where do you think you're going," demanded Randy.

"Bathroom."

"Get your ass back in here until I'm done," roared the coach.

"Why, we know what happened."

Randy was now in a full-blown rage. The team members sat in their stalls spellbound by what was happening. The assistants quickly got between the player and coach to make sure that no blows would be thrown. Accusations were tossed about between the proud player and the veteran coach until the assistants were able to drag Randy out of the room. Bob stayed with Rick and tried to diffuse the situation as best he could. Kevin meanwhile stood between Randy and the door, eliminating any escape route that could get the already frazzled head coach into a career ending mistake.

When the team and coaches arrived back at the hotel there was no meeting as usual. Bob sent the players to their rooms and told them wake-up would be at 8:00 am. The players carried looks of concern and murmured quietly to each other, unsure of how they were to handle this. It was unspoken but now known that the season was unraveling.

Back in his room Randy paced back and forth like a caged lion. He wanted to break something, anything. He felt the tension knot in his back and his jaws ached from the clenching of his teeth. Kevin and Bob, after getting the players back to their rooms, came into the head coach's quarters and sat down on the bed as Randy continued to pace.

"I think I'm going to toss the little jack-ass," Randy seethed.

"No, you're not," replied Bob quietly.

"I'm not, huh? And why is that?"

"He's your best player."

"We'll live," countered Randy.

"You won't," replied Bob. "Coach, I know you're under pressure though I'm not sure why, but you need all your bullets the rest of the way if you're going to survive…and you know that."

"Dammit Bob, there's more to a team than one player. We'll get by. Might make them have to rely on each other a little more," countered Randy.

"He bugs you because you're both alike. Be honest, how necessary was that speech you were giving tonight. You just wanted to hear yourself talk. Coach, you're going through the motions…he called you on it."

"He's a damn cancer," replied Randy intensely.

"He runs this team…it's his team, and I'm fine with that. The fact is, Randy, you and he are damn near twins and neither of you see it. Now go to bed. You always say not to make decisions when you're emotional. So don't."

Randy finally stopped pacing and sat down on the bed resigned to the fact that his assistant was probably right.

"I'll talk to Ricky tomorrow," said Bob. "Smooth things over and then you two hash it out under calmer circumstances."

Bob motioned to Kevin to follow him and the two assistants left the room and headed to their room. Randy continued sitting on the bed replaying the evening events in his head. He was scared. He was getting negative emails, letters were being sent to the president, the athletic director probably wanted him out, a petition was being circulated and now a full-blown crisis in a time when he needed his team to come together. God he was tired. Where was the joy he had once had with this sport? Everything had changed in the last few years and he wondered if maybe the game had passed him by. He realized he was terrified of the dark.

He reached for his phone and pulled up his contact list, pushing Brenda's name. He waited to hear her voice, longing to hear it for then all would be fine. She had always made it that way and he needed to know that it was still all right. At last, she answered, her voice immediately pouring some energy into his depleted body.

"Hi babe, it's me."

"Tough one tonight honey," she said quietly.

"Yeah, it got worse. Ricky acted up in the locker-room. I was going to run him but Bob calmed me down. How are the kids?"

"They're fine," she sounded tired. "Your daughter is excited about her party tomorrow."

"That's good," was his only reply.

"Sean's team won tonight."

Sean was their 15-year-old son, a sophomore at Saint Paul High School. As a youngster he lived on the ice but at the age of 12 he developed a love for the round ball. He was a member of the varsity basketball team, though he was well down the roster list.

"Did he play?" asked Randy

"He got in at the end of the game. Hey, he scored a basket, a nice three-pointer."

"How the hell did he end up in basketball?" Randy wondered.

"The world's a mystery," Brenda replied with a laugh.

"You're real funny."

"John called," said Randy, now speaking in a more serious tone. "Says my fan club is starting a petition against me."

"Oh honey," replied Brenda.

"It'll be alright."

"Is he backing you?"

"We'll see."

"I don't like him," replied Brenda. "He's a little smooth for my taste."

"He has a job to do and so do I…for now," replied Randy.

"Oh honey, don't talk like that."

"I'm sorry. I'm just tired, I guess. I miss you and the kids. I wonder if it's worth it sometimes," replied Randy woefully.

"I got another raise," Brenda said after a brief silence between them.

"You did? Congratulation's babe! How much?"

"Another $1,500," she replied with pride.

"Wow, you're making more than me now."

"You're not jealous, are you?"

"Nah…I'm happy for you. You deserve it."

"Thanks babe," she said happily.

"Well, I gotta get some sleep. We have a morning skate and I have to fix things up with Ricky."

"Alright honey. I love you."

He smiled. He still loved it when she told him that. He knew this woman was who he would grow old with from the moment he first saw her. He was thankful that after all these years he still felt the same way about her.

"I love you too," he replied wistfully. "I'll call you tomorrow night. Give the kids a kiss and have fun at the birthday party."

"I will," she replied and then the line went dead.

Randy lay back on the bed and stared at the ceiling. He glanced out the window and saw that snow was falling. He had always loved the snow. It was soft and peaceful and had a way of making him feel relaxed, even now in a time of stress. As he watched it, he began thinking about home, Brenda and the kids.

Was coaching really worth it? He did love the game and he loved forging relationships with his players. Suddenly he sat up and he could feel the color drain from his face. My God, he thought. I know these players better than my own kids. He realized that since he got on the bus early this morning he had not thought of Sean or Tisha once. He hadn't even realized that Sean had a game and he tried to think back to the last time he had seen him play. He couldn't remember.

Oh no, this was wrong. Somehow, he had lost his priority. He was more worried about some other parent's kid than his own. He worried about keeping them out of trouble, making sure they went to class, getting help when they needed it. Yet he never had these thoughts with his own kids. He knew somebody else's son better than he knew his own. It made him sick to his stomach.

But then those thoughts dissipated and his immediate problems returned. He tried to eliminate them from his thoughts and fall asleep but his mind refused to quit working. What would he do if he lost his job? His whole identity was wrapped up in being a coach. Slowly he began to realize that though he loved the recognition he no longer felt the same about being a coach.

My God, he thought, I've become just another guy collecting a paycheck. He vowed that on Monday he would refocus. He had to; the stretch run was upon him.

Chapter 2

FEBRUARY

Early Monday morning Randy unlocked the door to his office and sat down at his desk. Still tired from the previous weekend on the road he glanced at the schedule and saw that two more road series awaited him before the end of the regular season and more energy sapped out of him. He looked out of his office window and saw the snow start to flurry and wondered if spring was ever going to come.

The ringing of the phone bounced off the walls which were filled with awards, certificates and pictures of season's past. Randy finally took his eyes away from the flurries and looked down at the phone as the third ring began. He exhaled, knowing that it was probably his boss and picked up the receiver.

"Randy, come into my office for a moment?"

The words caused Randy's heart rate to increase and butterflies to awaken in his stomach.

"Sure John," he replied. "What's up?"

"Come on down, I'll talk to you here."

Randy set the receiver down and looked out the window. He sat back and pulled up his email. No reason to sprint to John's office for more bad news he reasoned. He saw that there were some emails from the fan club, but also some supportive notes and picked one that had been sent by a kid he had coached just four years before. He opened it and smiled as he read, remembering the kid's sense of humor. The note made him feel better and gave him a little energy. He was ready to face his AD.

"We seem to be getting a full court press from the alumni and boosters after this past weekend," John informed Randy as he sat down.

"What now?"

"I've got seven emails, nine phone messages and three letters."

"That's why they pay you the big money, John."

"Randy, you're putting us in a tough situation…"

Randy stood up and started to pace. He was agitated and John relished the moment. The cool one was starting to lose it.

"Look John," Randy said as he battled to retain his composure. "I don't like losing, but we are what we are. All we can do is work through it. I appreciate you keeping me up to date on all of this but it takes away from preparation."

John was doing all he could not to smile. He now had the upper hand on the one person who could derail his dreams for the department. He, the team manager, at last was gaining revenge on the star player who had made life so miserable in his younger years. It was time to start tearing down his coach.

"Randy, some boosters think you are losing your team. Apparently, word has it that you are losing your leaders on the team."

"I see," replied Randy, knowing he had just entered into a chess game. "In other words, there is now a mole in the locker room, helping with the propaganda."

"Be careful coach…" warned John.

"Look, I had a blow-up with one of our players after a tough loss," replied Randy. "This is not unusual stuff with competitive people. This is a game of passion and tempers flare during the course of a season. It's been taken care of."

"Has it really?"

Randy could feel the flush of anger building up inside of him. This guy was a damn administrator who pretended he knew all about coaching.

"I don't like where this is going, John…don't presume to tell me about coaching a hockey team. I've seen your resume and I didn't see any coaching experience, buddy."

Now John was on the defensive and it was his turn to try to control his anger. He felt insecurity creeping into his voice.

"Careful coach," the AD stammered, trying to regain control of the conversation. "I'm your superior and your best hope right now. I'm not the enemy. I need all the information I can get to defend you."

"Go grab a media guide then," Randy snapped but he realized he had just gone too far. "Ah hell, I'm sorry John. That was uncalled for. This is just very frustrating, that's all."

John visibly relaxed with the mea culpa, nodding in acceptance of the apology.

"I've talked to the President about this. He's obviously very concerned."

"Where's he stand?" asked Randy.

"Right now, he's non-committal. I can't really read him," replied John. "Where do you stand?"

"To be honest, Randy, I just don't know right now. I have some concerns but at the same time you have a wonderful history here."

"I see, well, you and he are going to do what you're going to do. All I can do is keeping working with this team. Are we done?"

"Yes, but we need some positive results, Randy."

Randy nodded, closed the door behind him and walked toward his office. He tried his best to appear as if everything was normal, but it wasn't and he knew it.

"Asshole," he said to himself softly as he thought of the man who would decide his fate.

Randy sat at his desk staring out the window for 30 minutes after his meeting with John. His mind was empty and his energy gone. He was completely helpless for the first time since he had become a coach. He knew the pressure was beginning to get the upper hand and he hated the thought of it.

Finally, he sat back up and grabbed a pen and pad and to make a list of possible jobs. He stared down at the blank piece of paper and finally wrote down 'athletic director'. Surely there were other things he could do but nothing was coming to mind. He wrote 'car salesman' down on the page and then put the pen down and turned toward his computer. He pressed the internet button and googled job search. The search engine spit out a page full of websites and Randy went to the first one on the page.

The website was colorful and assured the reader that there was a job for him. All he had to do was pay $9.95 to find it. Randy smirked but saw a browse button and pushed it. At the top of the page information was requested from him and he quickly filled out the web form and pushed 'next'. Another page appeared and asked him what type of job he was looking for. He scrolled down, looking at the different types ranging from administration, to media, to engineering, to sales. Finally, he pushed the administration button and a number of jobs appeared on the screen. He found one in Saint Paul and went to it but his heart quickly sank as he saw that he came nowhere near meeting the qualifications.

He sat back in his chair and started thinking about the early days of his coaching career. He had been so hungry and passionate and he wondered what had happened to that guy. He remembered the goals he had set for himself. He had been bound and determined to become a head coach by the time he was 25 and succeeded. He had taken a decent program and built it into a national power. But in recent years the fire had ebbed and he wondered why.

It had been so much fun building his program. He was determined to do it right and not take any shortcuts. The first two years had resulted in losing records but the third had been a breakout season. SPU had won the conference tournament and advance to the NCAA Division II national tournament. The next sixteen years had been nothing but success and he had become the dean of coaches at SPU. But the last three years had been different. He wondered why this was and what it meant about him. He was wondering if it was because he no longer liked what he was doing.

Randy knew that he was in uncharted territory and it scared him.

❧

Sitting at the booth in the student union building, Randy perused the school newspaper and munched on a ham and cheese sandwich. Most of the students had cleared out and headed toward their classes or whatever students do in the afternoon. He read an account of the previous weekend's games in the sports. A student writer was calling the team out, stating that their play was unacceptable for such a fine institution and Randy chuckled. He felt his cell phone vibrate and he smiled when he saw what name popped up on the small telephone screen.

"He shoots, he scores," shouted the enthusiastic voice of Adam Chatworth, his best friend from college.

"What are you doing," laughed Randy.

The two carried on an animated conversation and laughter filled the empty room. Adam was a successful car dealership owner in Salt Lake City. Randy and Adam had been both roommates and teammates in college at SPU. They had become fast friends and had remained so over the years. Every year they made a point to meet up with each other for a week, whether camping, gambling in Vegas, or sailing in San Diego.

"I'm thinking of making a change," Randy said, turning the conversation serious.

"Really, what's going on?" asked Adam.

Randy told him about the pressures from boosters and alums, the problems he was going through with the new athletic director and the frustration of the season. Adam listened dutifully and asked a few questions. Finally, Randy told him about the night in Iowa when he realized that he didn't really know his kids that well because of all the travel.

"You've been there forever," said Adam. "They're just pulling your chain…I'm sure they'll back you if you want to keep doing what you're doing. The question you have to answer is if you want to continue coaching."

"I don't know," replied Randy. "It's a different climate than before, bud. Things change everywhere I guess."

The two were silent for a moment.

"I'm just tired I guess," said Randy. "I'm tired of the travel, the politics, and the boosters. Hell, I'm tired of the bullshit, Adam."

"Why don't you come work for me," said Adam suddenly.

"Selling cars?"

"Yeah, you'd be good at it."

"Right," laughed Randy. "I just don't see that."

"No, seriously, you would be," countered Adam.

"I don't have the first clue how to do it," replied Randy.

"Jesus Randy, it's not rocket science. It's simple sales, which you've been doing for the past 22 years."

"What are you talking about?"

"You recruit don't you…isn't that sales?"

"C'mon Adam, that's different. Hell, I subsidize more than I sell. I have scholarships you know."

Adam was undeterred.

"No, it's not. I subsidize too, it's called a rebate. Consider it, O.K.?"

Randy chuckled, but what Adam was saying was making sense.

"Look, I got to get going," said Adam. "But I'm serious. You'd be good at it."

"I'll think about it," said Randy. "But don't hold your breath."

The two friends hung up and Randy looked down at the remains of his sandwich. Maybe what Adam was saying did make sense. He closed his eyes and pictured himself on a car lot, only this time he was walking out to the customer instead of seeing a salesman walking toward him. Somehow the picture didn't look right.

Randy opened his eyes and sighed. It would be fun working with Adam but he didn't see that happening.

It had been another disappointing weekend. The team had played hard in spurts but mental mistakes had seen two wins turn into a loss and a tie. Worse still, it had occurred on home ice in front of the home fans. On the second night Randy noticed hundreds of empty seats and he knew that this was just another bullet that John was putting in his gun.

On Monday Randy had met with John in his office so that the athletic director could let him know that the big money boosters were again calling with their concerns. Randy noticed that John seemed quite upbeat while delivering the bad news to him and started to realize that he was probably enjoying seeing him squirm. Unfortunately, with the losses piling up and home ice now gone for the playoffs Randy knew that there wasn't much he could do so he sat and took it with as much dignity as he could muster.

Later, in what had become another bad Monday, the athletic trainer knocked on Randy's door. The coach looked up from the paperwork he was doing and waved him in.

"Hey coach, I got some bad news for you," said the ATC.

"Of course you do," said Randy, only half-joking.

"We're going to have to keep Rick out."

The prima donna had gotten himself hurt this past weekend trying to be fancy with the puck. Instead of something good happening, he had been checked hard into the boards and had hurt his knee.

"The knee is sprained pretty well and there could be some ligament damage."

"How soon will we know for sure?" asked Randy.

"I called the doctor and set up an MRI for Wednesday. We should have full results by Friday," replied the trainer.

Randy sat back and nodded. Sooner or later his luck had to change he thought to himself, but obviously today was not going to be that day. The trainer stood up and headed toward the door.

"Hang in there, coach."

Randy merely nodded and went back to the paperwork in front of him.

The charter left the rink parking lot at Saint Paul University and lurched to the freeway. It was another weekend and another set of games to be played, this time with the University of Moorhead Eagles. Randy sat back in his accustomed spot on the bus and stared out the window.

The day was sunny and the rays bounced off the snow, giving the countryside a bright glow. The sun created crisp cold air, but it changed the way one felt. The dreariness of the winter season dissipated with the cheeriness the sun provided. He felt optimistic about this team though they would be going the rest of the season without their captain and best player.

The bus left the city and picked up speed as it headed west toward Moorhead. A movie played on the VCR and the players chatted quietly with each other while watching the comedy that played on the small monitors attached to the ceiling. There seemed to be a more relaxed attitude for this trip.

His cell phone buzzed and he struggled to get the phone out of his pocket before the message came on. He looked and saw that Adam was calling.

"What you up too, buddy?" asked Adam cheerfully after Randy had answered.

"I'm on the bus," replied Randy. "We're heading to Moorhead right now."

"Back on the road, huh? Listen, have you thought about what we talked about the other day?"

"Yeah, I have," Randy responded.

"Let me ask you a question," said Adam. "How much are you making right now?"

"Around 50," replied Randy.

"You work for me and I know you could make 100, I'm sure of it."

"Salary?" asked Randy.

Randy noticed that Bob was suddenly looking at him and he realized that he needed to lower his voice.

"No, commission buddy," replied Adam. "Listen, you're under a glass ceiling right now. I can break that glass."

Randy's interest was perking up. The thought of doubling what he was making was very enticing, especially considering the difficulties he was going through right now.

"You've been coaching for 22 years, right?" asked Adam.

"Something like that," responded Randy.

"You're probably making less than any high school coach who's been doing it for the same amount of time," said Adam, his sales voice now at full fever. "You work for me and the sky's the limit. People like their cars. Nobody wants to ride the bus to work. The best part of it is they are usually willing to spend more than they need to because you paint a vision in their mind of what they need. I make visions come true and you could do the same."

"Look," responded Randy. "I can't really talk now, but I'm giving it serious thought, Honest. You really think 100 is possible?"

"Hell yes," laughed Adam. "My worst salesman cleared 60 last year. He was worthless so I got rid of him."

"You have me thinking. I'll call you Monday," responded Randy.

"Sounds good," said Adam, and then the line was dead.

Randy put the phone back in his pocket and looked out the window, his mind racing. Double his pay, his friend really thought it was possible. No alums, no boosters, no prima donnas and no athletic directors. It had to be too good to be true, surely there was a catch.

"Don't pretend I couldn't hear what you were talking about," said Bob.

"What?" Randy asked with a sly grin.

"What's going on Randy?"

"Nothing, why do you ask?"

"Don't lie to me," countered Bob.

Randy leaned forward and nodded Bob over to the empty seat.

"You know this year has been difficult."

Bob nodded.

"I'm thinking about making a change."

"Better tell me everything," said Bob.

Randy started from the beginning.

It was a boisterous ride back to campus on Saturday. SPU had played well all weekend and had come away with a tie on Friday. The team had scored a late goal to knot it up and had nearly won it in overtime.

The momentum from Friday had carried over to Saturday and the team had put on their best performance of the year with a 7-0 shutout over the Eagles. Moorhead had gone into the weekend in first place and had ended in third. Though everyone felt better about themselves and the future, Randy only felt a void. There was no joy in victory, just a dread that another week would bring more problems, and he was getting tired of it all.

On Sunday Randy had made an effort to spend time with the kids and find out what was happening in their lives but this had only depressed him as he realized that he had no idea what was going on with them. He was stunned to find out that his son's basketball season was over and disappointed to find out that his daughter would be gone all afternoon to a birthday party. He realized that he was losing touch with his family. They were going on without him. Adam's offer was sounding better.

"Three points out of four," said John at Randy's door on Monday morning. "Not a bad weekend, coach. And without your best player to boot. Congratulations."

Randy really wasn't in any mood to be talking to his athletic director. He was fairly sure this man was doing everything in his power to get rid of him. Still, he was a professional and the face of his program. He was determined to act appropriately.

"Thanks, John."

"Wish we would have seen some of that earlier," replied the AD hoping to get a rise out of his coach.

"We normally get better as the year goes on boss. They're young, but they work hard."

"When do you think you'll get Rick back?"

"Trainer says he done for the year," replied Randy.

"That's too bad," said John.

"It is for him. I hate to see that happen to a senior, but it might be the best thing for the team. Youngsters have to rely on each other now. We'll see. What do you need John?"

"Look, I talked to the President and he really wants you back," said John. "But he has to have a solid argument to give when the boosters start howling."

Randy laughed and sat back in his chair. This guy was truly a piece of work he thought to himself. And the president was a damn joke.

"This isn't a laughing matter, coach," scolded John.

"No, it's not John. It's bullshit."

"Randy, I'm trying to help you. Don't go into a bunker by yourself."

Randy realized that in the past month their conversations had gotten much sharper in tone. He realized this was exactly the direction that John had wanted to take him. The guy was smooth and surgical, thought Randy.

"I know, I know," responded Randy. "I'm sorry, it's just that I like what I'm doing and I like where I'm at."

"I understand. I really want to keep you and I know the President does too," said John. "I know it doesn't seem like it too you but no one here at the university is out to get you. We want to provide everything possible for you to be successful."

Randy knew the game and he nodded. The AD and the President wanted a new direction but they had to have all their ducks in a row. Randy was intent on making sure that didn't happen.

"Look," John continued. "You don't have home ice so an argument can be made for you if you can get past the first round of the playoffs and make it to championship weekend in Minneapolis."

"That's the plan," responded Randy. "That's always the plan. The kids showed something this last weekend. If we can add to it this weekend here at home, we have a chance to get a streak going. Streaking teams are tough to beat."

"That's what I like to hear," said John. "Doing that gives the President an argument he can make for you."

Randy had finally had enough. He didn't want to play the game anymore, be the dutiful employee. These people were screwing with him. He may be going down, but he wanted them to know that he knew the game.

"Alright John, just stop," said Randy. "The President, and you for that matter, have a lot of arguments that can be made for me. My overall record, our post-season successes, our graduation rates…I could go on and on. This is about a supposed new vision that you have for athletics.

You're his man. He brought you in because he liked what you want to do. Let's cut to the chase. This is about wins and losses."

"Yes, it is, coach," the athletic director replied. "And you haven't had as many wins as losses the past few years. To be frank I think you're losing your desire. I hope I'm wrong but I don't think I am."

Randy wished he could argue but John was right, his desire and passion had faded the past few years. Still, he wasn't going to give him the satisfaction of knowing this.

"Then I know where I stand," replied Randy. "But listen, don't come into this office anymore or stand at our staff meetings and talk about loyalty. I think we both know that it's just a bunch of bullshit coming out of your mouth when you talk about that. In fact, I'm quite sure you don't have the first clue what loyalty means.

John was taken aback; he did not anticipate his coach talking to him this way. Randy prepared to stick the knife in.

"You can't..." said John, his face turning crimson.

"Look," interrupted Randy. "It's not your fault that you don't understand what loyalty means in athletics. You were never part of a team, and don't give me the bullshit about being a manager. Being part of the team is going through the practices, the highs, the lows, the pain, the joy, the development throughout the year, and the trust that develops from being a part of that. You'll never understand it so don't act like you do. I don't take joy in telling you this but it's time somebody told you that a spade is a spade, that's reality, not perception. And my friend, perception has never been 90% reality."

"Alright Coach, you want to be a straight shooter, let's straight shoot each other," bellowed John.

"It would be a nice change," replied Randy coolly.

"We'll start now," stammered John.

"Good," replied the coach.

"I'm pulling the rollover clause regardless of what the President decides," John said angrily.

"Sounds like you're letting your emotions get the best you," responded Randy coolly. "With your emotional state right now, I think we're probably done talking."

"Give him an argument to keep you coach. Regardless of what you think I still would like to have you back."

John stormed out of the office and headed to his as Randy sat back and snickered. For once he had held the upper hand and it had felt good. At the same time butterflies grew in his belly. He knew that this had put his job in serious jeopardy. Nothing short of getting to championship weekend could save him now. He was truly on a high wire and there was no net below him.

Randy stared at his phone and then picked it up and quickly dialed. At the other end, in Salt Lake City, Adam picked up.

"Hey, you really serious about me working for you?"

"Absolutely."

Chapter 3

MARCH

Bill Stanton had been Randy's coach in college and mentor in life. After giving Randy a scholarship out of junior hockey, he had taught him the nuances of the game as a player and then given him his start in coaching. When Bill retired, he worked tirelessly to make sure that his protégé would be his successor. On the day Randy had officially been given the job Bill called him and told him to meet him at Riley's for lunch.

Randy had walked into the restaurant and been given pats on the back and good luck wishes from the regular lunch patrons. The old coach beamed as Randy sat down opposite of him and excitedly talked about the future. After lunch had been eaten and Randy had picked up the tab the men made their way outside. As they prepared to leave each other the old man had given Randy a nugget of advice that he had never forgotten.

"Randy my boy," Bill had said. "I want you to remember one thing from me. Every season is broken down into a practice season and the real season. The practice season runs from October until February. The real season is in March. It determines how long you're going to be employed. If you're good, it's because you utilized the practice season to make you successful in the real season."

Randy knew that he had two strikes going against him going into the latest real season but he had a feeling there was a chance that the practice season was starting to bear fruit.

"Hi Randy," said John Bart, bringing John back from thoughts of his old mentor. "We need to talk."

Randy didn't feel like it and quickly thought up an excuse.

"Can it wait? I'm finishing up a strategy session," he lied.

"No," replied the athletic director doing his best to sound official. "This is the only chance I have today. Lots of meetings to attend."

Randy sat back in his chair as John walk into the office and plunk down in the worn chair in front of him. Randy thought he detected a slight edge about his boss.

"The President and I met last night," began John. "We haven't made any final decisions, but we're both thinking that a change might be good for all of us."

Randy remained calm but he could feel a fury building in his stomach. Years of coaching in pressure situations had taught him to never give away his feelings.

"I see," replied Randy dryly. "And how is that good for me?"

"Look Randy, I know this is hard to hear, and I want to reiterate that nothing has been decided…"

Randy put his hand up, silencing his athletic director. Outwardly he remained calm but his eyes now pierced through the messenger that was sitting in front of him.

"Sounds like it sure is heading that way pretty quickly," the coach responded, his tone even. "So much for the end of the season evaluation you were talking about."

"C'mon Randy," replied the AD with a slight squeak in his voice. "I came in here to tell you what's going on so you're not in the dark. I didn't have to, but I'm trying to be fair…"

Randy remained even and found that he was actually enjoying this conversation because his inclination was correct, John was uncomfortable.

"You still haven't explained how getting rid of me is good for me. I've made my life here. My friends and colleagues are here. Do you want me to go on? Now, I remind you because you said it, how is a change in the leadership of this program good for me?"

John fidgeted nervously in his chair. He had looked forward to this conversation earlier, but it was not going as planned.

"Sometimes we all need a change of scenery," he stammered.

"Then I think I should decide that," replied the veteran coach.

"We're afraid you may not see that," fired back the AD, struggling to gain control of the conversation.

Randy smiled but inside he was cursing himself. He had given the dumbass across from him an opening and he could feel his face warming, knowing that the crimson was letting his secret out.

"You're a piece of work," Randy finally replied, angry at himself for letting the AD off the hook. "I've got work to do and you have meetings to go to. Listen John, I want you to know we're coming together. I'm not going to make this easy for you."

John smiled. He knew that he was back in control.

"Randy, I would love nothing better than…"

"Good," replied Randy, grabbing a notebook full of plays. "I'll get back to work then."

John got up and walked quietly to the office door then turned back to his coach.

"Hang in there Randy, the President and I are pulling for you," he said and then he was gone.

"Great," muttered the coach as he sat back in his chair.

The team had one final series remaining in the regular season. On paper it was two meaningless games between teams that were at the bottom of the standings. Randy knew that in reality these were two very big games for his team. They had been playing very well of late, having won five and tied one in their last six games. Two more wins would give them serious momentum going into the playoffs.

On Friday evening the team continued their streak with an easy 5-2 win over the visiting Matadors of Northern Nebraska State. The team had been clicking on all cylinders and the crowd, though small, was loud and boisterous. It had been a fun night and after the game the coaches and players in the locker-room had enjoyed the victory.

Meanwhile, John Bart sat in his office with the phone to his ear. After two rings the phone had been picked up and the voice of Robert Jones, a very successful businessman and hockey booster, came on the line.

"Mr. Jones, John Bart here," said the athletic director into the phone.

"Hey big John," boomed the booster. "How are things at SPU athletics? Boys looked good on the ice tonight."

John agreed but quickly started discussing the direction of the program with the team's biggest financial booster.

"You want to get rid of ole Randy, huh? Got somebody else in mind?"

"Yes," replied John. "I can't give you a name, but he's a real up and comer and is an alumnus of the program. Also, he'd be a lot cheaper than Randy."

"How many years does Randy have left on his contract?" asked the booster.

"Three," replied John. "It would cost us $150,000 to buy him out."

"That's a few bucks. Listen, I'm not opposed to the idea. I won't pay the full 150 either. Randy's a good coach, but he ain't what he used to be. I'll make some calls and see if I can get some help."

"That would be great," replied John excitedly. "I really appreciate it. It's time to get Wildcat Hockey back up and running nationally."

"Listen John, just so you know. You and the prez are sticking your neck out on this one," warned the booster. "Randy's won a lot of games, brought in some pretty trophies, though never the big one. You screw up on the successor it could be you we're buying out next."

John felt his mouth go dry and butterflies develop in the pit of his stomach. Mr. Jones was sending him an unmistakable signal.

"I have to do what's best for the university, Mr. Jones." he stammered unevenly.

"Just so we understand each other. But I have no doubts that you'll bring in a good one. Bye John," he said and the line went dead.

John sat at his desk for another hour. He wasn't sure whether to feel good or scared, but it didn't matter. All that was important was to get rid of Randy. Everything else would take care of itself he reasoned to himself.

The next evening the Wildcats played even better and hammered the Mavericks 9-2 on Senior Night. Early the next day Randy drove to his office and pulled out a tape of an earlier game against Bismarck, their opponent for the opening round of the playoffs. He watched for tendencies of the upcoming opponent when the ringing of the phone brought him out of his concentrated thought.

"Randy, Everett Thompson here. What the hell is going on there?"

Everett was a big supporter of the program, though not the biggest. He and Randy had been friends since both had been players under Bill Stanton. Everett had made a fortune in hedge funds and found that giving money to his alma mater's hockey team was a fine way to beat the tax man.

"Hi Everett," replied Randy. "What exactly are you talking about?"

"Sounds to me like a coup is developing in the hockey program."

"I'm stuck in a bunker right now," agreed Randy. "What are you hearing?"

Everett told him about a call he had received from Robert Jones. Mr. Jones was looking for some investors for a buyout. Randy listened and felt his heart race. The little bastard was going to do it. He was going to get rid of him and the fix was now in. The evaluation and everything else that came out of his mouth was nothing but an elaborate hoax. Randy hung up the phone and felt an overwhelming desire to go over to John's house, pull the dumb bastard's sweater over his head and give him a good, old-fashioned beat down. He knew it was time to let John know what the game was.

Early the next morning John sat in his office with the phone to his ear when he heard his secretary start to speak in a loud voice.

"He's on the phone, Randy," Vivian Carter shouted as the door knob to John's office turned.

"I don't give a shit," replied Randy with a wry smile as he barged into his boss' office.

"I'm sorry Mr. Bart," stammered Vivian.

"It's alright, Vivian. What do you want, Randy?" replied John Bart coldly as he hung up the phone.

"How's the buyout going you piece of shit?" said the agitated hockey coach. "So much for the evaluation and the 'nothing's been decided' bullshit."

"Calm down, Randy or I'll have you removed and placed on administrative leave."

"Calm down? Are you serious? Sounds like I'm out. When were you going to tell me? I would imagine this would fall under not keeping me in the dark."

"That may be true," replied John, actually loving this moment. "We may go a different direction, and as AD I need to prepare for all contingencies."

John pointed to the chair in front of his desk and Randy sat down.

"We may also keep you. You're right about the team. They are playing very well right now. I believe they are 7-0-1 in their last eight games. Don't blow it all by saying something that will require action from me."

Randy nodded sullenly. John was in complete control of his fate right now and there was nothing he could do about it.

"You could have waited until after the season," replied the defensive coach. "Hell, you could have just kept your word about the evaluation. Right now, I can't trust anything you say."

"We're done now Randy," replied John, standing up from behind his desk and walking to the door.

Randy stood up and tried to regain his composure.

"No, we're not. Not by a long shot."

He grabbed the door knob and pulled hard. He smiled at Vivian as she looked toward the sound of the slamming door.

The trip to Bismarck was long but uneventful. The snows had finally decided to quit descending from the skies, and though the air remained frigid, signs were beginning to point to a change in season. The bus pulled into the arena parking lot and the team quietly unloaded and grabbed their gear which was stored underneath the bus. They trudged into the arena and changed into their practice outfits and made their way to the ice. Randy watched the players glide over the frozen water and smiled as the chatter picked up as the players became warm. He had a good feeling.

Twenty-four hours later, the feeling had changed as the Wildcats dropped the first game of the playoff. The team had been flat and seemed to react instead of controlling the play. Back at the hotel Randy and Bob quietly game-planned as they watched tapes of the game. Randy knew that the next game was probably the biggest of his career. Bob spotted some openings that could be exploited and added that into the notes that the coaches would give the players. Back in Saint Paul, John sat in the President's office as the two men look at the statistics faxed to them by those covering the game.

"Do you really think we can get Kincaid to coach?" asked the President.

"Yes, he wants to move up," replied Bart.

Allen Kincaid had been one of Randy's favorite players and was now a Division III coach. He had rebuilt Minnesota College from the ground up and this year had led them to their first conference championship.

"He and coach are very close," said the President.

"Kincaid will jump at the chance to coach his alma mater," replied John. "Randy won't do anything to sabotage his protégé."

"What about the buy-out?"

"Mr. Jones will cover $100,000 and has five others that will provide $10,000 each, so it's covered."

The President was silent for a minute. He liked Randy, but he had brought in John Bart to get athletics to the next level. He knew he had to give him latitude to run the department as he saw fit.

"Alright, you can make a change," he finally said soberly. "But not until the season is over."

"That should happen tonight. Looks like Bismarck beat us pretty good last night."

"Wait until they are back in town," replied the President. "Randy deserves that at least."

John nodded and got up from his chair and headed toward the door.

Back in Bismarck the Wildcats evened the series with a convincing 5-0 victory, setting up the deciding third game. The next night the two teams played a classic, neither willing to bend and after regulation were tied 1-1. In overtime both teams threw shots at the net but both goalies made spectacular saves to keep their teams alive. Finally, with less than two minutes remaining in the first overtime a Wildcat shot ricocheted off a Bismarck player and slid under the outstretched arm of their goalie, giving St. Paul a 2-1 win and moving them into Championship Weekend. Though excited, the Wildcats were exhausted from three games in three days and the ride back to Saint Paul was quiet.

As the bus pulled onto the campus Randy shook the sleep from his eyes and look at his watch. It read 7:17 am and he was looking forward to taking the day off and catching up on his sleep before coming back to practice later in the evening. He looked out the window of the charter and heard a groan slip from his lips. There on the corner was John Bart. John patted the guys on the back as they came off the bus and then pulled Randy over to the side.

"Randy, the President is still undecided, but this weekend certainly works in your favor," said the AD.

"John, I no longer care," replied a tired Randy. "Right now, the only thing I'm thinking about is the tournament."

"As you should be," remarked John. "I really mean this; we're pulling for you."

"Sure," smirked Randy. "I would think an athletic director would want his teams and coaches to do well."

"Well…of course," stammered John.

"Whatever," replied Randy, "I have things to do."

Randy grabbed his luggage and started walking toward his truck.

"You're done," muttered John under his breath.

As Randy was driving home from the school, he pulled out his cell phone and called Adam in Salt Lake.

"Hey, congratulations," said his friend on the line.

"Thanks…listen, what we've been talking about, I think I'm going to take it."

"You are? That's great," exclaimed Adam.

"It's not a done deal. I can't give you a final answer until the season is over, but right now I can't imagine a scenario where I come back."

"Sounds fair," replied Adam. "You sound tired."

"We just got back. Listen, I'll talk to you next week."

"Keep winning, bud."

On Wednesday morning Randy scurried around the athletic department as he prepared to leave for the Championship Weekend. His team had looked good in the practices and a buzz of excitement circulated through the hockey offices. He reviewed his to-do list for what seemed like the fiftieth time since he had arrived at six in the morning. Bob walked into his office and teased his boss about being a mother hen. Randy smiled and the two men began walking to the charter that awaited them to take them to Rochester for the tournament.

Randy's face soured as he saw John Bart standing at the door. The AD motioned for Randy to follow him and took him into his office. He told Randy now that he and the President would be flying in tomorrow for the tournament and tried to be conciliatory as he was giving his best wishes. Randy merely nodded and headed toward the bus. In truth, he no longer cared. John sat down at his desk and watched the team and coaches board the bus. As the large charter pulled out of the parking lot John grabbed his phone and dialed Robert Jones' number.

"Hi Mr. Jones," John said after Robert answered. "I still think we're going to need to make that change I spoke to you about."

"They looked pretty good this past weekend, Johnny Boy," replied the booster.

"Yes," agreed John. "We're all excited about Championship Weekend, but I don't think Randy is the guy to take us into the future."

"We'll know better after this weekend," replied a now non-committal Jones.

"I'm hoping you're still on board about the buy-out."

"Yes, I am, but the other investors have told me that they will withdraw if the team wins the tournament, and I'm inclined to agree with them."

"I see. Shouldn't that be my decision?"

"You can make any decision you wish JB, but if they win this weekend and you still decide you want a new guy you'll need new investors for the buy-out."

"Well, we're all hoping for the best," replied the subdued AD.

"Yes, we are young man. Cheer up…either way we win. Just remember that," replied the booster who was now controlling the strings.

"Thank you, Mr. Jones," replied John but the line was already dead and he realized that he nothing more than a puppet of his own making.

Randy looked around the visitor's locker room. In the corner sat Rick Jensen in his street clothes. The trainer told him that Rick would not be able to play and was doubtful if the team pulled the upset and moved on in the tournament bracket. Randy nodded and actually felt relieved. He had been pretty sure he was going to scratch his captain anyway but this took the pressure off.

The team went out and played spectacularly for two periods against host Moorhead, but despite playing so well they found themselves down 1-0 when they came back into the locker room for the second intermission. Randy diagramed some options on the whiteboard then he and the coaches left the players alone in the locker room, giving them some time for themselves.

In the third period the Wildcats fired shot upon shot on the Moorhead goalie but he managed to turn them all away until the final three minutes. SPU finally broke through with a power play goal from the point and then quickly followed that up with two more goals, the last being an empty netter. With the 3-1 win, SPU was advancing to the championship game against Southern Iowa.

Late that evening Randy picked up the phone and dialed his wife's number. A sleepy voice answered and the two talked quietly about the game and the kids. Finally, Randy picked up enough nerve to finally let his wife in on his conversations with Adam.

"Honey," he said a little apprehensively. "I might be making a change."

"What are you talking about?" inquired his sleepy wife.

He told her about his conversations with Adam and what that had led to. After telling her he could only hear her breathing through the receiver and he wondered how she was taking it.

"What do you think?" he asked her.

Again, only silence.

"Please honey, what are you thinking?"

"I'm not going to talk about this on the phone," she finally said sharply.

"All right," he responded but the line had already gone dead.

The next day the team played SIU for the championship and controlled the tempo throughout the game. They received solid goalie play and the offense was jumping, resulting in a 5-2 victory and with the win an automatic berth into the NCAA tournament. As the team celebrated on the ice Randy saw a smiling John Bart walking toward him. Randy waited for him and as John stuck his hand out in congratulations, John grabbed him and pulled him close.

"Either cut the rope or open the trapdoor, John," said Randy to his boss.

"Randy," John responded in surprise. "I told you we'd make a decision after the season is over."

"It's past that now," replied Randy, "You and I both know it. We're back in nationals and it's time to end the speculation."

"Look Randy, it's out of my hands," said John as he angrily pulled away from the coach. "The president wants an evaluation after the season ends."

The two men walked into the hallway leading to the locker room.

"Bullshit," replied the coach. "You lost your boosters who were going to buy me out when we won the conference. You're trying to find some new ones now. I'm not stupid, John. Now make the call."

"Only the president can," whimpered the AD.

"Fine," said Randy as he took his cell phone out of his pocket.

He went to the contact list and found the President and pushed the button, sending the signal to the president's cell. It was quickly answered.

"Mr. President, Randy here."

John Bart stood in front of his coach, seething.

"Am I in or out?"

The two men glared at each other as the President spoke to Randy.

"No Mr. President, it's your decision. I know this because John Bart, who is standing in front of me, said so."

Randy, still locked in a stare down with his boss, slowly smiled.

"That's great to hear Mr. President. But what about the rollover clause in my contract? John told me that regardless of what happens he's taking it away."

John eyes were piercing through his coach.

"That sounds fair," responded Randy with a smile. "I assume you'll tell John and I have no doubt your word is good."

Randy continued listening and. smiled triumphantly at his athletic director.

"Great, great," Randy finally broke in. "Thank you, Mr. President. I've got to get the boys ready for nationals. It was good talking to you."

"The president seems to have made a decision," he told the angry AD as they walked toward the entrance to the locker room. "By the way, this call may have been recorded. Have a good day, Boss."

The next week the team flew to the Final Five in Texas. St. Paul was the fifth seed and would have to play Massachusetts State in the play-in game on Thursday night. They arrived on Wednesday and went through their regular routine. Again, the trainers worked with Rick Jensen, but again his knee was not ready and they informed the coaching staff that the captain would again be unavailable for them.

On Thursday the team battled Massachusetts State but neither team could find an edge. The game was nip and tuck all the way to the final minute. Each team fought to control the puck in the final 60 seconds. MSC had the puck low in the offensive zone but the Wildcats managed to force a giveaway and had an odd man rush with 20 seconds left in the game. It was all they needed as the puck hit the post and ricocheted past the goalie, giving SPU a 2-1 victory and moving them into the semifinals.

Back in Saint Paul, John went to the president's office to try one final time to convince him that a change had to be made in the hockey program. He walked out twenty minutes later battered, knowing that Randy would not only be coming back but would be the coach probably for the next several years.

The next night Saint Paul took on Seattle State University in the national semifinals. The Wildcats played their best game of the year and knocked the tournament's number one seed out with a 6-1 victory, putting them only one victory from a national championship. The President called John and asked him why he wasn't at the tournament. John quickly made his way to the airport.

Late in the evening when Randy called home Brenda sounded ecstatic. She had watched the game on television and worked her husband for details about the win. He enjoyed her enthusiasm but he wanted to talk about next year, away from Saint Paul.

"Randy, our life is here," she replied, though not in an angry tone like the week before. "You've won the war. Why leave?"

Things have changed, honey," he replied. "I want to be involved in the kid's lives. I just need a change, and I think it would be good with Adam."

What about us, Randy? The kids and I have built our life here, not somewhere else. I just don't know."

"Well, we have choices now," he replied. "We'll talk about it when I get home."

"All right darling," she replied. "Win tomorrow and then have a safe flight."

"Can I come home if we lose?" he teased.

"I love you," she replied with a soft laugh.

"I love you too."

On Saturday, before a sold-out arena and a television audience, Randy and the team faced off against Michigan Poly for the title. Saint Paul played well but Poly had better athletes and they were just a little quicker to the loose pucks. The Wildcats stayed with MP through two periods, trailing only 3-2 going into the third, but the favorites finally pulled away in the final stanza, scoring three goals to secure a 6-2 victory.

The team trudged to the locker room and quietly began taking off their gear. Randy told them they would talk back at the hotel. The team got onto their charter and headed back to their quarters. It was silent except for some sniffling from the broken-hearted players. On the bus Randy ordered dinner for the team and as they arrived at the hotel, he gave them directions to the banquet room where they would eat.

After the team had eaten Randy stood up in front of them and began to speak.

"Guys, I'm very proud of you. You came together when everybody wrote you off and did something no one thought you were capable of…"

As he continued to speak his voice cracked a few times. He was so very proud of this team. He had almost given up hope on them earlier in the year but now they were national runner-ups, and they had done it without their captain. After he finished, he sat down in his chair. The players started to get up, but Randy again rose and had them sit again.

"I have one more thing to say," he began. "You may have a new coach next year. I'm tired and I'm at an age where I have to evaluate my worth to you. You deserve the best possible coaching and attention."

The players were stunned.

"I'm going to rest up and evaluate whether I'm that guy. I want you to keep this to yourself until I make up my mind but I felt that you deserved to know."

Randy stood up and quietly walked out of the room. As he was walking the team stood up and applauded their coach. He stopped and turned, a tear running down his cheek.

On the airplane the next day Randy stared out the window. He knew his answer. Tomorrow he would meet with John.

Chapter 4

CLOSING SHOP

Randy walked into the athletic offices and saw the national trophy sitting on a table in the middle of the entry way. With a smile of satisfaction, he made his way to his office as colleagues greeted him with congratulatory remarks. It was an exercise he had experienced before with other teams that had done well at nationals, but today it seemed extra sweet.

He unlocked his door and walked into the office and sat for a few moments and let the moment sink in before standing and taking off his jacket. As he hung it up, he glanced out his window into the gray day. Outside, students bustled to their morning classes as a light rain fell.

He sat down, clicked on his computer and put his feet upon his desk. He thought about the 22 years he had put in and wondered if he was really ready to give this all up. It had been a good run and SPU hockey had been all he had known during his adult life. It provided him with an identity and a decent living. It had given him friendships and the chance to shape lives. But it had also taken him away from his family and robbed him of watching his kids grow. This year it had nearly taken all his strength and endurance. Reluctantly, he knew that it was time to move on.

Randy hesitantly picked up the phone and as dialed Adam's number he felt his pulse quicken. After a couple of rings his friend answered and gushed about the tournament. Randy smiled as he listened to Adam's excited voice. For years his friend had lived SPU hockey vicariously through him and he had secretly done the same about what it was like to have money.

"So, let's cut to the chase," Randy finally said. "What are you offering me if I join you? Is there a salary?"

"You're going into your coach mode," Adam snickered good-naturedly. "All right, here's the deal. There is no salary but you don't need one. What do you make now, forty or fifty grand? You'll make twice that with me starting out."

"So, you're paying me commission?"

"That's how we do it in this business, bud," replied Adam. "I could pay you a salary, but that's a glass ceiling. You'll figure that out pretty quick and start looking for a better paying job. Here's what I'll do for you. I'll give you a salary to get started, get your feet wet. Three grand a month for three months then you're solo. No commission during salary and you can go off earlier if you want. Believe me, you'll want to."

Randy was quiet as he thought about the offer.

"How's commission work?"

"You get three points for every new car you move, two for used. You move an average of twenty a month. New sells usually are between twenty and forty grand, used between seven and 15. You do the math. People love cars. Your job is to put them into ours."

"You really sure I can do this?"

Adam laughed. "You serious?"

"Of course, I am," replied Randy.

"You'll be great at it, buddy, trust me."

"You're a cars salesman," joked Randy. "I not going to trust you, you need to sell me on why you think I can do this."

"That's fair," replied Adam. "Listen Randy, you're already doing it and don't even know it, and what's worse is you're getting paid shit while the university's making a ton off of you."

"I don't follow you," replied Randy.

"SPU costs twenty grand a year. You throw a kid some money, maybe five grand to come play for you. That's called a rebate in my business. You bring in ten kids a year. Working for me that nets you six grand, do those 11 more times you make $72,000 a year. You just got a big raise bud, only you're selling a car, not an education. Fact is, if you average one sell per day, you'll make over $150,000 per year. After one year I'll give you a sales team and you'll get an additional take from what they make. I made $375,000 last year and didn't sell a car."

"Damn, you are a helleva salesman. I'll do it."

Randy heard Adam clap his hands in celebration and he smiled.

"Wonderful. After the shit you've gone through you deserve a little bit of the good life," Adam said. "Welcome aboard, buddy, about time."

"Thanks," replied Randy, feeling a weight being lifted off of him. "I better get off now and let my athletic director know."

"Make the asshole squirm," replied Adam.

"I will, I'll talk to you soon."

Randy hung up the phone. The fire for next year had always driven him when the current season ended but there had been no fire for three years now. His kids deserved better and he knew that he deserved better. It was just time. He picked up the phone and called John Bart's office. Vivian offered congratulations as she checked to see when he could meet with the boss. After a moment she told him now was good. He quickly hung up and walked out into the hallway, oblivious to what lay ahead but excited about the prospects.

John was waiting at the door as Randy entered. He forced a smile but his stomach churned in this humiliating defeat. He loathed his hockey coach and it was driving him crazy that this simpleton had outflanked him.

"Randy, come on in stud," he said to his coach as he sat down behind his desk. "What a great job of coaching. I can't tell you how proud I am of you and the team."

"Really?" replied Randy politely with a hint of sarcasm. "How interesting?"

"Look, I want you to know that I've talked it over with the President and I'm getting that rollover reinstituted."

Randy smiled and nodded and decided not to bring up the phone call made after the conference championship game.

"Why don't we go further and talk about a new contract?" asked Randy.

"Now Randy, you've got a good one already. With the rollover back in you have four years guaranteed."

"What about a raise?"

"I believe you're paid top dollar for a Division II coach already," replied John, emphising the II. "I'd love to pay you Division I money but we just don't have that kind of income yet. No, I think you're fine where you're at."

"I see," replied Randy.

He stood up and started walking toward the closed door. John wanted to let him go but he knew that Randy was now the darling of the boosters and alums plus the spineless president was firmly in his corner.

"Wait Randy," he said. "Come sit down and let's talk about this."

"Doesn't sound like there is much to talk about, John," replied Randy. I just basically came in to see where I stood with you."

"I know your feelings are a little bruised after the difficulties you went through this year."

"You mean you trying to buy me out and leaving me hanging in the wind for the last three months?"

"Now Randy," replied John, relieved that his coach had returned to his seat. "I had every intention of bringing you back. Besides, it worked out well. That was tremendous coaching, best I've seen. You weren't just going through the motions."

Randy slowly stood up and placed both hands on his John's desk. He bent down and looked directly into John's eyes, piercing through them.

"I've never gone through the motions," he said in a menacing voice. "To be successful I've been willing to sacrifice being a fulltime husband and father. You wouldn't understand because you've never coached. If this was a game to you shove it up your ass."

"Calm down Randy, point taken. I apologize for the choice of words. Regardless whether you know it or not I had your back all the way."

Randy laughed and sat back down in his chair.

"You're a piece of work, John, but it doesn't matter much longer."

"What do you mean?"

"I'm ready for a change," replied Randy. "I got to thinking about what you said and surveyed the lay of the land. Come to find out there are other jobs that interest me and apparently I interest them."

John was concerned now. Randy was hot property and he could not afford to lose him. He had seen to many athletic directors become unemployed when hot properties got away.

"Now Randy, let's slow down a little," he said. "You love this place. You're a fixture here. There's no reason to pick up roots and start over somewhere else."

Randy smiled, enjoying the sight of his athletic director tense up.

"Actually, there is. I have an offer in hand that pays more and the boss doesn't interfere or play mind games like you do."

"Really, who is it? Maybe I can match their offer," John said, ready to negotiate.

"I already gave you that chance, John. Hell, you didn't even have to match it. Just show me a little something," Randy said as he stood up and walked to the window. He turned slowly and sat on the ledge.

"But no, you didn't have any extra income a few minutes ago. I was fine right where I was at."

Randy walked back over to the chair and put his hands in his pockets, staring at John. The athletic director could feel the color draining from his face. He silently prayed this was a bluff but he had a sick feeling he was losing his coach.

"See John, the problem with you is that you expect us to be honest and forthright, which we are, but you don't have to follow the same rules. I love this place, but I can't stand the thought of working for you any longer."

John was becoming desperate. This was not a hoax. Randy was serious and he knew that things would get very messy if he lost him.

"What about loyalty to your players," demanded John, "loyalty to the university that provided you with a good living for the past 22 years, or loyalty to the boosters and alums that have supported the program?"

Randy sat down and pondered these questions.

"Well, let's see. As you said I've been here 22 years so I think I've shown a great deal of loyalty to all three groups you've mentioned," he finally replied. "In return, I had a president give the athletic director the thumbs up to go to the boosters to raise money to buy me out. So now that we've finished second in the nation, you, who wanted to separate me from those players by firing me, is lecturing me about loyalty? You're something else, John."

Randy put his hand in his jacket and pulled out a letter he had written the evening before.

"I'm afraid my mind is made up," he said as he handed the letter to John.

John unfolded the letter and began reading. Perspiration developed over his upper lip and his teeth began to grind. He felt fear as he read Randy's resignation.

"Randy, you can't do this," he stammered. "There has to be something we can do to keep you. I'll get that raise. We can rework the contract. Please, you have to reconsider."

John knew that Randy now had him on the firing line. The boosters were solidly in his corner as well as the President. He knew that Randy was a 'shoot from the hip' type of person and would tell the media of the behind the scenes work he had done to get rid of him. He knew that in all likelihood if Randy left, he was gone.

"Have a good day, John," replied Randy with a smile and he rose and walked to the door.

"Randy."

The coach said nothing as he casually opened the door and walked out. John slumped behind his desk, not knowing whether to call the President now or later. He tried to remain calm but panic was overtaking him. His chest was tightening and breathes of air were becoming difficult to get.

❦

Randy felt like he was floating as he entered his office. He felt triumphant but drained. He had really done it. When he had gotten up this morning he had not known if he could really resign but he had and he felt liberated. He grabbed his cell phone out of his trousers and excitedly waited for his wife to answer. When he heard her voice, he collapsed into his chair.

"Honey," he said breathlessly. "I just resigned."

"You what?" she replied horrified. "I thought this was something we were going to talk about."

"Honey, I just can't do it anymore. I know because John offered a raise and the rollover."

"He what?" she screamed into the phone. "Are you out of your mind? You resigned? What are you thinking? So, what exactly are your plans now?"

"I told Adam I'd take him up on his offer," he replied meekly.

"You just expect the rest of us to stop our lives and follow you without discussing it first?"

"Honey, I…"

"I can't talk to you right now!"

He heard a click and the dial tone. He was stunned by her reaction. He had been sure she would understand and be excited.

"That didn't go as planned," he murmured to himself.

He closed his phone and thought about walking back to John's office but his pride would not allow him to. He had made up his mind, family be damned. Suddenly his cell phone rang. He looked at it and saw that it was Brenda. He wondered if he should pick up but knew that the consequences would not be good if he didn't.

"Can you still accept the school's offer?" she asked as he put the phone to his ear.

"I told you Brenda, I'm done. I don't want to make the sacrifices I've made anymore. I'm through," he replied evenly.

"Why are you doing this?" she moaned. "Explain it to me. I don't understand."

"Brenda, I know my athletes better than my own kids. I've never seen my son play basketball and I'm never at their birthday parties."

She remained silent.

"For seven months out of the year I'm gone on weekends, even when I'm here physically. You and I haven't done anything together in years. It just isn't worth it anymore."

As she listened her defenses reluctantly loosen.

"People might think it's about John or the boosters and maybe at one time it was, but it's not anymore. They just got me weighing whether this was what I wanted to continue doing."

Brenda grabbed a tissue and dabbed her eyes. Part of her understood but the other feared the change she knew was coming. They were comfortable now and that was worth something, wasn't it?

"Why didn't you tell me earlier?" she asked.

"That's just the point. This job doesn't give you the chance to have conversations like this. It's all consuming. At one time I was fine with that but I'm not anymore."

She loved him and what he was saying was true. She had long ago accepted that she was second to hockey. Maybe there was a chance that she could love this man without competing with the invisible mistress.

"So, we're going to Salt Lake City huh?"

"It's beautiful out there," he replied soothingly.

"What about jobs?"

"If Adam is right, we won't have to worry about both of us working."

She smiled. She wanted to believe him but she was a realist and he had made a living being an optimist.

"I hope he's right," she replied. "But in the meantime, I'm going to do some checking.

"Fair enough," he said relieved.

"From now on Randy, you talk to me before making any other life altering decisions," she scolded.

"I will babe," he snickered. "But this should be it."

"I have to go," she said. "We'll tell the kids tonight."

"I love you," he said.

She did not reply.

Randy and Brenda sat down with the kids after dinner and he told them the news. The children were quiet as the enormity set in.

Sean became angry. He was in high school now and had grown up with his schoolmates. The thought of moving away scared him and he lashed out at his parents. Randy knew that this was coming and patiently let his son spew his indignation. The boy came close to the line but did not cross it and then stormed off to his room.

Tisha was just the opposite. She loved adventure and moving would be a big one. She immediately started asking questions about Salt Lake City and then ran and grabbed her globe, demanding to know where it was. Her parents smiled and patiently answered her questions. She rose when she had no more and gave her dad a hug and a kiss on the cheek, then did the same with her mother. She ran to her room to begin planning the move. She had already decided there must be a garage sale and she rummaged through her things to find suitable sales items.

Hours later Randy and Brenda lay in their bed and talked quietly. Brenda was still worried about the change and what it would mean to her marriage, children and career.

"Explain the money situation to me again," she said.

Randy broke it down for her the way that Adam had done it earlier in the day. He talked about the potential earnings and his voice rose in excitement. She shushed him, not wanting to wake the children, but she did love seeing him this way.

"But they say the economy may be weakening," she said, the realist in her returning. "This housing thing is tightening things up."

"Remember honey, we're in a war right now. Every time we've been in one our economy has done well. World War I, World War II…"

"Randy," she scolded. "This isn't quite the same thing. You've been coaching for 22 years, what do you really know about the economy?"

"I know that recruiting is the same as sales. ABC, always be closing. I plan on doing that."

She turned and lightly put her hand on his face.

"Have you really thought this out? If you haven't, you're putting us in financial jeopardy so you can go to a birthday party or a basketball game."

"Honey," he said soothingly, longing to ease her fears. "You know Adam, he's always been successful. Why would things change now?"

She turned onto her back and looked up to the ceiling, only the silhouette of the moon providing light into the darkened room.

"Things are always changing," she replied. "You're coming off campus and into the real world. You're like a college graduate, grandiose plans with no thought of failure. Real life is different. It gives you challenges everyday."

"I know that honey," he replied but he was hurt that she was treating him like a child.

"Have you really thought this out?"

"I have honey, I promise you I have. Now let's get some sleep. I love you."

"I love you too Randy, but I want you to really think about this. There's still time to change your mind, and there is nothing wrong with that. As you know it is a woman's prerogative. I don't see why it can't be a man's too."

He laughed and she smiled.

"Honey, I have, I promise you that I've been thinking about this for three months now. I believe it's the right thing. Now go to sleep."

They kissed and rolled to their sides away from each other. He was nearly asleep when he heard a strange sound. It was Brenda silently wiping tears from her eyes as she quietly wept.

He pretended to be asleep.

Both the president and John Bart tried to talk Randy out of leaving but his mind was made up. It was time to turn the shop over to someone else, whoever that may be. Meanwhile, the boosters, who had just two months before had been calling for Randy's head now wanted the blood of the athletic director who had let their beloved coach get away.

Randy enjoyed the spectacle as the embattled athletic director fought to retain his job. No longer were the calls and threats coming into the president's office about him but the man who had tried to orchestrate the coup. Now the alums were running the show and John was trying to outrun the mob.

Randy knew he had played a large part in John's downfall. In his final press conference, he had felt the freedom to speak his mind. He told the media of the sleepless nights wondering if he would have a job next year and the hurt of finding out that supposed supporters were having clandestine meetings for buyouts. He talked about his loyalty to the SPU, but the hurt that those in the administration had caused in their clumsy attempt to oust him.

He had received an outpouring of support from the community as well as other coaches. Meanwhile John had bunkered down in the athletic department, not believing what was being said by his former coach. He now understood what Randy had endured and he privately planned his revenge but the boosters were louder and soon Saint Paul University was not only looking for a new hockey coach, but an athletic director. The purge had been completed four weeks later when the president announced that he would be retiring at the end of the year. Though he put on a happy face inside he seethed at the quiet result of the board of trustee's vote.

Randy continued with his duties. Though he had retired from coaching there was still recruiting calls to make and scheduling to be done. He talked to each recruit and explained to them that SPU was still the place for them, with or without him. Each recruit had questions about the future and he made sure they understood that the program was ready to take off, they being the only missing link.

The head of the search committee asked Randy to help with the selection and he agreed to have breakfast with the finalists and to give the committee his take on each candidate. In his short meetings with the hopefuls, he told them about the returners and gave insight to how he had run his program. Though they of course wanted to give a positive impression, they were genuinely interested in what he told them. In the end he gave the committee his assessment of the candidates. He was comfortable with whomever they would choose but gave them a rank order at their request.

Randy's office was now bare of the mementos of a 22-year career and he sat at a desk that would soon belong to somebody else. He thought back of his time here and smiled. It had been good and he had been good. It dawned on him that this was all he had ever known professionally. At times butterflies would enter his stomach and hot pins stab his upper back as he wondered about the future. Doubts would inevitably creep into his mind but he knew that there was no turning back. The net below him had been removed.

∞

The press conference had been exciting. He had sat in the back row and watched the enthusiasm of his former player who was now taking over the program. He smiled when his name was mentioned and felt the hope and excitement that comes with every new hire. He was glad his protégé was taking over and he looked forward to the future for both himself and his former team.

As the months went on and the new coach moved in Randy spent less and less time at the school. He wanted to give the new guy his space, put his plan in motion. But mostly Randy no longer felt a part of the department. He was now the past and the future had arrived. He found other things to do until he stopped coming in at all.

As his tenure wound down the going away parties picked up. First it was his coaching staff who threw a humdinger where the liquor flowed and the lies flourished. Then it was the athletic department staff and coaches where new hijinks to be remembered and legend making were performed. Finally, there was the university's formal going away party where the guests drank wine and quietly socialized about the state of education within the tyrannical clutches of the federal financial aid overseers.

Finally, the last day of Randy's employment of SPU arrived. He planned to put in just enough time to take out the remaining boxes of books and mementos left in the office. He shed a few tears with his secretary and spent some time thanking those who helped him outside of the limelight.

After the last box was loaded Randy sat in his truck and took one last drive around the campus. As he was driving his cell phone went off. He looked and saw that it was Adam. His friend was jovial and excited and Randy found it to be contagious.

"Hey buddy," said Adam. "I can't wait to get you here. It's going to be great."

"I know," replied Randy. "I'm excited, but scared."

"Really?" said Adam incredulously. "There's nothing to be afraid of. This is a gold mine you're coming to."

"I hope so," Randy said quietly.

"Listen buddy, it's a gold mine because we don't rip people off, just give them a good deal. You'll be fine."

"You really think so?"

"I do," replied Adam. "And so does everybody I talk to and everybody that you talk to. Just trust yourself."

Randy smiled. "All right, I'll see you soon."

Randy clicked his phone shut and continued driving around the campus. It was beautiful and peaceful, the sounds of birds chirping and the smell of freshly cut grass. He loved this place. It had become a part of him.

That's what scared him.

Chapter 5

SETTLING IN

Randy looked out the plane window in awe. Below him lay Salt Lake City and the Wasatch Mountains that served as its backdrop. It was late May and yet these mountains still looked as though it were the middle of winter. He smiled to himself and felt the excitement as the wheels touched down on the runway. He yearned for the change that was coming.

As he exited the aircraft, he felt youthful and the joy that came with all things being possible. He wanted to run down the corridor but he controlled himself as he made his way to luggage. As he was coming down the escalator, he saw Adam waiting and both men broke into grins as they embraced.

"Welcome to Salt Lake City, buddy," Adam exclaimed.

"It's great to be here," replied Randy. "I see you're still uglier than hell."

The two men laughed. For a moment they were college students again, happy to see each other yet always ready to crack upon each other.

"True, true," Adam replied. "But fortunately, I'm still better looking than you. I still can't believe Brenda chose you over me."

"Adam, you were never in the running," laughed Randy.

"Let's get your luggage and let's get out of here."

"So, what are you driving this year?"

"It's a surprise, but you'll love it," replied Adam.

The two friends made their way to pick up Randy's luggage, laughing as they strode through the room. Randy grabbed his bag and the two made their way to the parking lot. Adam led him to his latest car, a brand-new silver Dodge Challenger and Randy laughed at the irony. Back in the '80s when then roomed together Adam had driven a '72 Challenger. Some things never change, thought Randy.

After the two men ate a lunch of eggs and hashbrowns they drove to Adam's dealership. Adam had a Dodge and Chrysler dealership. He had always been a Dodge man and his friends always teased him that he was the third Dodge brother, only he had been born 100 years too later. Adam pulled into his personal parking spot and the two men jumped out and headed into the showroom of the huge dealership.

"Follow me, you're going to like this," instructed Adam as they entered the building. "Here's your office. I think you'll be pleased."

Randy's jaws dropped. It was a huge office, much bigger than the closet that had served as the hockey office, but what caught his eye was the life size poster of him from his playing days in college.

"It's beautiful," stammered Randy. "But shouldn't I be out there with the rest of the salesmen?"

"They didn't just finish second at nationals. Only the best for you bud."

"You going to show me how to do this or am I just a pretty face?" asked Randy after thanking Adam.

"Well, I definitely can't use you as a pretty face so let me show you how this is done," replied Adam.

Adam took Randy to Terry Kennedy, his best salesman, and gave Terry some quick instructions.

"I'm going to leave you in Terry's hands. He'll show you the ropes and get you going."

Terry gave Randy a quick tour and explained the nuances of spotting and selling. Randy listened intently and followed Terry as he worked some customers. In three hours, Terry already had two sales and was working on his third. Randy was amazed with how Terry quickly earned the trust of his customers, wondering if he could do the same.

While cooling a customer Terry grabbed Randy and pointed to a man looking at some trucks.

"There's a bird. Time for you to get a sale," he told Randy.

"You really think I'm ready?"

"Sure, you are; remember, find his interest. Get to know him first. Don't try to put him in a truck, let him ask you to get in the truck for a ride. Become his best friend and then close the deal."

"Here goes," replied Randy as he walked out to the customer.

Randy remembered the things that Terry had done and played the role. He found out that the man was a racing fan so he started talking IndyCar with him. Soon they were debating the CART/IndyCar merger and whether that was good or bad for open wheel racing. Before he knew it, they were driving down the freeway in a sparkling Dodge Ram 2500.

They drove back to the lot and Randy took him inside to a desk on the showroom. Terry pulled Randy aside and told him to take him into his office.

"Use the trappings of the office, bud."

Randy took the customer into his office and soon they were discussing hockey and coaching. Randy could sense the sell nearing and they began negotiating. They went back and forth but the customer said that he wanted to sleep on it. Randy got up and shook his hand. As the customer walked out Terry walked up and asked Randy what had happened.

"He wants to think about it, but I think he'll come back tomorrow," replied Randy.

"Never let the customer walk out. He liked you and trusted you. Now you'll never see him again," replied Terry.

"Really?"

"Yeah, but don't worry about it. You did well, you're a natural, just have to work on the close."

An hour later Adam and Randy left the office and headed to Adam's house. Randy relayed his story of his first sales attempt and Adam smiled.

No sale but a promising start, thought Adam.

Brenda looked at Maria, who shared an office with her at TaylorTronics headquarters. She had worked for the company for the last six years and loved her job. Maria slightly nodded her head toward her friend as she continued to speak on the phone and Brenda forced a smile. Today was her last day and it was taking a toll. She continued cleaning out her desk and tried to keep a cheerful façade for the co-workers but she realized that it was becoming a losing battle.

After Maria got off the phone she quietly got up and left the office, pushing the lock knob in and quietly closing the door. Brenda remained in the empty office and buried her head in her hands and began to let the tears escape. She loved this place and the people that worked here with her but in a matter of hours it and they would only be a memory and it brought heaviness to her heart.

The tears were liberating and seemed to cause some relief. She wondered how she would get through this day but knew it no longer mattered. She silently thanked Maria as she grabbed some tissue and dabbed her eyes. She opened one of her boxes that contained things that had previously been in her desk and pulled out a mirror and fixed her face. She was determined to make this a good day so she rose and unlocked the door and walked out. Waiting were her co-workers who came over and took her to the conference room where a surprise going away party was prepared for her.

The rest of the day was wonderful. Work could be done on another day and the co-workers instead enjoyed each other's company, reminiscing about past clients and jobs. They talked about family and summer plans and the enjoyment of little things. It was a wonderful day for Brenda and she was truly sorry when her shift ended. Tears fell again, but she had made it through.

The weekend came and Brenda worked on packing and preparing for the move. The kids tried to be helpful and at times actually were but, like all kids, eventually the stress of moving affected them and they bickered over small things that to them were big. Brenda hoped that by ignoring it the kids would either grow tired of fighting with each other or would work it out. Besides, she had much to do with little time to complete it. She finally realized that ignoring it would not work as the fights grew in volume and intensity.

"Stop fighting," she bellowed, succumbing to the annoyance of the bicker. "You both have things to do so go do them!"

Both kids tried to blame the other for the problems but Brenda had had it and she raised her forefinger to put a stop to it.

"I do not want to hear anymore raised voices," she demanded. "Go into your own rooms and pack everything. When you think that you are finished, come out to get me and I will inspect it. If I concur, I will immediately have more work for you. Now go."

The kids initially protested but the bickering stopped and Brenda relished the cessation of raised voices. As she worked, she again began to stew over the decision to move. Why had Randy acted so compulsively she wondered? They had always discussed major decisions and it was hurtful that he had not talked to her before resigning.

Worse, this decision did not feel right. It seemed as though he was looking to run away from something. Sure, Adam had been a good friend all of these years but was this really the right time to make this move? Randy didn't understand signs that the economy was now slowing. He had lived in the academic world which was a world of theories. Real life, she thought to herself, was so much different than anything he knew or understood. She was scared but she knew she had to put on a brave front.

Randy flew home the next day and was bubbly as he met his wife at the airport. He grabbed his bag from luggage and talked excitedly about Salt Lake City. She smiled as she listened to him and tried to bury the fears that seemed to be enveloping her.

"I'm going to really like this job babe," he said to her as they drove toward their home, which was now on the market but had not had any takers yet. "It's fun. I almost closed my first sale but I screwed up and let him sleep on it. I promise you I won't make that mistake again."

"That's good dear," she replied.

"Did anybody look at the house?" he asked.

"No," she said with a tinge of concern. "They say that the market is having problems."

"I'm sure it short-term," he replied. "How's the packing going?"

That was Randy, always the optimist.

"It's coming along. I'm glad you're home. The kids are starting to drive me crazy."

"They'll be fine. They're just excited," he responded.

"I hope so."

"Don't worry babe. I was made for this and it is so much fun working for Adam. I love it and you're going to love Salt Lake City."

She smiled but she wasn't sure. They arrived at the house and the kids ran to Randy and he told them all about the new city that would soon be their home. After lunch the family went back to work. Brenda told Randy she had some things to do in the basement and gave him instructions of what needed to be loaded into the moving van that was in the driveway. He nodded and she kissed him on the cheek and smiled. He looked so happy, so relaxed and she felt it was her duty to be as cheerful as well.

She walked down into the basement and began putting jars into boxes. After filling one box she stopped and walked into an empty room and sat down in the corner. She could no longer contain her tears. She cried quietly but her chest heaved as she struggled to contain the sound coming out of her. She couldn't help herself. This was the wrong move, she knew, yet there was nothing she could do to stop it. A feeling of helplessness had overtaken her.

As day passed into night the family continued loading until there was nothing left. They slept on the floor in sleeping bags and at dawn rose and pulled out of the driveway, heading west. They drove through the day, stopping only for the obligatory potty breaks and meals that were eaten in haste. They finally stopped after they had driven over 500 miles. They found a hotel in Mitchell, South Dakota that had an indoor pool and Randy took Tish swimming.

Brenda and Sean stayed back in the room. Brenda was exhausted and immediately fell asleep while Sean munched on some chips and washed it down with a Dr. Pepper. After 45 minutes in the pool Randy and Tish came back into the room and within thirty minutes the lights were out and the four travelers were soundly sleeping.

Morning came early and they took quick showers and were back on the road before the sun had risen. It was another long day of driving and they did not stop until they arrived in Rock Springs, Wyoming. There another hotel awaited them and the previous night's ritual was repeated. After a short night the family was up early in the morning and again hit the road, only this time they knew their final destination would be Salt Lake City.

They drove through the day and early evening when at last their destination came into view. Brenda and the kids admired the scenery as they came closer. Salt Lake was truly breathtaking with the mountains overlooking the city. The area was green and so clean. She could see why Randy was excited. There was a sense that anything was possible but still her concerns would not go away.

Brenda pulled in behind the moving van that Randy was driving and he led them to Adam's house. The moving van came to a stop in front of a beautiful home with an immaculate yard. Randy climbed down from the moving van and waited for Brenda to park. Adam came bounding down the steps and immediately grabbed Tisha as she got out of the car. Brenda walked over to Adam and received a big hug. She smiled as he talked and laughed.

She was here but still it felt all wrong.

❧

The day was hot and muggy for Salt Lake City standards as Brenda and Tisha climbed into the car. The daughter jabbered to her mother about her expectations of a new house and the mother smiled and nodded. Today they would begin the process of finding a permanent home, Brenda's first attempt at bringing consistency back to family life. For four weeks they had lived with Adam and though she appreciated his patience and giving nature she needed to have her place to reset the roots.

She had called a realtor that Adam recommended and had met with her to discuss the specifics of what she was looking for. In this computer age she was able to pare down the houses to five and today she and Tish were to look at them and decide if any would make a suitable home.

Brenda met the realtor, Barbara Jackson, at the offices of Thompson and Sons Realty. Barbara was friendly enough but Brenda could tell that the woman saw her in terms of dollar signs. After some small talk at the office, they drove to the first of what would be five houses. Tisha sat in the back loving the fact that she and her mother would be spending the day in the search of the perfect home. Tish knew exactly what she wanted and was hopeful that she would be able to provide her mother with the adequate guidance to meet the specifications.

They viewed the five homes but neither mother nor daughter was happy with what they saw. While these houses had looked promising on a computer screen, they were lacking that certain something when seen in person. Barbara, undeterred, diligently took notes of her clients and pulled out her list of properties, knowing that somewhere was the right house for this family.

It was important to find the right place for these clients, thought Barbara. Clients were becoming few and far between because of the slowdown in the economy. She had actually begun looking for a second job because she had not made a sale in over two months. But this mother and daughter had just moved into the city and they had to have a place to call home. Barbara was determined to find that place for them.

Everyday Randy became a little bit more confident about his abilities. Terry Kennedy continued to give him pointers and Randy knew that it was just a matter of time before that elusive first sale closed. There was always traffic coming through the showroom but he noticed that Adam seemed somewhat concerned about something, yet still put on the happy warrior face. Terry was always busy but some of the other salesman seemed to have more time on their hands than they liked and would quietly congregate with each other by the coffee pot. Whenever Randy came near them, they would smile and be pleasant but the conversations would stop until he walked away.

Randy continued to work the customers that came into the showroom. There always seemed to be some type of problem…not the right color, price a tad too high or simply in to kick a tire and dream. But the most common problem that Randy encountered was that though the customer seemed to meet all the financing expectations, for some reason the lender would not agree to the financing terms. This was beginning to cause him some concern but still he viewed it as being inexperienced.

Late in the day the perfect customer came in. He knew what he wanted and Randy was determined to meet his needs. They looked at a number of options and the customer found one he liked. Randy negotiated a price and presented it to Adam, who nodded approvingly. Randy came back out and congratulated the customer and they went back to the financing department to complete the deal. Randy stood nervously as the financing was figured but this time it was accepted. Randy had finally made his first sale and he could not stop from smiling.

Brenda and Barbara had spent four days looking for the right house but thus far had been unable to find what they wanted. Barbara suggested another house that had sat vacant for over a year. It was a little small but had promise. Brenda walked through it and loved the wooden floors and mahogany that was tastefully utilized in the dining area. She saw the potential of the yard that had long overgrown but had potential areas for gardens. The large trees provided shade in the summer and peacefulness to the property. The more that Brenda looked at it the more she liked it. She and Barbara agreed to meet the next day to work on price but first she wanted Randy to see it.

"I got a gift for you bud," Adam told Randy.

"What is it?"

Adam handed Randy a check. Randy could not take his eyes off the figure that was staring back at him.

"You're kidding," he stammered.

"How do you like it?" asked a beaming Adam.

"This is half of what I usually make in one month," replied Adam, his mouth dry.

"Get ready for a lot more of those."

Randy looked up from the check and smiled. He felt as though he were floating. Adam was happy for his friend but also worried. Sales were getting harder to come by because of this credit thing. But more than that, something deeper was troubling him. He had heard some rumors and if true they could be devastating to him and his friend.

Brenda and Randy drove through the quiet neighborhood as she excitedly described the house he was about to see. Randy smiled when he saw the house. It was perfect, just as he had pictured it and it seemed to make Brenda happy. He had become concerned about his wife. He knew she was still hurt that he had not included her in his decision to come out here but this house seemed to be the tonic she needed. Though it was a little smaller than he had hoped for it was still beautiful and the yard had many possibilities. As they were looking around Barbara drove into the driveway.

The couple talked quietly and then went to their realtor and told them they wanted it. The sat down on the porch and began discussing prices until all agreed upon a fair offer. Barbara recommended a broker for a loan and gave them his card. They shook hands and Barbara left them alone.

"I think I'm going to like this place after all," giggled Brenda.

"I told you," he replied with a smile.

"Do you really like the house?"

"I love it babe. I can't wait to see what you do with it," he responded.

"I have a lot of plans," she laughed. "I think it can be so cute."

"Are you happy, babe?" he asked her as he grabbed her hand.

"I am Randy."

They embraced and he stroked her hair tenderly.

"It is beautiful here," she said softly as she gazed into his eyes. "I love the mountains and the air is so fresh here."

"I think this was a good move for us," he replied.

"I do too," she said as she kissed him tenderly on the lips.

"Let's go celebrate. I have a big check in my pocket that's burning a hole in it."

"Oh Randy, I'm so proud of you. You got a sale."

"Was there ever a doubt?" he asked teasingly.

She laughed and they embraced again. He led her to the car and they drove toward the city. The sun was turning into a brilliant orange hue that shined across the countryside. They found an intimate restaurant and went in and were seated at a corner table lit only by a candle. They absorbed the atmosphere and enjoyed each other's company for the first time in ages.

"How long has it been since we've gone on a date?" he asked.

She laughed softly as she thought.

"It's been a while," she replied dreamily.

"I have an idea," he said. "Let's get a hotel room and take a bubble bath together. Adam can watch the kids. Come on babe, I don't want this to end."

"Neither do I," she replied lustfully. "Make the call."

He called Adam and soon they were downtown Salt Lake. He found the hotel he had in mind and went in and got them a room. They virtually ran down the hall and he stuck the card in the keypad, opening the door. As soon as the door closed behind them, they were in each other's arms, lovingly kissing and feeling the contours of bodies that had once been familiar.

He tenderly carried her to the bed, his hands gently moving up and down her upper-body and arms. She arched her back as he delicately kissed her neck. His hands softly touch her skin and he deliberately tempted her with his motions and built the excitement of the woman he loved.

She groaned in ecstasy and placed her hands on his waist, reveling in the anticipation of what was to come. Their lips met and slowly opened, allowing the tongues to delicately circle each other. As their excitement grew clothes fell to the floor until they were completely nude. She took him inside of her and their bodies began to tremor together as they felt the joy of their act. She gently bit upon his ear as he continued to provide her pleasure. It had been so long since they had made love and she felt as though it were the first time all over again.

He looked down at her, admiring her beauty as he continued to love her and she returned his gaze with a slight smile filled with the enjoyment of the moment. All too soon the lovers felt the rush of the climax which brought the wondrous feeling of exhaustion brought from the act. They collapsed upon each other and held tightly. They were in a place they had not been in ages and they did not want to leave.

As they lounged together under the bubbles and warm water, they continued to touch each other as new lovers do. They laughed and felt joy and soon realized that this place had brought them back to the love they had felt before but had forgotten as the years passed. The made love one more time then fell asleep, entwined together in each other's arms.

The morning light awoke them after a sweet slumber. Randy walked over and looked out the window as Brenda admired him from under the sheet.

The sky was cloudy on this morning.

Chapter 6

OVERCAST

Brenda hung up the phone and slumped down in her chair. The house in Saint Paul had still not sold and even more alarming was that no one had even looked at it for over a month. It was crazy, she thought, the house was still relatively new, had a big yard and was in good shape. How could it be that in a metropolitan area of over one million people not one person had looked at it? She tried to quell the uneasiness inside of her but it was proving to be impossible.

She wondered about the new house. The offer had been made and accepted. Everything had seemingly gone smoothly with the broker but now the closing deadline was fast approaching and still there was no word on whether the loan had been accepted. She and Randy had good credit but she wondered if the house in Saint Paul was affecting the loan application. Deep down she knew it couldn't be good. She ran scenarios through her head and tried to figure out how they would be able to make two payments, even if the Saint Paul payment was relatively low.

The phone rang and Brenda answered it quickly before it went to message. Barbara Jackson told her that she needed to call the broker quickly because a problem had developed with the financing. Brenda's heart sank and deep down she knew that the house was slipping from her grasp. Though Barbara tried to sound reassuring Brenda wasn't sure if the realtor was really just trying to quell her own fears.

Brenda quickly called the loan officer and was invited to his office. She got into her car and quickly drove to the office building that housed the mortgage company. He greeted her politely and led her into his office. Behind closed doors the house broke away from her grip and disappeared.

She stood in the parking lot numb and helpless. She unlocked her car and got in as tears began to fall. Inside she grabbed her phone and pushed her husband's number.

"Randy, I just had a meeting with our broker. We've been turned down."

"What? Why? How can this be?" he demanded.

"He says we have a number of problems and that the federal rules have changed," she replied. "First of all, the bank said because you changed your profession, we can't get a loan for two years. Also, because the house in Saint Paul has not sold, they don't want to give us a second loan."

"What? That's ridiculous. I'll call him. There has to be some mistake. Banks always loan to people with good credit. We should at least be able to get an ARM."

The phone went dead and Brenda started the engine and drove back to Adam's. She went into the house and walked into the bedroom, lying down and stared at the ceiling. She hoped that Randy would be able to persuade the broker but she knew there was no chance. Her phone rang again and she answered, knowing by his tone that all was lost.

"This just can't be," he said in a resigned voice. "I'm sorry babe."

"You should have known," she lashed out.

"Brenda, how the hell should I have known?" he asked irritably.

"You and your damn plans," she replied angrily. "Things were just fine in Saint Paul. You had won the war and…. Why didn't we stay? We had a good life there."

"We've already had this conversation, Brenda," he responded angrily. "Right now, instead of assigning blame we need to come up with plan B."

"I wanted that house," she replied, breaking into tears. "Who knows what will be available in two years, assuming we sell the house in Saint Paul!"

"Brenda, stop it," he commanded.

"And who knows where the rates will be. It could be up around eight or nine percent in two years."

"It could also be lower," he replied.

"I don't want to talk to you right now," she said angrily. "Good bye!"

Randy heard the click and thought about calling back but realized it would do no good. She needed to calm down and arguing with her would be counterproductive. He set the phone down and walked into the showroom. It was time to make a sale.

Brenda spent the next week looking for rentals. She tried not to think of the house she had just lost or the house that she loved in Saint Paul. Surely, she would be able to find a suitable place to live for the next two years but her heart wasn't in it. As she looked, she felt embarrassment as she tried to explain to her daughter why they would not be moving into the house they had found and this made her angrier with her husband.

The drive calmed Randy's nerves. A favorite song from the past blared on his radio and he opened his window, letting the wind blow against his face. His upper back muscles loosen up and his problems with Brenda seem to dissipate with the warm air blowing into his face. Ahead of him he saw the dealership and for a moment he thought about passing by and just driving. As he debated his hands took over and the car turned into the lot. He smiled to himself and realized that since he was running low on funds this was probably best.

He waved to a group of salesmen who were congregated out front. The nodded back and he made his way into the showroom and walked toward his office. In Adam's office were two men in suits and a cop. He wondered apprehensively what was going on and caught Terry's attention, motioning him to come into his office.

"What's going on?" asked Randy as Terry closed the door behind him.

"I don't know but they've been in there for the past hour."

"Are we getting any traffic today?"

"Not so far but I'm sure it will pick up."

Randy nodded but he realized that there had been a lot of days without traffic. No more salary, only commission and he still only had one sale under his belt. The men finally left and Randy walked into his Adam's office and immediately felt a gnawing in his stomach. Adam didn't look so good. His color was drained from his face and he didn't seem to have any energy. He sat slumped in his chair staring into only a place he could see.

"Adam, what was that about?" asked Randy.

"I'm sure it's nothing," replied Adam unconvincingly.

"You don't look so good. What is it?"

"Apparently I'm being investigated for fraud."

"Fraud!" exclaimed Randy. "What are you talking about?"

"They say I've committed a number of offenses through our financing department and they suspect I'm embezzling also."

Randy slowly sat down as nervous perspiration began to form on his upper lip.

"It's nothing to worry about," replied Adam though he did not sound confident. "They have nothing on me, only suspicions."

"Adam," Randy said slowly. "Is it true?"

Adam did not answer nor did he look at his friend. Randy's chest began to hurt and he wondered if this was what a heart attack felt like.

"Damnit Adam, is it true?"

Adam finally looked at his friend and seemed to find some energy. "No."

The men sat silently, both trying to comprehend the turn of events that had hit them.

"I think somebody is trying to set me up," Adam said finally.

"You're talking crazy," responded Randy.

"I know," agreed Adam. "Everything will be fine. I gotta go for a while. You mind the store. I'm going over to my lawyer's."

"Adam," began Randy, but he had nothing more to say.

"Just mind the store," he said quietly. "I'll be back in a while."

Randy watched his friend leave and walked back to his office. Terry walked over to Randy's doorway but was waved away. Randy needed time to let this digest. Suddenly, his phone rang. It was Brenda and he wasn't sure whether to answer it but finally did on the third ring.

"I think I've found a place," she said.

Randy spent the next hour in his office pondering the situation and wondering if he should let Brenda in on what was happening. On one hand he still felt guilty about not including her in his decision to leave SPU but on the other she had been pretty unapproachable since the loan for the house had fallen through. He finally decided not to decide and walked outside.

He scanned the lot and saw that it was not only missing customers but the salesmen seemed to have disappeared also. He went into the showroom and saw Terry sitting at his desk playing a game of solitaire on his computer.

"Terry, where is everybody?"

"They left."

"Left, what for?"

"We're not stupid Randy, two guys in suits come in with a cop and then Adam leaves chalk white. Nobody wants to be on the ship when it goes under."

"What are you doing here?"

"I've been with Adam for fifteen years. He's been good to me so I figure I at least need to hear him out."

Randy walked into his office and sat down. The dealership phone rang and he picked it up.

"Chatworth Chrysler and Dodge, this is Randy."

"Hi Randy, this is Bob Jackson from the Wasatch Daily. I'm looking for Adam Chatworth."

"Adam's out of the office right now. Can I take your number?"

"Where's he at Randy, his lawyer's?"

"Why do you ask," demanded Randy, immediately regretting asking the question.

"Rumor has it that you folks might have a little legal problem brewing over there. Something about promising one thing, delivering another thing and pocketing the extra cash. I just want to get his side of the story."

"Again, if you give me your number, I'll be sure to give it to him."

Bob knew he had a guy that he might be able to open up so he kept working the pigeon on the other end.

"Aren't you the hockey coach," he asked.

Randy remained silent.

"Come on, I just want to brag to our sports editor that I'm talking to the guy he won all those hockey games for Saint Paul. How do you like Salt Lake?"

"I'm a cars salesman," Randy finally replied.

"Got any comment? You and Adam played together in college, didn't you?"

"I have none to give. I'm just a simple cars salesman. I'll be sure that Adam knows you called."

"Come on Randy, I'm not a bad guy," said the man with ink under his nails. "I'm just a working stiff like you. What's going on there? Help me get Adam's side of the story out."

Randy laughed. They were all the same, wanting to be your best friend until the story was written.

"I'll let him know you called."

Randy hung up the phone and walked out of his office into the empty showroom.

A strange thing happened after the newspaper article came out. People starting stopping by the dealership and the few remaining salesmen found themselves busier than they had been for awhile. Brenda had found a place for the family to live and they moved out of Adam's house two days after the visit from the cop and two men in suits. Though there wasn't a shortage of people on the lot, Randy was still having problems closing the deal. There always seemed to be something wrong, whether it was credit history, wrong make or lack of interest. It didn't help that gas prices were continually rising and were now well over three dollars a gallon. Randy and Terry sat in his office after closing and discussed the current clientele coming in.

"All I'm getting is tire kickers," said Randy.

"I'm getting a lot of those too," agreed Terry. "But there's a few live ones there everyday."

"I need to find one pretty soon. My bank account isn't looking so good."

Terry nodded. His sales had dropped over fifty percent from just six months before and he was thankful that he had put some aside for a rainy day.

The next day Randy finally had someone who was in the mood for more than just kicking a tire. He showed him the latest models and talked about how good the gas mileage of the cars they were looking at were. The customer test drove three cars before finally settling on the one he wanted. Randy took him into his office and they began filling out the necessary paperwork to make the deal work.

They traded prices and finally found one that would give Randy a nice profit, yet also provide the buyer with a sense that he was a hell of a negotiator.

Randy took the offer to the back and was quickly approved. The two of them went to get financing. Randy pulled the credit and it was beautiful. The buyer had a decent score and not a lot of outstanding bills. Most important, there were no non sufficient funds. But there was one red flag.

The buyer was thirty days past due on his current mortgage payment. Randy asked him about it and the buyer explained that he had been out of town for a period of time and had missed the payment. He promised to get it fixed. Everything seemed to be fine and the two men went back to Randy's office while they waited for the approval. In the finance room the officer tried a number of things but the lender continually replied with a denial. At last, it became apparent that the sale was a no go and he called Randy to let him know.

Randy excused himself and walked back to the finance director and demanded to know what had happened. They tried some more tricks but the sale was lost and Randy had no choice but to go back to the buyer and break the bad news. As another lost customer walked out of the showroom Randy slumped in his chair. What did he have to do to finish a damn sale?

In the coming days gas prices continued to soar and went over four dollars a gallon. The salesmen were hopeful this would increase sales in economy cars. Customers continued making their way into the dealership but it seemed as though every deal was torpedoed once the financing came back. Those that did get loans were saddled with high interest rates. Word began to leak out that it was virtually impossible to get financing at Chatworth Chrysler and Dodge and soon the customers were drying up. After a near mutiny by the salesmen Adam finally called his lender. He needed answers now.

"Bob, what's going on?" demanded Adam on the phone with his lender he had worked with for over twenty years. "We've had eight straight sales torpedoed because either the buyer can't get financing or the rates are sky high."

"Adam, expect more of the same. We have some problems here right now," replied the lender.

"What are you talking about?"

"Nobody's loaning anything right now, from housing to business to cars to furniture. It all has to do with housing. Nothing is selling and people are going into foreclosure. We're seeing all sorts of defaults so we have to tighten up."

"But Bob," argued Adam. "You guys have to open the doors a little or we've all got big problems. People want to get out of their SUV's and trucks and into economy cars. Gas is sky high. You stop loaning and we could go under very quickly."

"I can't help you Adam, we have to watch out for ourselves right now. We're hearing some disturbing news about Fannie and Freddie. Keep that to yourself, but we may be seeing a crash pretty soon."

Adam was stunned. He had bills to pay and payroll to meet and now his lender was telling him that the banks weren't going to help. Worse, there could be a crash on the horizon.

"Well, until then I need you to send some help for our customers," stammered Adam. "If you can't we'll have to go to someone else."

"Look Adam, we don't want to lose you, but to be honest you are poisoned right now. You're under investigation and the over/under has you going out of business by the end of the year. You do what you have to do. Believe me, we're not the exception right now, we're the rule."

Adam didn't know what to say so he just hung up. How had this all happened? For the last twenty years he had led a charmed life. Now he was under investigation for fraud, couldn't make the payments on his house and was in grave danger of losing his dealership. What had he done to make this all happen and what was he going to do now?

"Adam, turn on your television," yelled Terry.

Adam did as he was told and his mouth dropped. Fannie and Freddie were on the verge of implosion. It was all over the news. The news report gave the details of the near destruction of the two companies and the only question remaining was whether the government would come in and save them.

Outside his window rain drops had begun to fall.

⚮

Randy pulled into the dealership and saw four police cruisers with lights flashing and he knew that this couldn't be good. He parked his car and ran into the showroom. Adam was sitting at Randy's desk while two police officers hovered over him. His office had been overtaken by men in suits who were putting papers into boxes and hauling them out as another man in a suit was unhooking Adam's computer.

"Adam, what's going on now?" Randy asked, realizing he was no longer surprised by anything.

"I've been served," replied Adam bitterly. "Randy, they're charging me with fraud."

Randy saw that Adam was handcuffed.

"Listen," Adam said calmly. "My lawyer's number is in the top middle drawer of my desk."

"Adam, they're cleaning out your desk."

"Alright, take down this number."

Randy wrote down the number that Adam gave to him as the lead detective came into the office and motioned for the officers to transport the prisoner to headquarters.

"Call and have her meet me at the police station," Adam instructed Randy.

"All right," stammered Randy.

"Randy, run the shop until I get back. Keep everything normal."

"I'll try," a concerned Randy replied.

"You've got to do this for me Randy, please," and he was gone.

Randy watched as Adam was loaded into the car. The media was outside and television was streaming it for its internet sites live. He didn't know what to do, how to act. He looked back into the shop and saw the salesmen congregating together. He turned back to the cars that had lights above them flashing and watched them disappear into the city and then he walked back into the show room.

He looked at the crew that had started a meeting without him. He demanded to know what was going on and Terry filled him in. The mutiny was now on and Randy was charged with quelling it. He tried to speak but was drowned by angry voices of young salesmen. Soon they started heading toward the door.

"I can't believe you guys," Randy shouted to the departing workers. "We have to stick together."

"It's going down Randy," said a young salesman. "If they're charging him, he's done and this place will be closed within a month. Who we going to follow? You?"

"Adam will be back. You know he's innocent."

"We don't know that," another said.

"He's been there for you," shouted an enraged Randy.

"Shut up 'coach'," chimed another sarcastically as they walked through the door.

"Let them go," said Terry.

Randy broke away from Terry and ran to the door. He swung it open and stepped out in a full rage.

"Fine, go you bastards. Good luck! I promise you this, we'll survive and I'll make damn sure he knows who walked out on him."

The men laughed at him and soon they were gone. Terry sat at his desk and toyed with his computer as Randy walked by him and glanced at the computer screen. On it was a job search site.

"Not you too, Terry," he said sadly.

Terry only shrugged.

Adam staggered into the showroom. His tie was in his pocket and his collar button was undone. In his hand was a paper bag that contained a fifth of Jack Daniels. Terry walked up to him and patted him on the back then walked out of the dealership. Adam saw Randy standing at his office door and smiled. He walked to him, gently brushing by him as he entered the office and sat down on the couch. Randy walked to the coffee maker and grabbed two cups. Adam poured one cup half full and handed it to Randy, and then took a swig from the bottle.

"How you holding up, buddy?" asked Randy.

Adam smiled and took another swig. Randy put the cup to his lips and let the liquor enter his mouth. It burned going down.

"They think they have a pretty good case against me, buddy," replied Adam. "It's all bullshit, but…it looks good."

"Well, explain it to me," replied Randy.

Adam talked about the case that had been built. They said that he had changed information on loan papers, giving false information about clients to make sure that the financing would pass. Because he had used a computer it was now a felony because it had gone over wires which made it all the more serious. He was also accused of falsely advertising loan prices that were never meant to be met as well as a number of bait and switch schemes. All told, Adam told him, he was looking at a maximum of 115 years if convicted on all counts.

"That sounds bad, Adam," replied Randy, putting his cup out for more whiskey.

"Ya think?"

Randy kind of snickered. The alcohol was moving into his bloodstream.

"I know," sighed Adam. "But I'm innocent."

Randy nodded.

"I haven't hidden a damn thing. They're making a circumstantial case."

"We're losing crew," said Randy.

"That's to be expected," replied Adam.

"It pisses me off," said Randy fiercely.

"You can't take it personal, buddy. Right now the important thing is to get drunk. Stay here and drink with me. I need you, both now and tomorrow."

Randy nodded and picked up the phone, letting his wife know that he wouldn't be home until late. She started to protest but he just hung up. He didn't want to fight with her right now. She called back but he merely silenced the ring as the men took another sip of the whiskey.

"I don't know," Randy said finally. "There has to be somebody better than me to run the store. Why not Terry? He's been with you forever."

"There's no one else I trust. I'm innocent, stick with me, please."

"All right," Randy finally said after thinking on it with an alcohol filled brain. "But I'm scared."

"Me too, bud, me too

Chapter 7

A COLD WIND

Randy sat quietly in the living room as the light of the barely audible television flickered in the darkness. It was twenty minutes into a new day and all were sleeping except for him. In his hand he had a bowl of cereal and he slowly twirled the spoon in the milk as he wondered how he could have made such a tremendous mistake in judgment.

The war had been won decisively at Saint Paul University. He had been offered everything he had asked yet had turned it down. The joy of watching both the president and athletic director go down was tempered now that he found himself lower than them. He was quickly running out of money and working at a place that could be shut down at any moment. As these thoughts raced through his mind, he stared forlornly at the local news channel that was explaining the downfall of the Adam Chatworth's Chrysler and Dodge dealership.

The previous day had seen Adam make his first appearance in court. The judge determined there was enough evidence to proceed and ordered Adam to stay away from his dealership until the case was adjudicated. The prosecutor had demanded that the dealership be shutdown but Adam's lawyer had countered that a number of employees who would be adversely affected if it were closed. The judge had agreed with the defense and the dealership remained open.

The days moved forward as the season changed from summer to fall. Foot traffic continued to decline steadily at the dealership and Randy spent most of his time in the office talking to Terry as they debated whether to stay or move on. For the time being they decided to stick by Adam but both knew that the day was probably coming when they would have to fend for themselves.

One early fall evening after the shop closed Randy called Adam and updated him on the latest. There were still had four salesmen and four mechanics. Randy had tried to get a couple more salesmen but there had been no interest. Adam stilled stubbornly reasoned that the business could be kept going because people wanted their cars. If he gave the best price, they would come in and buy the product. He asked Randy to come to his house. It was time to schedule a sale, product had to be moved and he had a plan. Randy hoped he was right and it was good to hear a lift in his voice. He locked up the dealership and sped over. As he drove, he tried to believe that this sale would be the answer they were looking for but lingering doubts continued to persist.

The friends planned into the night for the sale. Adam would put what little money he had left into advertisements on television and radio. Prices would be slashed to just above cost. They had to move the cars right now and somehow become a factor in the market again.

The following days saw Randy and Terry preparing for the sale. Banners were put up and commercials were made. The word was out and on the night before the sale Randy and Terry spoke to Adam on the speakerphone making sure that everything had been accounted for. After the meeting the two men at the dealership walked to their cars and headed for their homes to get rest for surely the next day would be a busy and profitable one.

Early the next morning an optimistic Randy headed back to the dealership. On the way he stopped and grabbed a newspaper out of a newsstand. His mouth dropped when he looked at the metro section. It was an expose detailing the alleged crimes committed by Adam, who was now facing trial for frauding the good people of Salt Lake City. A large picture of the dealership was above the story with Adam's picture inset against it. Randy crumpled the paper and angrily threw it in the garbage and he silently fretted over the affect he knew this would have on the sale.

The banners fluttered in the wind and the salesmen stood ready but traffic only drove past the dealership, none stopping in to check out the deals. As the day wound down the salesmen became disgruntled and complained among themselves. Randy watched them as they banded together and finally walked over to join them and as expected they clammed up. When he asked what they were talking about none spoke. Instead, one by one, they walked over to the door and left the dealership. Only Terry and Randy remained in the shop and there were still two hours to go.

"Might as well close it up," Terry said sadly.

"We still have two hours."

"The story killed us," responded Terry.

"We still have two hours," repeated Randy.

"No, you have two hours. I'm going to a bar."

"You be back tomorrow?"

"I dunno."

"I'll see you tomorrow."

"We'll see," and Terry walked out of the showroom.

Randy slumped in a chair in the empty showroom for the next two hours as cars passed by the dealership. He wanted to cry but he was a grown man who had picked this path. Now there was no choice but to follow it and he was afraid. At closing time, he walked to the doors and began locking up when a car pulled up. With newfound hope he quickly unlocked it and walked out to greet the customer.

But it wasn't a customer. It was the reporter from the Wasatch Daily.

"How'd the day go?" ask the beat man.

"Fuck you," responded Randy as he walked back to the showroom.

"Maybe I want to buy a car," the reporter shouted after him.

"Oh well," Randy said sarcastically.

"You don't want to make the media mad; you know that, don't you?"

Randy walked in and locked the door and headed to his office. He turned and watched the newspaperman smile and get back into his car and drive away. He walked into Adam's office and found the bottle of

Jack Daniels that he kept hidden in his bottom drawer, grabbed a cup and poured a stiff one and then dialed Adam's number.

"How'd it go?" asked Adam, devoid of hope.

"Bad."

"No way," he replied sarcastically as he looked at the article for the umpteenth time.

"Adam, we're getting killed in the press. We had maybe three people stop by today and all they did was kick the tires and ask about the case. Then, to top it off, the guy that wrote today's story in the daily came by to gloat."

"Three?"

"That's it," replied Randy.

"After all that advertising?"

"Three."

"This is bad," lamented Adam.

"I would say we lost more salesmen too."

"How many are left."

"Me for sure. Probably Terry, although he's pretty down. Outside of that it's a crapshoot."

"Shit," Adam said in a low voice as if he had just been hit in the stomach.

"Maybe you should close down," said Randy quietly.

"I can't," he responded fiercely. "That would be saying I'm guilty."

"No, it wouldn't."

The men quietly pondered their quandary.

"Randy," Adam finally said. "It's all I've got left. I've given all my savings to the lawyers."

"How bad are your finances?"

"What finances?" laughed Adam sadly.

"Oh Adam, what are we going to do?"

"I need you," pleaded Adam. "Don't leave me. Please, I need you now more than ever."

"Adam…shit…I'll talk to you later."

Randy hung up the phone and rubbed his temples. He had a splitting headache. In another part of town, a man sitting on his couch broke down. His world had caved in and he was quickly losing everything.

❦

Randy drove to the house and saw Brenda at the kitchen sink through the window. He didn't want to go in and tell her that the day had been a bomb but there wasn't any choice. He turned off the engine and walked into the house as Brenda looked up from what she was doing.

"Randy, we have to talk," she said.

He nodded.

"How was the sale, did you make any?"

He nodded no and told her about the day and her face hardened.

"You know I love Adam," she said after he had finished. "But we can't keep going on like this."

"Honey, he needs me," replied Randy.

"We need you too," she replied tersely. "Randy, we're nearly out of money."

"We can't be," he said stunned. "What about our retirements."

"Mine's gone and yours in dwindling quickly."

"How?"

"Randy, we were making $125,000 a year between the two of us. That's about $10,000 a month, minus taxes that makes it around $7,000. For the last three months you've brought home $2,000 after taxes and I don't work anymore. We've had to dip into our retirement accounts just to keep up."

"It'll be all right," he finally responded through this latest shock. "We're just in a slump right now."

"No, it's not," she said sharply. "We're in a recession that isn't showing any signs of getting better. Honey, this isn't working. We have to make a change."

He sat down and put his head on the kitchen table. What was next to hit? How could everything have gone so wrong? What had he done to deserve this? It wasn't right or fair.

"Maybe we could get some unemployment," he said finally.

"We can't Randy. We quit our jobs; we didn't lose them."

"Maybe the rules have changed."

She laughed at him and didn't care if his feeling were hurt. He had made his choice, she thought. He had won the war and thrown the spoils away.

"Come back to reality, Randy," she said in a sarcastic tone.

"You'll see," he responded angrily.

"Fine, go…I hope I'm wrong," she replied as she got up from the table and walked to the bedroom. She was tired to the bone from worry and trying to figure out where the man she had married had gone. This imposter was nothing more than a child who was bound and determined to bring her and the kids into the abyss he had made for himself. She did not want to be around him right now so she closed the door and locked it. She lay down and stared at the ceiling and felt tears begin to form.

No damnit, she said to herself. He's not going to make me cry tonight.

"You'll see," he said quietly as he sat at the table.

The next day he walked out of the house without speaking to Brenda and drove straight to the benefits office. He knew there had to be a way to get something. He had been a faithful taxpayer his whole adult life and surely now, when he was down, the government would give him some aid to get back on his feet.

He confidently marched into the office and was shocked to see the length of the line of people. He had always viewed these folks as deadbeats but as he waited in the line his feelings began to change. His pride left him and, in its place, only a feeling of hopelessness. He waited more than an hour until he was summoned to the desk of Daisy McGregor according to the name plate she had placed on it. He sat down and told her his plight but she had no response until he had finished.

"I'm sorry," she said. "You're not eligible for anything. You quit your job. These benefits are only for people who have lost their jobs."

He tried to argue but it was no use. Brenda had been right all along and now he tried to gather what was left of his dignity as he stood.

"Next," shouted Daisy.

He walked away from the desk. It had been a cold and embarrassing experience. He felt like he was nothing. He was no longer a championship coach or a great salesman. He was simply another loser looking for a handout and the government had shot him down. Brenda had warned him but he had known all. Well, turns out that he was really just another down on his luck deadbeat. He walked to the car and climbed in and drove to the house.

"You were right," he said quietly to his wife as he walked into the kitchen.

"I know," she said without looking up. "I'm sorry you had to go through that."

"God, what have I done?" he said, slumping down in a corner and putting his head in his hands.

"We'll get through it," she said quietly.

"Oh God, what have I done?" he repeated and he lightly pounded on his head. "It was pride. I just wanted to see his face when I left."

She finally looked up. He looked so small on the floor, so broken. All his life he had come out on top but for the first time he was in a tailspin and he didn't know what to do. She walked over to him and sat beside him, pulling his head over to her.

"Honey," she said soothingly. "It doesn't matter anymore. We just need to figure out what we're going to do now."

In the next room Sean and Tisha strained to hear their parents. They had sensed for a while that something was wrong. Sean stood up and walked into the kitchen, determined to find out what was happening.

"Mom, dad, are we broke?" he asked apprehensively.

"No honey," Brenda lied. "We're fine. Don't worry about it. Everything is all right."

"Then what were you talking about?" he asked.

"It's all right son," said Randy unconvincingly. "We're just planning. Times are a little tough right now, but we're fine. We just want to make sure we stay that way."

Sean nodded but he did not believe his parents.

He turned and walked to his room. Tish watched her brother and looked back toward the kitchen. Her brother seemed afraid and that frightened her. She looked toward the kitchen and then went to her room and crawled under her bed. Something was wrong.

"Shit," said Randy quietly as he looked at his wife.

"Don't swear," she admonished him.

"That was close."

"Too close. Randy, we have to figure something out."

They had tried to put their best face on but Randy knew that the secret was out. Sean didn't believe them and why should he? They were living in a rental and cutting back on everything. The kids weren't stupid. It had been dumb of him to think they wouldn't know. He had only been kidding himself.

They lay in bed and talked softly late that night. Their world was spinning out of control and they were desperate to regain control. Something had to change and quickly.

"Honey, I'm going to put out resumes," she told him.

"I guess it's time," he agreed. "I'm sorry honey. I really hoped that it wouldn't come to this."

"I want to work," she lied.

"Thanks," he whispered.

"Honey," she said to him.

"Yes?"

"I know that Adam is your best friend, but you can't save him."

"I can help him though," he said resolutely.

"No, you can't," she replied. "It's time for you to watch out for us. We need you to bring in real income."

"I will honey, I promise."

"You need to be realistic Randy. It's time to look for something else."

He was silent.

"Randy?"

Still, he did not speak. She turned away from him and felt her anger rising. His pride had once been his strength, but now it was a fault.

"All right," he finally said softly.

She turned back toward him but this time he turned away. She put her hand on his shoulder but he did not respond. Finally, she turned back around as he stared into the darkness.

⁂

The day had been uneventful. A few customers had come by but more out of curiosity than interest in buying anything. The good news was that Terry had shown up to work and had actually closed a deal and three cars had come in for tune-ups, but more days like this would spell doom for the dealership.

Randy drove to Adam's house after closing shop and pulled into the driveway. Adam was out on his front porch nursing a beer and saluted his friend as he got out of the car and walked toward him. He offered a beer but Randy shook him off.

"Adam, I'm broke," said Randy.

"How bad?"

"Bad. Brenda's retirement, savings, everything. It's all gone. I still have a little in my retirement, but it will be gone after this month."

"I'm sorry," said Adam.

"No one's coming into the shop. It's over."

"Not yet, it's not."

"Adam," Randy said intently. "I've got to find something else."

"I need you," pleaded Adam. "You're all I've got. I promise you that it will work out, but I need you to keep us going."

Randy let out a sigh. He was tired of this. What could Adam be thinking? Terry was the man to keep things going. He had only sold one car since moving while Terry had been moving them for years.

"Adam..."

"Please Randy, you're all I've got. I'm begging you. I promise you I'm innocent. Please."

Randy looked at his friend. He had never seen him in such a desperate plight. This man had survived much and thrived but now everything was being taken away from him. Randy knew Adam was innocent and it was obvious he needed his help. He sighed and slumped in his chair.

"Damn," he said finally. "Brenda's going to kill me."

Brenda had perfected her resume and was sending them to local firms and companies. Most of the jobs she was highly qualified for and some even over-qualified. She followed up with phone calls to the human resources departments and waited for the phone to ring to set up interviews that she knew would be coming.

But the phone never rang. She continued poring over want ads and jobs on the internet, sending resume after resume. But the phone never rang.

Bills piled up and soon the last of Randy's retirement was gone. She kept tabs on the money but it was quickly slipping away. She prayed for Randy to make some sales but every day he came home empty. On the night before rent was due, they sat in the family office and tried to figure out how to turn $400 into the $1,200 due for rent. Finally, Randy knew that he had no choice but to make a call he abhorred.

"Dad," he said over the phone. "I need help…"

Randy explained their situation to his dad and mom. As he told them he felt ashamed and weak. He was groveling and he knew it. He hated himself as he explained the brilliant decisions that had led him to this place.

"Son," his father said softly. "You need to get out. There are other things you can do. You can get back into coaching. That's where you belong. I still don't understand why you left it. If not coaching, something, but the car business is dying. I see they're all going bankrupt. I watched the hearings this morning."

"I don't know dad, Adam needs me."

"Son, it's not working out. Your first priority has got to be your family. You have to take care of them, not your friend."

"I know."

"I'll help you out, but I want you to consider it, OK?"

"OK," he replied. "Thanks dad."

"I love you son."

"Me too," replied the son.

He hung up the phone and wiped his eyes.

Brenda continued calling potential employers but no one was interested in her qualifications. She was over qualified for most jobs now and she knew that it was killing her chances. Companies did not want to hire these types of prospects for it would be only a matter of time before they would be looking for a better paying job. They wanted someone long term and she didn't fit that bill.

After another disappointing phone call, Tisha walked into the family office and handed her mother a list. Brenda looked at the childish writing and smiled. The list was long and well thought out.

"Momma,"

"Yes dear," replied Brenda.

"I made my Christmas list for you."

"Have you been good this year?"

"Very good," responded the child.

"It's quite a long list."

Brenda's heart was breaking for she did not know how they would be able to buy presents this year.

"I know," she responded. "I don't expect to get everything. You can use it for my birthday too."

Brenda smiled. "That's very nice of you honey."

"Thank you," she responded with a smile.

"All right," said Brenda as she carefully put the list on the edge of the desk. "Mommy needs to finish some things up."

"Mommy?"

"Yes."

"I also mailed it to Santa."

"I thought you didn't believe in Santa anymore."

"Just in case," the child responded.

"OK sweetie," the mother replied. "Let me finish this now."

"OK. I love you mommy."

"I love you too," she said as she watched her child walk out of the office.

When the child had left the room Brenda picked up the phone and began dialing the number of yet another firm she had sent her resume to. The phone began to ring on the other end and soon was answered by an automated answering service. As the voice on the other end gave the caller directions Brenda stared at the list her daughter had just given her.

She felt her chin begin to tremble and she hung the phone up. She quietly rose and walked to the door of the office and softly closed it and locked it. She sat down and leaned against the door as tears began to drop. She felt powerless, unable to move and soon her breathing increased as she struggled to muffle the sobs that were now freely flowing out of her.

She was completely broken. No one in the world wanted her right now and because of that her children were going to suffer. She had failed them. Randy had failed them. They were awful parents and she was devastated that the children had to pay for the mistakes of those who should know better. It was their job as parents to protect and provide but now they were failing and it was nearly killing her. Her cries were becoming louder as she continued to struggle to muffle them. She mustn't let the children know. She had to put on the façade of strength but she knew she was weak. She had failed them.

Behind the door Sean listened to his mother. He hated his father at this moment more than anything. He was responsible for this. He wanted to break the door down and hug his mom but he was afraid and the fear froze him. He quietly backed away from the door and went outside. He didn't know what to do so he began to run.

As he ran the hate for his father continued to grow with each step.

Chapter 8

SNOW FLURRIES

Randy sat in his car at the dealership, his eyes staring at the first flakes of the winter season but his mind elsewhere. This just wasn't working. His accumulating debt continued mounting uncontrollably. He and Brenda had worked for over twenty years and now they had almost nothing to show for it. Her retirement was gone, his nearly, and their savings had long since disappeared.

How could he have let this happened? The call to his father had been brutal. Never in his worst nightmare could he imagine having to call his dad for money. He knew the old man was right. It was time to watch out for his family, but Adam felt like family and right now he had nobody. Could he really walk away knowing that Adam would stand by him if the roles were reversed?

He started the car and realized he was cold and wondered how long he'd been there. Brenda and the kids had to come first, he knew, as he turned onto the roadway and drove toward Adam's house. It was time to have the talk he had been dreading. He stared at the road ahead of him that was slowly turning white from the snow falling on it and soon Adam's house appeared in the distant. He felt the now familiar knot in his stomach tighten.

He pulled into the sullen driveway and saw the flicker of the television through the darkness of the window. He stepped out of his car and trudged through the new snow to the front door and rang the bell. After a moment Adam opened the door, gave a sad grin at seeing his friend but it quickly disappeared.

"Adam, it's over," Randy said.

Adam walked back to his chair in front of his television.

"I had to call my dad and ask for money for rent. For rent!"

Adam stared at the screen.

"I'm 48 years old and I'm asking my parents for money. I'm done!"

Adam looked up and motioned for Randy to sit. Randy reluctantly walked into the room and plunked down on the couch, rubbing the bridge of his nose.

"Slow down Randy," Adam finally said.

"Adam, I would love to help you but I can't anymore," replied Randy with remorse. "I have to watch out for my family."

Adam laughed slightly without smiling. He understood his friend's plight but also knew things that Randy didn't. In the business world his friend was a newborn and did not yet have a grasp of the ever-changing marketplace.

"So what's your plan," he asked Randy. "Coaching? It's the middle of the season right now. We're still open which means that every day we have a chance to make some money. Every day we have a chance to sale some cars."

"Right," replied Randy sarcastically. "We've done so well lately. I have to find something, anything."

"Who do you think is hiring right now?" asked Adam.

"Somebody has to be," murmured Randy.

"Randy, I need you. I've told you that and I'll continue to tell you. Without you I'm sunk. If I'm making money I can help, but right now I need you so that I can help you in the future."

"C'mon Adam. We're done. Nobody's come by. Nothing is going on. We're done, let's just move on."

"Look, I got nowhere else to go. I don't know why this happened, only that it did," replied Adam. "You are the only one I can trust."

"I don't care," replied Randy. "I really don't. I can't take it anymore."

The two men were silent but Adam's eyes hardened. He couldn't lose Randy, not now.

"Randy," he said quietly. "You called me, remember?"

"Don't throw that at me," hissed Randy.

"Damn right I will," replied Adam, his voice rising. "I didn't ask for all this to happen but it did. When you asked for help, I was there. When you needed a donation for the program I was there. When you asked for a job, I was there. Now I need you and you give me a sorry ass 'I can't take it anymore' story."

"That's bullshit Adam. Don't try to guilt me. You enticed me," roared Randy.

"Kiss my ass, friend," replied Adam.

"$175,000 a year, remember that? Since I've joined you, I've made $10,000 in five months. Nine thousand of it was in the first three months with the salary. You could have told me about the credit problems, the investigation, but no…don't you think that might have played a part in my decision making?"

Right," said Adam, standing up and walking toward Randy. "Before you joined me it was John Bart this and John Bart that…I can't take it anymore you said…. hmm, I knew I had heard that before."

Randy stood up as the men glared at each other.

"You wanted out and I was your opening," growled Adam. "I'm sorry things haven't worked out as you planned! Welcome to real life where business is a risk! You can do everything right and still lose you stupid bastard!"

They glared, imaginary daggers shooting through the other. Finally, Randy looked away and sat back down but Adam continued to stare hard at his friend.

"How's the search going anyway?" asked Adam, already knowing the answer.

"There's some interest," lied Randy.

"Good, where at?"

"All right, all right, there's no interest yet."

"How about Brenda?" ask Adam more softly.

"Same," replied Randy.

"If we're open, we have a chance," Adam said firmly.

"Not much of one," retorted Randy, but he was now softening and Adam knew it.

"I'll take anything right now. Randy, you know I'm innocent. I need you, please…"

Randy stared at the television screen. He wanted to walk away but he couldn't. He knew he couldn't turn his back on his friend and he realized that it would probably cost him dearly.

"My lawyer tells me things are happening," Adam said, breaking the silence. "I don't know if that's good or bad, but I have to believe good because I'm innocent. Please keep the shop open, then, whatever the outcome you can do what you want after."

Randy sat silently deep in thought. He still wanted to walk out but he knew he couldn't turn his friend down. He was all he had and he knew he had to hang in there with him. Truth was he had nowhere else to go. He was hitched.

"Shit, all right. But I'm going to keep looking," he said finally to Adam.

"Fair enough, thanks buddy," replied Adam with a relieved voice.

He looked at his friend as he rose from the couch. Adam looked so small, so vulnerable. He had to be there for him but he shuddered at the consequences he knew were coming.

"I'll talk to you tomorrow," he said quietly as he made his to the entryway.

Adam nodded and hoped it was so.

Two salesmen walked around the dealership lot waiting for someone, anyone to drive in. Inside the showroom Randy stood at the large plate glass window and stared toward the street as cars zoomed back and forth. It had been two weeks since he had agreed to give it another try and still, he was searching for a sale. The two remaining salesmen and Terry had managed to make some sales which produced enough income to keep them coming back and Adam to pay enough bills to keep the dealership doors open, but there was nothing else.

Adam was virtually broke, all of his money going directly to the dealership to keep it alive. Bills and franchise fees were coming due and he realized that he was going to be short. On top of this his lawyer fees were piling up and it had become apparent to him that something was going to have to go.

Adam rechecked his math for the seventh time and still the numbers came out the same. He was significantly short for next month's bills which were already behind and loans which kept the business going were coming due. He had to have cash and it had to be fast. He wondered what he could do, where he could go but no answers came to him. He walked into his living room and slumped down on his couch.

He had not made any payments on his house for six months now and it was only a matter of time before the bank foreclosed on him. He could do a short sale but houses, like cars, weren't moving. But one thing was…furniture.

He walked around the house and took inventory of what he had. He had beautiful antiques and expensive furniture. He had artwork on the walls and a marble bar in the basement. He quickly figured how much he could charge for everything and if the numbers would cover the bills coming up. He walked to his computer and looked up prices and put a price on each piece of article he had. He no longer saw furniture and art in his house, he saw assets. Assets that could be sold quickly to produce the capital he needed to last at least three more months.

He smiled and blocked out the pain of losing the things he had spent his business life collecting. He had been poor growing up but had lived the American dream. He had used his skills acquired at a youthful age to procure a scholarship to college. He had parlayed his education into a business degree. Taking that degree, he had revamped a struggling dealership where he had been hired out of college and turned it into the top sales shop in the region. He then climbed the ladder to larger markets until he had put enough away to start his own shop.

Adam had taken his dealership from nothing to the most successful in the western United States and his dreams of having money had been reached. Now, twenty years after starting this odyssey, everything he had built up was nearly gone, but he still had a trick or two left to play. Survival was now the game and though he had few cards and fewer chips he knew that he was in until the hand played out.

He advertised on Craigslist and soon his phone was ringing and sales were being made. He hated to see his property walking out the door in the hands of a new owner but he knew if he survived, he could always replace what he was now losing. The one thing he couldn't lose no matter what happened was the dealership and he kept remembering this as his house became more and more bare.

Adam knew the day was coming but it still sent a wave of shock and trepidation through him when he saw it. He pulled into his driveway after returning from his lawyer's office and there it was, attached to his house with duct tape. He got out of his car and walked over to it. It was in a clear plastic bag presumably to protect against the weather. He pulled it off the wall and reached into the bag. On the front of the envelope was CERTIFIED MAIL stamped in large red letters.

Adam felt self-conscious and looked around to see if anyone was looking. He knew what the contents inside would say. No one was looking as he walked through his front door into his now bare house that was devoid of pictures and most of his furniture. He went to the kitchen bar which now served as his dinner table and fingered the envelope. At last, he ripped it open and pulled out the papers. They were official looking and the words were cold, to the point. He was out. In 60 days, this would no longer be his house but the bank's and soon after it would be auctioned at a fraction of its worth.

That night he sat on a folding chair in his den. His house was gone. He was still in it but it was gone. At least I get two months of free rent, he mused to himself. But it did not comfort him. He knew it was just an object but it signified so much to him. On the day he had bought it he felt that he had arrived. He loved the house not because of the structure but because of how it made him feel. Now it signified loss. It was now the symbol of the fall he had taken. It hurt and he wept.

The cell phone sitting on the desk rang early the next morning at the dealership. Randy was the only one there as he prepared the coffee. He jogged back to his desk hoping against hope it might be a customer. He picked it up and saw Adam's name across the screen and flipped it open.

"I hear your house is pretty bare right now," Randy said.

"Yeah. Still got a bed and TV though so I guess it isn't all bad."

"Also read in the paper you got a certified letter," responded Randy.

"Yeah, I get to live rent free for a couple of months anyway. How's the shop?"

"Lonely. I swear, how the hell do you keep finding silver linings?"

Adam laughed softly.

"Just a glass half full kind of guy, I guess. Look, I've raised enough capital to pay bills for the next two months but we still need to cut back," he replied.

"Cut back what? There's nothing left to cut back," replied Randy.

"Yeah, there's still some overhead in the form of salaries. All the mechanics have got to go except for George."

"You can't do that. What about our guarantees."

"George can handle it."

"Adam…"

"Damnit Randy, I don't have a choice."

"This is bullshit," replied Randy.

"Yes, it is, but I still don't have a choice."

"I'm not going to do it. It's your shop, you do it."

"I can't," responded Adam. "Judge won't let me go there, remember?"

"All right," sighed Randy. "But you owe me."

"Get in line," chuckled Adam.

Randy saw George come in but he couldn't get himself to go talk to him. Soon his three assistants arrived and they sat in the empty garage area chatting. Randy finally found some courage and called for George to come to his office. The chief mechanic came in and Randy broke the news. George started to protest and Randy told him it would do no good but that they would have to figure out a way to continue to move forward.

George paced around the office and outside Terry and the two remaining salesmen watched and wondered. George began spewing invectives against Adam and Randy let him vent, hoping that soon it would end and the two of them would go out and take care of the awful business at hand. Instead, George quit. He was done and would be taking a job that was being offered by a rival dealership. Randy tried to dissuade him but to no avail. George marched out of the office muttering under his breath and soon the mechanics were driving away from the dealership.

Terry asked what had just happened. Randy recounted his morning conversation with Adam as Terry listened. Once he had finished Terry told Randy to call Adam and let him know that he was leaving too. Randy started to protest but Terry walked away from him and motioned for the two salesmen to follow him. The men put their coats on as Randy tried vainly to get Terry to change his mind.

At the door Terry turned and patted Randy on the shoulder then walked out into the cold morning and was gone. Randy stared in disbelief. He was all there was left. He, the one who couldn't sell anything was Adam's last remaining hope and he was there only because he couldn't get anything else. What was he going to do? He could feel all hope slipping away.

Suddenly the phone rang.

"Hi Randy," said the voice. "Bob Jackson from the Wasatch Daily, miss coaching?"

"No comment," growled Randy.

"Yeah, I can imagine," replied the reporter. "Anyway, I hear you guys are closing ship. That true?"

"Who's your source?" asked Randy.

"Randy, a good reporter never reveals his source."

"Better get a new one. We're still kicking. We expect Adam to get exonerated. I gotta go. I have another customer."

Randy hung up the phone. They would survive he swore to himself. This bastard reporter had given him the kick in the ass he needed. He phoned Adam. It was time to get serious.

Brenda was tired of rejection. She could feel herself reaching a breaking point and she wondered how close she was to the bottom. She was tired of the cold voices of human resources departments that would not give her any answers. She was really tired of the rejection letters that arrived in the mail informing her that she wasn't what they were looking for. She needed a warm voice, someone who would offer some hope. She went to her purse and found a business card for Sherry Jackson. Sherry had been her best friend at her previous firm. She punched the numbers on her keypad of her phone and heard ringing. Soon Sherry's familiar voice answered.

Sherry was excited to hear from her and they happily chatted for a few minutes about their kids and the latest office gossip. Finally, Brenda told her about her struggles. She confided to Sherry about her anger at Randy, the frustration of not being able to find a job, the fear of running out of money.

Sherry listened, her heart was breaking for her friend and she wished she were there to hug her. Brenda apologized for ranting but told her that she had no one else to talk to and Sherry understood.

"You just have to have faith that everything will work out," said Sherry.

"I try," replied Brenda. "But every month we're getting deeper and deeper in debt. Adam has a strange hold over Randy. I've told Randy he has to get something else, but he keeps telling me its going to work out. I just don't know what to do."

"Something will come up," said Sherry. "You just have to push through this. Remember the old saying…this too shall pass."

It was good to finally unload on someone and now that it was at the surface Brenda felt a lump in her throat and her eyes began to water. She tried to stifle it but then decided to let it go. She lied down on the floor and let the sobs grow into a painful wail.

In the adjoining room Tisha heard her mother and ran to her. Seeing her cry like that was terrifying and she began whimpering in fear and anxiety. Brenda made no attempt to stop. The tears had control of her. All the tension was coming out and she had lost control. Tisha couldn't take watching her mother like this and ran to her room. She didn't know how but she knew that her mother was crying because of something her daddy had done.

She found her crayons and grabbed some drawing paper. In red lettering she scribbled in large letters I HATE DADDY FOR MAKING MOMMY AND ME CRY. Her tears rolled down her cheeks as she grabbed another sheet and drew a picture of the family. She, Sean and Brenda had sad faces, but Randy's had an evil smile on it. She made teardrops falling out of her and Brenda's eyes. Still, the picture was not complete. She grabbed another crayon, this one fire orange, and put a big X over the picture of her father. She hated him but she didn't know why.

She only knew that he was making everybody cry.

Randy walked up the driveway with the mail in his hand. He looked at the envelopes and saw four bills. The fifth envelope interested him. It was from his retirement account and he opened it. Suddenly, he stopped in his tracks. The balance was zero. The latest swoon in the stock market had taken what little was left. He had nothing. He had been relying on using it to pay rent, but that was now out.

Wait, he thought, maybe it had already been deposited into the bank account. He turned his key and opened the front door. Nobody was home right now. Brenda must be at the store with Tish and Sean was probably at practice he figured. He walked into the office, now sure that he would find the remainder of his retirement already in the bank. He went to his bank's website and signed in and waited it for it to come to his account.

He sat horrified. It couldn't be. He was destitute. He had nothing left. Twenty years of coaching, watching his finances, keeping tabs of everything and seeing it build up had been lost in only five months.

He looked again, making sure he was truly seeing what he knew he saw. He had $1.42 left in savings and $17.26 in checking. He picked up his phone and called Brenda. If she was shopping, he had to stop her. She picked up at last.

"Where are you," he asked.

"The store," she replied.

"Brenda, don't buy anything. We have to talk."

"What's wrong," she implored alarmed.

"We only have seventeen dollars in checking and a buck fifty in savings!"

"But your retirement, what about that?"

"It's gone. It's zeroed out."

"Oh my god," she said feeling faint.

He hung up. He could feel outrage building inside of him. What had she done, he wondered? She must have wasted all the money spending it on something they didn't need. Now rent was coming due again, bills were continuing to pile up and they had roughly nineteen dollars to their name.

With Christmas coming he had to figure out a way to tell the kids that they would be without a tree or presents. There would be no turkey dinner, no gifts from Santa, nothing! In fact, he suddenly realized to his horror, there may not be a roof over their heads. Where was he going to come up with money for rent? He could call his dad again but he knew that his parents were living on a fixed income and it was doubtful they would have the extra money. What were they going to do?

He looked at the family phone and saw there were seven messages. He pushed play and heard a creditor asking for his money. He erased it and then listened to another, and then another, and then another. Had she not paid anything he wondered? He knew their finances were bad but he never dreamed that they would sink to this level.

He heard the car pull into the driveway and walked to the door, waiting for his wife to come through. It had to be her fault. She had better have some answers. Brenda walked in and Tisha followed close behind, whining that they hadn't bought anything at the store.

"Go to your room," Randy said harshly to his daughter. "I have to talk to your mom."

Tish looked apprehensively at her mother who nodded reassuringly. Tish quietly walked by her dad and made her way to the bedroom and crawled under her bed.

"What have you done!" he demanded.

"What are you talking about," she retorted.

"The money, what have you spent it all on. I know its not bills, there's seven messages from creditors on the phone. Where the fuck has it all gone?"

"Don't talk to me like that. I'm not one of your hockey players. It's gone to paying rent and electricity and internet and food and car insurance and our house payment in Saint Paul, you know, the one that hasn't sold yet!"

"Jeez Brenda…" he stammered.

"Remember when you were going to make all that money selling cars? Well Randy, you haven't sold any. You haven't brought any money home. Did you think retirement was going to last forever? Our retirement was built upon stocks and bonds. I don't know if you've noticed but the stock market has gone down 5,000 points since September."

"I know you've wasted it on something! Tell me what you've spent it on, tell me now damn it! It couldn't have just disappeared."

"I told you! God Randy, come into reality please. If you don't bring anything home, which you haven't since you got here and I don't have a job, how long did you think we were going to last. You shouldn't have quit coaching. You shouldn't have let your pride get in the way…"

"Go to hell," he huffed as he grabbed his coat.

"Where are you going?" she demanded.

"I'll be back!" he snorted as he slammed the door behind him.

He walked to his car and jumped in. The engine roared and the tires spun in the compacted snow as he backed out of the driveway. He jammed it into drive and felt the back start to slide but he didn't care. He corrected and the car straightened out.

He didn't know where he was going and didn't care. Right now, his world was crumbling and this seemed to be the only escape. He couldn't be in the house right now. He wanted to hit her. Belt her across her smart mouth and these thoughts scared him. She had always been the love of his life but right now he hated her. He hated her because what she said he knew was true. He had let his family down but it was her fault. She should have stopped him before he had gone through with his plan. She should have put her foot down. He would have listened to her, but no, she had let him screw up and now they were in peril.

He had nothing to do and nowhere to go. He had no prospects and now he was singlehandedly running a dying dealership. What had he done? Why hadn't she stopped him? God, he hated her right now.

Under her bed Tish prayed that her dad wouldn't come back.

Chapter 9

HEAVY SNOWFALL

"I'm sorry honey, I know you're not wasting money."

He stood in the dimly lit bedroom, his wife's back to him. He still had his coat on and snowflakes were stubbornly clinging to his collar.

"I'm just scared I guess," he said sorrowfully.

She turned and faced him and he could see that she had been crying. Her cheeks were stained and her eyes puffy but she still gave a sense of strength and dignity through her vulnerability. She slowly rose and walked to him and they embraced and a tear stole from his eye. She saw it slowly rolling down his face and tenderly washed it away.

"I know babe," she said softly. "It'll be all right. We'll figure something out."

He sat down on the bed, still in his coat which was now wet about the collar. She knelt down in front of him and he held both of her hands, yet he was too ashamed to look her in the eyes.

"What are we going to do?"

"You could sale some cars," she said softly and they both laughed.

"Yeah, that could work."

He pulled her upon him and lay back in the bed. They were both exhausted from the stress and their fight and soon fell asleep, she atop of him, he still in his coat.

Light broke into the room and he began to stir. She had since crawled under the covers and he sat up and looked at her. The light from the early morning sky gave the room an eerie feel as though in a fog. He quietly took off the still damp coat and walked out of the room and into the kitchen.

It was a new day but his financial problems were still waiting for him as he quietly filled the coffee maker with water. He pulled the can of Folgers out of the cupboard and put three heaping spoonfuls into the machine and switched it on. The darkened water began to drip into the carafe and he stared at it, his mind blank but no longer sleepy.

He poured himself a cup and sat down at the kitchen table as she walked in. He smiled at her but it had a trace of sadness to it and she returned it as she filled a cup with the fresh brew and pulled the milk out of the refrigerator. She tipped the carton and the liquid in the cup turned from black to a chocolate brown. She walked to the table and sat next to him and they quietly sipped.

They began talking quietly about the financial pitfall they were now in. Randy told her that Adam had sold most of his furniture on Craigslist and that he had used the money to pay the bills of the dealership. She nodded and then looked at him, her eyes alive.

"Why don't we do the same?"

Randy thought about it and shrugged.

"Do we really have anything of value?" he asked.

"Does it matter?" she replied.

"All right," he said finally. "You figure out what we should sale and how much to charge. I'll take pictures of it tonight and we'll put it on tomorrow."

She nodded and giggled.

"What's so funny," he asked.

"So garage sales have come to this, on the internet."

He laughed quietly but both were trying to mask the pain of his latest failure. He stood up and went to the bathroom and showered. After drying and getting dressed he kissed Brenda and left for the dealership. She got the kids up for school, thankful they wouldn't be there for what she had to do.

The next day calls came fast and furious. The furniture and office equipment sold quickly which amazed them and soon they had $3000.00 in cash. The crisis had been averted and they still had the television and computer but the living quarters had become bare. They went together to the bank and put the money into their checking account and drove to the rental company and paid their rent early.

"Let's get the kids some Christmas gifts," Brenda suggested.

Randy nodded and smiled but first he turned into the grocery store parking lot and drove to the trees that were for sale.

"We'll need something to put them under," he said and she smiled.

After picking out a decent tree for only $35.00 they drove to the nearest mall and began shopping. The bustle of the crowd and the colors of the decorations along with the relief that they had survived another month lifted their spirits as they shopped for the gifts that they hoped would bring smiles to Sean and Tish.

"This was a nice," she said to him lovingly as they completed their shopping.

"Yes, it was," he agreed. "You know, it doesn't have to end just yet."

She looked at him with a mischievous grin as he tried to look innocent.

"Really, and what exactly do you have in mind?"

"Well…we have time for a little date."

"Sounds heavenly," she replied. "What do you want to do?"

"Let's go get a dessert," he suggested.

"But my figure," she protested jokingly.

"I'll take the chance," he responded with a sly smile as he pulled her to him.

They walked to a darkened restaurant and asked for a corner booth. The hostess led them to their seats and they ordered a piece of chocolate cake and two decaffeinated coffee mochas. They talked quietly, enjoying each other's company like old times while conversing on Christmas' past and their hopes for the future. For a while they were back to where they had come from, no longer dealing with their desperate financial struggle and holding their family together. For a while it was no longer about

Adam's struggles and lack of sales at the dealership or the hopelessness of the job searches. For a short time, things seemed normal.

But reality found a way of working its way back into the conversation. He told her of an article he had read of a murder-suicide in California where a recently laid off man had murdered his wife and three kids. Though they wondered how anyone could do such a thing to ones they love, they now understood how the desperateness of the times could lead to this and though unspoken, both prayed that at some point they did not become that story.

Though they did not say it out loud they knew that their world was imploding.

Sean stood at the window, seething. He watched the headlights of the cars going by the house and as each passed by, he felt his anger grow. He didn't know his parents anymore, didn't trust them. All of his life he had felt safe but the last seven months had been a free fall brought on by his father and sanctioned by his mother. Why had they done this, he wondered angrily? They had always been very practical people, not ones to take chances. His father had always told him that there were never any guarantees but preparation and careful consideration improved odds of success. So why had he jumped into this car selling thing without properly preparing? Hadn't life been good at Saint Paul?

Now he was standing in an empty living room. The furniture was gone. He went into the office and though the computer remained it was on the floor because the desk and chair were gone. Books were piled up against the wall because the bookshelf that had once housed them was gone. The only things that remained intact were the bedrooms and he wondered how long that was going to last. They had gone mad and they had lied to him. Never lie, he had been told, but apparently that didn't apply to them.

Finally, he saw the car headlights pull into the driveway and he ran to the door, waiting to ambush them and find out the truth once and for all. As his dad had told him on the occasions he was in trouble, the games were over and it was time to pay the piper. He just never dreamed that he would be the piper.

"Where's all the furniture?" he demanded as they walk through the door with the bags of presents they had bought earlier.

"Watch your tone, son," his father scolded him.

Sean didn't care. His anger had built up to overtake his fear of his father. He wanted answers and he wanted them now.

"Where is it?" he demanded. "We're broke, aren't we?"

Neither Randy nor Brenda responded as they stared at their son dumbfounded.

"Thanks for ruining my life," spat out Sean.

Brenda sat the bags down and walked toward her son but he backed away. He didn't want to lose this anger for in a strange way it felt good. He didn't want to forgive them right now. He knew that eventually he would but it would have to wait.

"Sean, honey, please calm down. You're overreacting," she said compassionately with a hint of defense. "Things are tighter right now but we're all right."

"You're lying," he growled.

"Son, calm down," Randy responded sharply. "Our furniture is getting old so your mother and I decided to sell it and get some new ones. That's where your mother and I were, as well as doing some Christmas shopping as you can see. If we were broke, would we be bringing in bags from the mall?"

Sean couldn't argue that but still he couldn't get himself to believe his dad. In his gut he knew that he was being lied to. He wouldn't let go of the anger and it provided him with courage to continue.

"I don't believe you! I'm not stupid you know. We're going to be homeless, aren't we? Just be honest with me."

"Son," stammered Randy and Brenda looked at her husband with concern.

"I hate you," yelled the boy. "Why did we ever move? I hate you!"

Sean turned and stormed out of his room and slammed his bedroom door behind him before collapsing on the bed. His rage felt good but at the same time he felt completely drained. They were lying to him, he was sure. Soon they would be out on the streets and it was his father's fault. He no longer held any feeling for him.

"Well, that went well," Randy sighed.

"He's right Randy," said Brenda. "Maybe we should be honest with them."

"Honey, let's let them be kids. We'll figure something out to keep getting through. I just know our luck is going to turn around," he said without much conviction.

"I hope so," she said in a monotone voice.

"Trust me," he said but he knew she didn't.

In her room Tisha sat in her closet and drew another picture. She drew a picture of a man with an evil smile and scary eyes. On top of the picture, she wrote D-A-D over it. She carefully colored it and then looked at what she had made. She could feel her eyes watering and tears trickled down her cheeks. She looked at the picture more deeply and then reached for a pencil. Suddenly she jammed the pencil down on the face that she had just drawn. She did it again and again, feeling the anger but not knowing why she felt this way. She jammed the pencil through the paper one more time than carefully put it on top of the other pictures she had drawn.

One picture was of her mother, another of her brother. The third picture was of her. Each of them had sad faces and a tear coming out of their eye. She wiped her face and quietly walked to her bed, crawling under the covers and closing her eyes when she heard footsteps coming toward her room. She wanted them to think she was asleep so she didn't stir when the mother bent down and kissed her on the forehead.

The bedroom light went off but her mind remained awake and frightened.

❧

Randy sat at the stoplight, tired from another day of no sales. He hated being at the dealership now that all the employees had left. He missed his conversations with Terry and his phone calls with Adam were becoming more and more antagonistic. But still, they were open for another month and that meant there was still hope, however dim.

The light turned to green and Randy was glad to be away from the shop as he continued toward his house. He wondered how Brenda's job search had gone. He had called her a couple of times today but there had been no answer. Hopefully she had finally found something in her job search and he decided that not talking to her had been a good thing. Ahead he saw the driveway and he slowly turned into it, home for the day.

As he walked toward the door, he heard Tish crying and Sean's voice. He was tired and he didn't want to deal with the drama that was becoming his family. He thought of turning and getting back in the car but trudged forward instead, putting his house key into the lock. He opened the door and walked in to face the latest tempest.

Sean and Tisha were standing in front of the bathroom door. Tish was crying uncontrollably and Sean was knocking on the door, begging for it to be opened through his tears.

"Hey, what's going on," shouted Randy, immediately concerned. "Where's your mother!"

Tisha continued to wail uncontrollably as Sean's tearstained face turned toward his father who he completely loathed at this moment.

"She's in there. She won't talk to me," screamed Sean.

Randy ran to the door and frantically began testing the doorknob. It was indeed locked and he tried to think, though it was nearly impossible with Tisha's high-pitched wail directly behind him.

"Honey, open the door," he implored.

"I hate you daddy," screamed Tish through her sobs. "You scared mommy. She hates you too and now she hates us."

Randy turned around and reached for her.

"Come here baby," he cried to his daughter as Sean continued begging his mother to open the door.

Tisha backed away from him, fear enveloping her of this imposter who had taken over her father's body.

"No, I hate you, I hate you!" she screamed.

Randy turned back toward the door, still trying to turn the locked doorknob.

"Honey, come on, please open the door. You're scaring the kids."

Sean pushed his father away. Randy was stunned at his son's strength and looked at him in astonishment.

"Leave her alone!" the boy screamed.

"We hate you," his daughter bleated through her tears. "You're a bad man!"

"Tish, I need you to calm down," Randy shouted through the chaos.

"She's right dad," Sean screamed. "It's your fault!"

Randy's head was swimming, what could have happened to lead to all this? He had to get control of the situation, get everyone on the same page, but how?

"Sean, I need your help…" he said while coming back to the door. "Honey, come on, open the door."

"Leave her alone dad," Sean said as he pushed his dad away from the door again. "You've ruined our lives!"

"Sean," Randy shouted, the situation now completely out of his control.

"I hate you daddy, I hate you," the frightened little girl screamed.

Randy again moved back to the door, desperately trying to figure out how to get it open. The screaming of the child grew in volume and Sean again attempted to push his father away.

"God damnit Sean, get your sister and get into the other room!"

"No, I won't let you hurt mom anymore," Sean screamed as Tisha grabbed Randy's leg and tried to pull him away from the door.

"Hurt mom? What are you talking about?" demanded Randy.

Inside the bathroom Brenda sat in the corner, her arms wrapped around her knees which were up to her chest. She stared at the door and tried to shut out the chaotic events of what was happening behind it.

Earlier today she had suddenly felt the walls closing in on her and after yet another rejection from a place that she was over qualified for. She had picked up Tisha from school and sent her down to watch television. With the child taken care of she had thought about taking a bunch of pills and going to a permanent sleep. She had even written a note saying good-bye and was ready to do it when Sean had arrived home. When she saw him, she felt ashamed and had run into the bathroom with the pills. Now she sat crying softly and wondering whether or not to go through with it.

"You've ruined our lives!" shouted Sean in the chaos outside of the bathroom to his father as he again tried to push him away.

Randy grabbed his son by the collar and angrily pulled him close. His eyes were aflame and the grip hurt Sean's neck. Fear overtook both of them and Randy let go as Sean stared at his father in stunned silence.

"Get your sister and get into the other room. Don't make me ask again," Randy said intently.

Sean did as he was told as the young girl screamed in confusion and panic. With them out of the way Randy turned his attention back to the door.

"Honey, open the door, please baby."

There was still no response.

"Please open the door," he begged his wife.

No sound, nothing. Randy realized that he had to break down the door so he backed away and came forward with all his strength. The door splintered, but did not break. He did it again but still the door held. He tried a third time and finally the door gave and he tumbled into the bathroom.

His wife stared into oblivion and continued to cry softly. Randy saw the pills and grabbed them, making sure that none had been taken. His wife looked at him with blank eyes as he gingerly pulled her close to him. She seemed to be uncomprehending and had a pitiful look about her. His eyes filled with tears as he stroked her hair and hugged her tight. He stood up and lifted her into his arms. He had to get her help.

"Sean, get your sister, we're going to the hospital," he shouted.

They got into the car and sped to the hospital. Tisha sat in the back with her mother, tearfully hugging her but Brenda only responded with a vacant stare ahead, her hands down at her side. They drove into the hospital and parked in front of emergency. Randy lifted his wife out of the car and ran to the ER with the kids a step behind.

Inside they waited in the lobby area. The kids refused to sit next to their father but at this point he no longer cared. His thoughts were behind those doors where Brenda was. He couldn't lose her; she was the love of his life and he was terrified. He wanted to go back with her but the doctors had instead led him over to fill out paperwork. He had been as efficient as possible, hoping that once finished they would let him join his wife, but they had refused. So now he sat and waited while his mind raced.

At last, a doctor emerged from behind the doors and called Randy over. He told him that his wife had "shut down" and inquired about their current situation. Randy told him of the struggles they had gone through and the doctor told him that it appeared that his wife had gone through a nervous breakdown and needed to be watched. The pills were a major concern for it appeared that she had a plan for hurting herself. Randy listened, his head spinning.

"We're going to release her to you," the doctor said.

"You're letting her go? Doctor, you just said she's unresponsive and in danger of hurting herself. You can't release her," he admonished.

"I'm sorry, but I don't have a choice. If she would have taken the pills, we could have taken her, but by not taking them it tells us she had second thoughts. You don't have any insurance Mr. Albertson so we can't keep her unless it is life-threatening."

Randy stared at the doctor in disbelief. His wife was sitting in a wheelchair and being wheeled to him. She looked so small and vulnerable that it stunned him. Her eyes had dark circles around them and her cheeks had no color. She simply stared, not responding to anything, not even the children who ran to her as she was brought out. Randy looked at the doctor once more with pleading eyes but it was to no avail. He turned and grabbed the wheelchair and the broken family went back into the bitterly cold evening.

At home Randy carried his wife into the house and laid her on the bed. He saw the note she had prepared and opened it and felt his breath leave him as he read it. He looked at her but her eyes stared into nothing. He finished the note and folded it and put it into his pocket and covered his wife up with a blanket and walked out of the room. She quietly rose and with the blanket wrapped around her walked to the chair by the window. She sat down and stared into the dark evening, thoughts no longer entering her mind.

"Sean, I need your help," Randy said softly to his son.

"I don't care what you need," replied Sean. "I hate you."

"Son, calm down," the father admonished. "I have my hands full just with your mother."

"You tried to get rid of her," the boy accused.

"No, I tried to get her help. Ah hell, think what you want," he replied. "You want to be a man? Grow up then. Pitch in and help or get the hell out of the way."

"I won't let you hurt mom anymore," the son responded stubbornly.

"Fine, get out of my way then," replied Randy crossly.

"Stop fighting," said the soft voice of Tish, trying to be brave.

"Come on sis," Sean said, grabbing her hand as he glared at his father.

In the bedroom Brenda heard nothing. She had withdrawn deep inside of herself and was merely trying to survive. She stared unknowingly out at the darkness. Randy looked at her and wept quietly.

What had he done?

The teacher led the little girl to the office. She had started crying while at her desk and was unresponsive to the question of why. The teacher was concerned, something was wrong. Something was affecting the little girl for this was not the first time it had happened. The child continued to whimper as they came closer to the office. She was afraid that she was in trouble.

So was the teacher.

The teacher walked the child into the office and gingerly led her to the school counselor. The counselor and teacher conferred softly outside her door as they stared with concern at the crying child.

The teacher left to return to her classroom as the counselor walked into her office. The child tried to be brave but continued sniffling. The counselor spoke to her in reassuring tones and coaxed the child to speak.

"My dad is bad," she said finally.

"Why is he bad, what has he done?" the counselor asked softly as she wrote down what the child said.

"He hurt mommy. He's bad."

"How did he hurt your mommy?"

"He's bad," the child said with more conviction.

"You can tell me, honey."

"He hurts all of us. He's bad."

"Please tell me how he hurts you."

"He's bad," murmured the child.

The counselor picked up the phone and dialed some numbers.

"I think we have someone here you need to talk to," she said into the receiver.

Randy saw two police cars at his house as he slowly pulled into has driveway from another worthless day at the office and he immediately feared the worst. My God, he wondered to himself, had Brenda hurt herself? Horrible thoughts passed through his mind as he jumped out and ran to the door where a police officer waited.

"What's going on," he exclaimed. "Is my wife all right, the children?"

The officer led him into the empty living room where a man waited for him. He was wearing slacks, a tie and a white shirt with the sleeves rolled up.

"Who are you?" demanded Randy.

"Mr. Albertson, I'm Henry Taylor from Child Services. That is Officer Davis and Officer Jenson. We have some concerns about your children."

Randy stood uncomprehending. He could see his daughter peaking out at him with a fearful face. He glanced around the empty room, trying to shake the cobwebs from his head.

"What are you talking about?" he finally replied meekly.

"Sir, where is your furniture?" ask Henry.

Suddenly another man, dressed almost identical to the Henry walked out of Tisha's room.

"Henry, could I speak to you for a moment?"

"Sure. Tom Anderson, this is the father, Mr. Albertson."

Tom nodded and put out his hand. Randy stared at him as he moved his hand toward the outstretched hand and shook. Randy's hand had become cold and clammy and he felt perspiration forming on his forehead.

"I think it would be best if Mr. Albertson waits here with the officers," said Tom and Henry nodded as the men moved toward the child's bedroom.

In the bedroom the two men from Child Services conferred and then Tom handed Henry some childish drawings. Both men looked at them with concern and then to the small child that sat stoically on her bed. They continued to talk quietly among themselves as Henry looked at the drawings.

Randy started to snap out of his haze and began to walk toward his bedroom to check Brenda, but the officer put his hand on him, stopping him in his tracks.

"What's going on here," demanded Randy. "I want to see my wife and kids."

"You need to stay here, sir," responded the officer.

"Where's my wife, is she alright? What the hell is going on here?" he said in panic.

"You need to stay here," repeated the officer.

"I'm not under arrest, this is my house, I'll go where I want," retorted Randy.

The officer grabbed Randy by the elbow. His grip was hard and Randy felt as though a thousand needles were shooting through it.

"Sir, I want you to calm down and let these gentlemen finish their work. Your wife is awake, she's in the bedroom but she seems to be unresponsive."

The two men from Child Services walked back over to Randy and he looked at them wildly. His head was spinning and his elbow hurt. He needed to get his bearings but he felt as though he was on a merry-go-round that was spinning ever faster and he couldn't get off.

"Mr. Albertson, we have some serious concerns about your children's welfare," Henry said to him.

"What? Why?"

"We don't feel this is a safe environment for them. We'll be taking the two minors with us."

"No you're not," Randy replied angrily.

"Sir, I'm going to put this to you bluntly. We have reasons to believe that they have been abused by you physically."

"Based on what?" Randy demanded.

"Sir, you will have the opportunity to read the complaint, but right now I'm obligated to remove the kids from here immediately for their own safety."

Two other officers walked by with Sean and Tisha. The kids didn't look at their father. They appeared to be zombies, just following.

"Sean...Tisha," screamed Randy as a second officer came to help restrain the distraught father. "You can't take my kids!"

Randy struggled to break the grip of the two officers but it was to no avail. The kids walked through the front door and into the darkening night. Randy fought but he couldn't reach them. He couldn't save them.

"Sir, please calm down," said Henry in a controlled voice. "You don't want to escalate the situation."

"I haven't done anything," pleaded Randy. "Oh my God, please don't take my kids...please, I'm begging you."

"I'm sorry sir," replied Henry as two police cars holding his children sped off into the night.

"Oh God, Oh God please...Oh my God," cried Randy, tears streaming down his face.

The officer and remaining Child Service man walked out of the house and Randy collapsed onto the floor. He lay in a fetal position and sobbed, his chest heaving. His world had now completely come apart. They had taken his kids. They had walked right in and taken them. He had been helpless to stop them and now he had no one to turn to. He sobbed uncontrollably.

He stood up at last, realizing that Brenda was here. God, he prayed to himself, please give me some strength. I have to be strong he kept repeating to himself. He walked into the bedroom and saw his wife. She was in the chair staring into the darkness of the night. He walked to her and she continued to stare. She was in another world and he didn't know how to bring her back. He had lost everything. His wife was here physically, but no longer emotionally. His kids had been taken by the state. All was lost.

He grabbed her hand.

"Honey, please, come back to me, please."

No response, only blank eyes staring straight ahead.

"Please baby, I need you so."

Still there was nothing.

And then he saw it, a single solitary tear beginning to form in the corner of her eye. He watched it grow until finally it broke away and slid down her face and he smiled.

"Oh thank God," he said softly. "Brenda, we'll get them back. I'll figure something out, I promise. I love you so much, please, come all the way back. I love you…"

Brenda continued to stare out the window, but more tears fell from her eyes. Randy kissed her on the cheek, tasting the salt of her tears. She wasn't gone after all. It was a start, it was hope. It was all he had.

Sean and the officer talked quietly at the police headquarters. For the first time in ages Sean felt safe. He was afraid but he knew that tonight at least he was safe.

"Sir," he said respectfully but with anxiety. "Don't make me go back to him."

"It's all right son," replied the officer.

"Please sir, don't send me back. I'm afraid of him. I don't want to hurt anymore."

The officer nodded.

"You're safe now, son."

Chapter 10

BLIZZARD

She stared out the window and began to see the colors of the winter day. Her head cocked slightly to the side in wonderment of the brilliant white that covered the ground. She realized she felt as though she had been under this cold covering and wondered how long it had been. She knew bad things had happened while she had been sequestered to this chair. The house was quiet and dark and her hazy mind tried to remember the others…there had been others.

"Randy," she whispered hoarsely, suddenly remembering the name of her husband though the fog would not allow her to remember his features.

Again, she croaked out his name and she sensed someone stirring in the bed behind her. He sat up, not sure if he had really heard his name being call, but hoping fervently it had.

"Randy," she said more clearly.

"Brenda…oh Brenda," he said as he flew toward the woman that stared out the window. "Thank God, oh thank God."

"My babies are dead…" she murmured, remembering that there had been a commotion in the house at some distant point.

"No, they're not," he exclaimed excitedly. "We'll get them back; I promise you we will."

"My babies are dead," she said, her voice rising as the feeling of helplessness overtook her. "They're gone! Randy! Why, why has this happened?"

"We're going to get them back," he sobbed, tears streaming down his haggard face. "I promise Brenda, we'll get them back."

She suddenly sat up straight and her chin rose. She felt the strength of a mother who must save her children and she stood up from the chair.

"No Randy," she said methodically. "Not you. You are responsible for all of this."

He looked at her pleadingly, helpless.

"Why did you bring us here? Why did you ruin our lives?"

"Brenda…"

"No," she said firmly, maintaining her composure. "I don't want you to do anything. You've done enough and now I must bring my babies back."

"Brenda," he again pleaded.

"No Randy, no more," she hissed at him. "You've done enough. You let those people take my babies. You are a coward!"

"Brenda," he said through his sobs of guilt. "They're my kids too, please let me help you."

She slapped him across the face.

"Get out!"

He slumped over.

"Get out now!"

His tears now uncontrollable, he looked at her with pleading eyes but she was unmoved. He had lost them all, he realized, as she pushed him through the doorway. He collapsed to the floor once the door slam behind him. He was now all alone.

Two days later Randy and Brenda sat in Family Court though she would not sit with him. The two parents had issued a petition for the return of their children and Brenda spoke to the judge, begging him to allow her to have the children back. After she spoke Randy broke down as he told the judge of the misfortune he and his family had experienced since leaving Saint Paul. The judge listened thoughtfully and then retired to his chamber.

Randy attempted to sit beside Brenda in the gallery while the judge was away, but she stood up and walked away. Soon the judge returned from chambers. He called Randy first and told him that based upon the allegations of abuse he was issuing a no-contact order and that he was barred from seeing or being with his children. Randy buried his face in his hands, wondering how it all had come to this.

The judge then spoke to Brenda and told her that at this time he could not release the children to her care because she was still living with Randy. In addition, without a means of providing support financially for the children he had no choice but to keep them in foster care. He did give Brenda an opening, providing her the steps she would have to take in order to gain their custody. She nodded stoically as the court was dismissed.

"You hurt my babies, you lost them you bastard," she said out in the hallway.

"Brenda, those accusations aren't true. You know I would never hurt the kids."

"I don't care if it is or not anymore Randy," she hissed. "I will do whatever they ask to get the kids back. Whatever! I'm warning you, don't get in my way."

He looked at her pleadingly. Where had his wife gone and who was this woman?

"Brenda," he said hurtfully, "we can do this together."

She laughed at him as he felt his heart breaking.

"Are you out of your mind," she said. "Only I can get them back. You're barred from them. If I can get a job, I can get them back but I can't be with you anymore, nor do I want to. You lost them. You lost them you bastard."

Randy watched her walk away from him, his head spinning. What could he do? This was madness. How could anyone think he would abuse his kids? He slowly walked out to the parking garage and got into his car. He turned the key and began driving aimlessly but soon he found he was at the dealership. Randy was numb and sat at his desk after arriving. No one came to the lot while he was there and he doodled, his mind trying to comprehend his situation.

Brenda arrived home and walked into the empty office, turned on the computer and immediately went to the internet. She typed in the web address of TaylorTronics and went to the contact section. She found the number she was looking for and dialed. After two rings a familiar voice came over the line.

Twenty minutes later Brenda was no longer unemployed. She walked out of the house and climbed into the car and as she drove, she felt joy again. She had taken control of her life and soon the children would be back.

"I got a job," she said as she walked into his office.

He continued to doodle and did not look up.

"That's great," he said in a monotone voice. "Who hired you?"

"It's my old job back in Saint Paul."

He looked up, his facial expressions giving away the stunned feeling he was experiencing.

"What?"

"I took it," she said defiantly.

"I see," he felt his face turning red and anger building inside of him. "What about us? Brenda, we're a family…"

"A family?" she exclaimed, her voice bouncing off the empty walls of the showroom. "My dear, we are not a family anymore. The kids are in foster care and you're not allowed to see them. You've ruined everything. Now, I'm going to try to fix it."

"So, you're going to Saint Paul, huh?"

"Yes."

He looked down at his doodling and felt tears forming but he decided to somehow be strong and stifle them. He had to give her a reason to stay.

"Brenda, don't go. Please," he said but his fortitude was disappearing into panic. "There will be a job here. I haven't done anything wrong and this will pass, I swear it will."

She stood at the doorway of his office and he noticed how cold she looked. There was no expression, nothing.

"I can't do it anymore Randy," she said, again showing no emotion, only resolve. "I have to get my kids back even if that means I have to eliminate you from our lives."

"Please Brenda, listen to me…"

"Maybe things will change, but for now I'm doing this and you can't be a part of it."

"Brenda…"

She turned and walked out of the dealership. Randy ran to the door but it was too late. Her car turned onto the street and she was gone. He walked back into the dealership and into Adam's office. He found the whisky bottle and took it to his office. There was no need for a cup. He unscrewed the lid and took a swig. It burned going down but the hurt remained.

His car weaved into the driveway and stepped out. He staggered as he walked, the whisky controlling his motions. He fumbled with his keys and managed to get the front door open. He walked to the bedroom but the door was locked. Attached to the frame was a note. He opened it clumsily, ripping the edge. He read it and kicked the door.

"Bitch," he growled in his drunken state.

He stumbled to Sean's room and collapsed on the bed. His head was spinning but he wasn't sure if it was from the booze or not.

⚮

Brenda walked into the gray office building that housed Children's Services. She displayed a confident air as she made her way down the dank hallway that led to the overcrowded offices of the protectors of the youth. A young and underpaid receptionist met her and directed her to a harried looking man with a balding scalp and a day's worth of whiskers. His people's skills were lacking but Brenda wasn't looking to make friends.

She handed him a fax copy documenting her new position back in Saint Paul, complete with salary and perks. He looked at the paper before him and picked up the phone, dialing the numbers on the letterhead. After talking for a few minutes to someone in human services at TaylorTronics he hung up. Brenda then handed him a sealed envelope. Inside was the latest psychological result of the woman from the state's preferred doctor. The man opened it and briefly scanned the document and nodded approvingly.

"Mrs. Albertson, it appears that all is in order. We will forward this to the judge with our recommendation to release the children to your custody with conditions," he said.

She nodded.

"I'll be out of town for the next few days to get a place in Saint Paul," she said. "We lost our home earlier this year, among other things."

He nodded but did not say anything. He had heard hard luck stories for the past thirty years and had grown hardened. He led her to the door but stopped her before she left.

"Remember Mrs. Albertson, your husband is to have no contact with the children without prior permission from the court. If we find out he has, the order of custody will be rescinded."

She nodded and walked out. She looked at her watch as she waited for the elevator and saw that she still had four hours before her flight. She drove to the airport and checked in. As she entered the gate of her plane, she heard her phone ring. She looked at and saw it was Randy. She turned it off.

She settled back in her seat as the wheels sped down the runway and smiled. Her luck was changing. For the first time she felt something that hadn't been there in ages. Hope.

At the dealership Randy slowly nursed a whisky and water. Screw life, he thought as he took another sip. He was alone again at a dealership that no longer had any type of life. There were no salesmen, mechanics or customers. He lamented to himself of his plight. This time last year his team was starting a run that would eventually lead to a national trophy. Since then, he had lost his house, his income, retirement, kids, and now his wife. He had experienced losing streaks before but this was ridiculous. He took another sip and thought about the accusations of abuse.

The accusations were the worst part. He wanted to crawl under a rock, disappear. He felt as though people stared at him as if he were a horrible monster. In truth they didn't know who he was. It didn't matter though, he was branded.

Then he sat up. He was tired of feeling sorry for himself. All right, he thought, he had lost everything. He had royally screwed up and it had affected the ones he loved. But he had not abused his family. If nothing else, he had that and it was something worth fighting for. God, it had been so long since there had been fight in him, but suddenly, in the darkened showroom it had found him. He screwed the lid on the whisky and dropped it into the garbage. He was going to fight. He didn't know how nor where it would lead to and he doubted it would make a difference, but he didn't care. He was going to fight, and he was going to get Adam in the same fighting mood. It was time to strike back.

A week later in a dank courtroom Brenda hugged the kids after the judge awarded her custody. She led them to the car as they talked excitedly about going back to Saint Paul. They were going back to where it was safe and normal. At the dealership Randy paced as two Child Service representatives waited in his office with a police officer. Soon he would be seeing his kids though only for a few minutes. He had to make it right.

Brenda and the kids pulled into the dealership and they slowly walked into the showroom. Randy was smiling broadly and started to run to his kids before the police officer gently reminded him that he could not touch them.

They walked in and Brenda looked at her watch impatiently. She didn't know why she had agreed to this. Perhaps she still had some love for her husband, or maybe just seeing him look so pitiful had moved her. Whatever it was she was now regretting it. Randy and the police officer walked over and the kids looked at their father apprehensively.

Randy couldn't contain his smile but he felt scared at the same time. What could he say to them? He looked at them and his mouth went dry. Finally, he tentatively walked toward them as the two representatives from Child Services watching intently.

"Son," he said to Sean though the boy would not look at him. "I know you're mad at me and I'm sorry. I never dreamed we'd be in the fix."

Sean just stared at the floor. He had been upset when Brenda told him they had to see their father before leaving.

"Look son, you're going to be the man of the house for awhile," continued Randy. "Help your mother. She's going to be really busy and will need your help. Take care of her and your sister."

Sean still would not look at his father but seemed to be softening. Randy hoped that the boy would say something but he knew he couldn't push it.

"All right son. I understand," he said after a few moments of awkward silence. "I love you and even though you're mad and hurt I know you love me too."

Sean looked back at his mother, his eyes watering.

"When you're ready to talk, you can call me. I'll be waiting and no matter what I'm doing I'll take it. I love you son…"

Sean wiped his eyes and Randy bent down on his haunches and smiled at his daughter.

"Sweetie, I love you. Don't forget that," he said to her as she nodded. "Everything will be all right. Soon we'll be a family again."

"I love you too, daddy," Tish said.

"I'm so sorry you have to go through this, baby. I want you to be brave and help mommy, OK?"

"I will daddy, I love you."

"OK baby," he said as the representatives started gently nudging the children toward their mother. "I love you."

Tish suddenly broke away and ran to her dad, throwing her arms around his neck and he grabbed and squeezed her. The younger representative reached toward the child but the police officer motioned for him to stop.

"I'm sorry Daddy," she said as she began to cry. "I'm sorry I drew those pictures and got you in trouble. I'm sorry I said you were bad."

He gently rubbed her back and he felt a lump growing in his throat yet her words also brought untold joy to him.

"Tish, Tish it's alright baby," he said with his voice breaking. "I know you're sorry."

He gently grabbed her head with both his hands and looked into the little girl's eyes.

"In a way, maybe I was bad. I thought about me before you, mommy and Sean. But not anymore, honey, not anymore."

"I'm sorry daddy, I'm sorry," she pleaded. "Please don't hate me, please."

"Tisha, look at me. I could never hate you. I love you little girl. You're my sweet daughter and I'll love you no matter what."

"I'm sorry," she whimpered.

Randy stood up with his daughter clinging tightly to his neck. He slowly walked over to Brenda and gently put Tish in her mother's arms. Brenda looked at Randy with a bewildered but thankful expression. He kissed Tisha on her forehead and stepped back, the police officer lightly patting the emotional father on the back.

Brenda turned and walked to the door as Tisha lifted her delicate hand and lightly waved. Randy smiled through teary eyes and walked to the door, watching them get into the car and then seeing it pull away. The officer again patted Randy on the back and walked to his car. Randy continued to stand at the door, tears falling from his eyes but his heart, though broken, now filled with hope.

His daughter still loved him and he was thankful. He forced a smile. He was no longer totally alone.

⌇∞⌇

Randy smiled as the customer walked out of the showroom. He had done it. He had made a sale and it hadn't crashed at the end. He hoped there would be more of the same, but he knew it was highly unlikely there would be many more coming in wanting to pay cash. Still, he would take his small victory because it had been a while.

He thought of Brenda and the kids, wondering how they were doing and if they missed him. As he thought of the kids, he could feel his body heating up from the frustration he was feeling. Abuse…it was bullshit but it was what it was. All he could do now was find a way to move forward but he knew it was going to be a painful and long crawl.

He went to the computer and logged onto his bank account. Rent was due and he hoped that magically there would be money to pay for it but he knew better. The website appeared before him and he put in his password. Just as he had thought there was no money. He sat and stared at it but no longer felt fear. Not having the kids, in a strange way, was relieving. With them he was terrified of being evicted. Without them it wasn't such a concern.

He plodded on for another week sitting at his desk playing solitaire on the computer, hoping a customer would walk in but the lot remained empty. He tried to find different ways to occupy his days and spent much of it going to college hockey websites and following his old team. He was pleased they were doing well.

Sometimes he would pick up the phone and call Bob, his old assistant. They would talk and he would tell him how well he was doing. His old friend knew he was lying but would play along anyway. He missed coaching, not because he wanted to do it anymore, but because it provided steady income which in the current recession, that was saying something.

He would go to the empty house at night. The only thing that remained was the television which flickered snow since cable was now a long-gone luxury, a few dishes and a mound of dirty clothes. At night he would roam through the house, walking into each room and imagining everything being fine. He could see his kids and they were smiling. His wife would be planning for the next day, so many things to do she would say to him. He smiled but he hurt because he knew that it was likely that those days were a long way off, if at all.

After another day of few customers who chose not to spend their money Randy drove home. He pulled into the driveway and saw what he knew would be coming at some point. Taped to the door was a certified letter. He grabbed it as he walked into his house. He didn't need to open it for he knew the eviction notice had arrived.

He called Adam and his friend sympathized.

Adam packed up what remained into the car and headed to his friend's house. They were roommates once again. He now accepted that bad luck would find him. He had become numb since his family left and he no longer felt the energy to fight.

He pulled into Adam's driveway and walked into the house. Adam was watching the big screen of his television and nodded.

"Seems like college again," Adam said, his eyes staring at the television.

"What do you mean?"

"We're rooming again and we didn't have furniture or money then either."

"Yeah," responded Randy. "Good point. Say, do you have any extra tires?"

"What for?" asked Adam.

"We could make a tire man again in the middle of the living room," laughed Randy softly.

"Oh yeah, that's right."

"So, what do you think?" asked Randy, turning serious.

"Not good," replied Adam.

"Nope," agreed Randy.

"I'm due to get booted out of here pretty soon," said Adam.

"So, you're saying that I shouldn't make myself too comfortable?"

"That's what I'm saying," chuckled Adam. "Say, how you holding up?"

"I'm still in the game but I've been beaten up pretty good," replied Randy.

"What about this abuse stuff?"

"Well," mulled Randy, "I guess I know how you feel now."

"We'll get past it," replied Adam.

"I hope so," replied Randy.

The men sat silently as they watched the muted figures on the television screen. They had gone through a lot and they knew that there was still more to come. It was unspoken between them that it would probably get worse before it got better but they wanted to believe that they were strong enough to persevere.

"Hang in there, buddy," murmured Adam.

They sat silently; each man enveloped in his own thoughts. The world was caving in on them, a world that they had for so long felt they controlled.

"What are we going to do, Adam?"

"We have some money, enough to get us through another month or two. Somehow you have to find a way to sell some cars," he replied.

Randy sat back on the couch and watched the figures on the screen. His mind was pondering, trying desperately to figure out a way out of this current malaise. He and Adam needed each other right now. They were all each other had.

"When I was coaching," Randy said quietly, "I always looked for the worst guy on the team and coached the shit out of him."

Adam looked at his friend.

"I knew at some point he'd be getting a lot of ice time because of injuries, kids quitting…whatever. Anyway, I knew that at the most inopportune time I'd need him."

Adam continued gazing at his friend. He wondered why Randy was talking this way.

"Well," said Randy, now staring intently at his friend, "I'm that guy and you're the coach. So, how do I sell cars?"

"All right," replied Adam, now smiling. "I hear you. You want Sales 101.

"Now's as good a time as ever," replied Randy.

"You're right, let's get started."

Adam shut off the television and the men grabbed a beer. Class was now in session.

The Sheriff's deputy sat patiently in his cruiser outside of Adam's house as the two men packed the last box into the truck Randy had brought from the dealership. They had known this day was coming and had been preparing for the past week. What little Adam had was now in storage in the back of the dealership and this would be the last load.

Adam and Randy walked through the house and Adam talked quietly about each room as they checked to make sure they had everything. Adam had loved this house. It had signified that he had made it but now it showed his fall from grace. When he walked out the front door it would be gone. It was only a house, he told himself, but he knew that it would be a long time, if ever, before he would be in position to buy another one. His credit was destroyed, reputation ruined and his business failing. He could feel his dignity abandoning him as the neighbors looked out their windows in curiosity.

"Let's go," said Randy quietly. "You don't need to be the spectacle anymore. Fuck them."

"Thanks buddy," Adam replied. "Let's begin starting over now."

Adam tossed the house keys to the deputy and climbed into the driver's side of the truck. They slowly pulled out and headed to the dealership to dump the furniture and figure out what was next. As usual the dealership was empty when they pulled up.

Adam walked in to his office and called his lawyer. He told her that he was now out of his house and homeless. He had nowhere to go and asked her if he could stay at the dealership. She told him she'd call him back.

She called the DA, which irritated him since he was in the midst of an outstanding round at the private golf course he was a member of. He initially refused her request to let Adam stay at the dealership but she persisted in her argument. He was wasting time with this dumb bitch, he thought to himself. He had to get back out to the links. He finally relented but made the condition that Adam could not be at the shop during business hours.

"Anything else?" she asked him.

"No," he replied hurriedly.

"I'll send you some papers tomorrow for the court," she responded.

"Fine," he replied. "I'm busy now. I need to go."

She smiled as he hung up. He had made a huge mistake, one that might lead to her client's survival. She called Adam and let him know that it was all right to stay. After she got off the phone, she hurriedly began putting together the paperwork. The DA had given her a gift and she did not want to give it back. She loved the dumb bastard right now.

She finished the paperwork and drove to the golf course. She explained who she was and why she was there and soon she was in the passenger seat of a golf cart in search of the very important man. She found him on the 14th tee and he signed the papers with much aplomb, impressing the other three members of his foursome. She thanked him and headed back to the clubhouse.

Soon she was at the Judge's house explaining the situation. The judge had better things to do and the paperwork was in order so he signed it, making it official. She thanked him and apologized for the inconvenience which he gruffly accepted. She left his residence and smiled as she drove away. Men were so easy on weekends she mused to herself.

She drove to the dealership and told Adam they needed to talk in his office. Randy nodded and told Adam he would get the rest of his stuff stored. Adam followed his lawyer into his office while admiring her figure. She didn't have the best face but did have a nice ass, one that he would love to learn more about.

She sat him down and showed him the paperwork, explaining what exactly it meant. Adam looked at her stunned and thrilled. He couldn't believe it but she seemed sure. He smiled, stood up and grabbed her, pulling her close to him and hugging her tight. At one time he had been distraught that this girl would be representing him. Now he realized she was a woman, and a damn conniving one at that. He was instantly attracted.

She left the dealership and Randy walked into the office, everything now put away.

"So what's the story?"

"I can stay here, but only after business hours."

"Where are you going to go when we're open?"

"The Salt Lake University library, it's free and it has internet access," replied Adam smiling.

"Internet access?"

"Yep, you're going to call me when you have a live one and then we'll negotiate together via instant messenger."

"Adam, I don't think you can do that," replied Randy.

"Yes, I can, Candace just got us clearance by the judge and DA, though they don't realize they just did that," he replied.

He explained to Randy what his lawyer had just accomplished.

"Damn Adam, that might work and we're not breaking any rules."

"It'll work," replied Adam. "I'm also going to advertise via email. You're going to send me the lists. We either step up or we're done."

"I love it," replied Randy. "You're sure this is legal?"

"That's what Candace just told me. Say, I also talked to her about your situation."

Randy frowned at his friend.

"Adam, I don't have any money for a lawyer."

"Look, hear me out," replied Adam. "Candace knows someone who has a hard on with the juvenile system. She thinks he might take it pro bono. He's apparently a big hockey fan and knows who you are."

"Who is it?" asked Randy.

"She wouldn't say, only that she'll talk to him."

"Thanks buddy," replied a hopeful Randy. "But how come you get the girl and I get a guy?"

"I'm better looking and have far superior taste," teased Adam. "Look, don't thank me. You stuck with me when everyone else left. I'm not going to let your family get away from you without a fight."

"You're a better friend than I deserve," replied a touched Randy.

"I know," replied Adam with a smile.

"Well, maybe I exaggerate a little."

The men laughed and hugged. They could sense that things were changing.

They just didn't know if it was for the better but they allowed themselves to hope.

Chapter 11

YOU'RE NOT QUALIFIED

Brenda looked at her phone as it vibrated in her hand. Randy's name appeared on the screen and she quickly debated whether to answer. Being back in Saint Paul had given her a sense of freedom, an independence that she had not felt in years. Seeing his name was a past she was no longer sure she wanted.

The phone continued to vibrate and finally Brenda flipped it open. Randy tried to act as if everything was normal but they both knew that things had changed significantly. They talked quietly though there was no warmth in the woman's voice.

He asked about the move back, work, and their new place and she replied with curt answers. She realized he made her feel weary. He was no longer the man she had married, the man who had dreams and was willing to chase after them. Now he was twenty-seven years older and afraid. She realized she didn't want him anymore. She wanted adventure and found that it was possible if he was not in the picture yet at the same time it scared her. She still loved him and her marriage vows had meaning to her.

She told him about the incoming bills and that she needed her first check badly. He laughed softly. He was no longer thinking of a first check. Any check would be good now. He wished that somehow he could help her financially. He had thought about asking her for help but now he knew that even though they were a thousand miles apart, he needed to help her. He needed to provide in some way for her and the kids and he quietly vowed that he would find a way.

They spoke a little longer but he soon realized that she didn't want the conversation to continue any longer. He knew he signified all the toils and struggles of her life. He silently hoped that her thoughts toward him would change and he vowed make that happen. They were past words now. He needed to do tangible things. He had to or she would be gone for good.

He closed his phone and his heart hurt. He missed the kids but right now he mostly missed her. He had taken her for granted, assuming she would always be there. Now she wasn't and he knew he was at a crossroads. He could give up and let her go or fight and find a way to win her back.

Randy decided to take a ride and he thought of the conversation that he was going to have with Adam. He knew it may cause hard feelings but what he was fighting for no longer involved his best friend. He pulled back into the dealership and took a deep breath. He wanted to go in and get it over with but he was afraid. He was scared he would back down, take the wrong path. He took another breath and walked through the garage door and into the shop. He heard the television and walked toward it. Adam sat in his darkened office lit only by the flickers that came from the screen. He smiled when he saw his friend, but it was a weary grin.

"Adam, I have to start looking for a second job," said Randy and Adam's smile disappeared into concern.

"Why?" he asked suspiciously.

"Brenda needs some extra help financially. She can't pay for everything. It's more expensive in Saint Paul than here."

"But if we're selling, we should be fine," replied Adam.

"So far that's a big if," answered Randy as he sat down on the couch, his eyes staring up at the ceiling.

"Look, if our plan is going to work you have to be here all day. If you work nights, when are you going to sleep? I need your full concentration if we're going to get out of this," argued Adam.

"I understand that Adam, but I have to help Brenda and the kids. When things pick up, I can back off and come back full time."

Adam stared straight ahead and slightly shook his head, partly in anger and partly in desperation.

"What if you get an offer for something full time?" asked Adam.

"We'll deal with that bridge when we come to it," replied Randy.

"Alright," shrugged Adam. "I think it's a mistake, but alright."

"Thanks Adam," Randy said as he got up from the couch and walked to the break room.

Neither man spoke to each other the rest of the night.

Randy looked at the cars on the lot as he walked around the shop. He was bored and tired of spending his days at the 'ghost town' as he now called the dealership. Everyday he would come and wait for the customers that would rarely stop by. He had no one to talk to beside Adam on the phone and now he had no desire to do so. He needed to find something to do. Something to pass the time until the funds keeping the front door open dried up, which he knew would be sooner rather than later.

He walked out into the cool February air. Brenda and the kids had been gone for a month now and he had no luck finding that second job. He had been ashamed so he had stopped calling Saint Paul. It didn't matter. When he did call, she was always busy and could talk only for a short time.

Randy searched for things to do around the shop. He had spent one day washing all the windows. Another day he drove each car into the garage and gave them thorough cleanings. He explored the whole shop from top to bottom. Now there was nothing left to do to pass the days.

He watched the traffic go past the dealership. It was a busy road and he started counting the cars that he would see in one minute. He remembered seeing a guy out with a sign in front of the pizza parlor advertising. Maybe it would work for him. Hell, he had nothing else to do so he decided to give it a try. He went into the back and got some markers and a poster board. He spent the rest of the day making the perfect sign, one that could be seen from all the lanes of the road. Surely someone would take pity on him and come in. Tomorrow he would give it try.

The next morning, he stood out in front of the dealership with his sign, waving to all the passing cars. He smiled when honked at and gave thumbs up to others. After standing and waving for an hour he saw the blinker go on a car. It was an actual customer. He hurried toward the car as the driver parked it and started conversing with him as soon as he opened his door. They looked at what he had but it wasn't what the buyer was looking for. Though discouraged, Randy realized that he might be on to something so he went back out in front of the dealership with his sign.

Within another hour three more cars pulled up and Randy started working them all. They seemed interested and Randy started feeling hopeful. But the customers soon realized he was the only one there and became suspicious. Who only had one salesman on a lot, they wondered? Must be some scam they figured and they left.

Randy walked into his office and stuffed the sign into the trash can. Nothing was working. This place was as good as dead. He had to do something quickly. If this place went down and he didn't have another job he would be homeless.

He made some calls to places he had sent his resume but there was no interest. Some places told him he didn't have the right qualifications while others said they would get back to him. Randy had heard it all and he felt the familiar panic seeping back into him. He would be out in the streets soon. There was little doubt about it.

The high school hockey season was coming to an end and he had heard that there may be some openings. He called the athletic directors of the local schools to inquire about them but received little information back.

He walked across the street and bought a newspaper and headed back to his office. He tossed most of it except for the want ads. He went to the employment section and started looking to see what was available. One advertisement caught his attention. The new community center being built was looking for an athletic manager for the sports activities they would be offering. He read the qualifications and realized that he met each one. He thought about it and realized that he should be an extremely attractive candidate, especially considering his past success coaching. He quickly pulled up his resume on the computer and began tweaking it so that it enhanced his qualifications needed for the position.

He smiled when he finished his letter of application and faxed it to the number listed. At last, he might have some luck coming his way. He was perfect for this job. He waited for Adam to show up as it was now closing time. He wasn't going to keep this a secret from his friend. He owed him that much. When Adam pulled up Randy met him at the door. He knew this probably wasn't good, there were no cars missing from the lot.

"Adam, I think I have a pretty good chance at a job I applied for," began Randy excitedly.

"You do?"

"Yes. You know that new community center that's being built downtown? They're looking for a guy to run the athletic side of it. I fit all the credentials they're looking for."

"I see," said Adam warily.

"It will be full time also," replied Randy.

"I figured," replied Adam testily.

"If I'm offered it, I'm taking it," said Randy defiantly.

"That'll shut me down," said Adam without looking up from his desk where he was now sitting.

"It could or you could get Terry back to run it," countered Randy.

"I've already talked to him. He's not interested," replied Adam, finally looking up. "He's doing great at another dealership, or so he says. He's running the shop."

"Oh," replied Randy, surprised by this news.

"Look, you have to do what you have to do. It's business. I understand that. You've been there for me…"

"So, what are you going to do?" asked Randy, softening.

"Probably sell if I can," he responded. "I'm getting close to not being able to pay Candace anymore. If I lose her, I'm dead but at least I'll have three squares and a roof over my head."

"I'll keep you updated," replied Randy, now feeling a sorry for his friend. "In the meantime, I'll keep plugging away. We had some customers today, but no sales."

"Thanks," replied Adam in a resigned voice as he got up and walked past Randy.

"Where are you going?"

"I don't know, I'll be back in a while."

"Need company?" asked Randy.

"Nah, I'll be back later."

Randy watched him go out the door and into the night.

Randy re-read the letter in his hand for the tenth time. It couldn't be he kept thinking to himself. It had only been two days since he sent in his resume with hopes that he was finally coming out of his own personal hell and now this letter was sending him back.

He read it again. It was real and stark. The community center had no interest in him because of the potential abuse charges against him. Potential abuse charges! He had never raised a hand toward his wife or kids and now he was an untouchable because of potential abuse charges. He was feeling as if he had been kicked in the gut over and over again.

No, this wouldn't do. He had to put an end to this nonsense. He ran out and jumped into his car. His tires screeched as he pulled out of the parking lot and headed to Child Services. He had to convince them to drop it. He hadn't done anything. His crime was being stupid enough to leave a job that was offering him a raise and accepting a sales job just as the worst recession in memory had decided to batter the country.

He parked and ran into the building and went up the stairs instead of waiting for the elevator. He ran down the hall until he came to the door that said Child Services. He charged in and demanded to talk to the head honcho.

A woman came out and invited him into her office. He sat down and started telling her about his plight and she listened without interrupting him. After he had finished, she explained their policies and procedures. Fifteen minutes later Randy stormed out of her office and headed across the street to the office of the District Attorney. He told the receptionist he needed to talk to the DA who was handling his case.

She dialed and spoke quietly into the phone, then looked up and told Randy to have a seat and that someone would be out soon. Randy sat and waited and thought of the joke this situation had become only it wasn't funny but instead was on the verge of destroying him.

A smart looking middle-aged man in glasses came into the sitting area and asked for Randy. He rose and followed the man into his office. On his door was JACK TAYLOR, ASSISTANT DISTRICT ATTORNEY. Jack politely asked Randy to sit and also sat down behind his desk, pulling out a folder and reviewing it. The two men were silent while Jack looked at the material before him. Finally, he sat back and looked at Randy.

"Mr. Albertson," he said, again politely but without feeling. "My name is Jack Taylor. I'll be handling your case..."

"These abuse charges are untrue," blurted out Randy but Jack put his hand up to silence him.

"Let me continue please," he responded dryly. "Mr. Albertson, you shouldn't be talking to me. Anything you say I can use against you."

"I haven't done anything though," pleaded Randy. "I think you know that."

"I don't know any such thing, Mr. Albertson," responded the assistant DA. "In point of fact there is very compelling evidence to suggest that you abused both your wife and kids."

"This is a witch hunt," cried Randy. "You have no evidence. I know this for a fact because I've never abused anybody."

"Look Mr. Albertson, there is no use continuing to talk. There is an investigation going on and we'll make our decision after the completion of that investigation."

"Then speed it up!" roared Randy. "Charge me so I can defend my name or clear me so I can move forward."

"Be careful what you wish for, Mr. Albertson. Now good day, we are finished."

Randy stormed out of Taylor's office and slammed the door behind him. He could feel himself coming unglued. How had he reached this point? What had he done? He kept asking himself questions that had no answers, making him want to lash out but he knew he couldn't. Somehow, he had to figure out a way to get through this crisis.

On his way back to the office he called Brenda and told her what had happened. For once she wasn't in a hurry to get off the phone with him. He told her about the letter from the community center and that he figured that must have something to do with the lack of interest of the other places he had applied to. She offered condolences, but had no advice.

He went back to the office and pondered some more about his situation. It just didn't seem possible this was happening to him. Suddenly he finally understood what his friend was going through and felt shameful for trying to ditch him. When Adam came in that evening the old friends talked and then went out for a dinner at the nearby McDonalds. They laughed and pretended that everything was going fine and for a short while they felt normal.

The next day Brenda called and told Randy that she and the kids had just returned from a lawyer's office and sent affidavits stating that he had never abused them. Randy was touched and thanked her when he received another call. He told her he had to take it and switched over to the other caller.

"Mr. Albertson, this is Jack Taylor from the District Attorney's Office," said the voice on the other end.

"What can I do for you Mr. Taylor?"

"I'm just calling to let you know that the investigation is complete and we have decided not to pursue a complaint against you," he replied.

"I told you Mr. Taylor. So how do you suggest I get my reputation back? Are you putting out a press release? It's been all over the paper you know."

"That's not my responsibility Mr. Albertson, and quite frankly I don't care," responded the assistant DA. "The fact is that with the affidavits from your wife and children I can't make a case but, in my experience, where there's smoke, there's fire. I have no doubt that you are indeed an abuser. I just can't prove it, sir."

Randy was smoldering as he listened to this self-riotous asshole. If the DA's office was doing this to him, he could only imagine what Adam was going through.

"So, I can assume that the smear campaign will continue then?" and angry Randy asked.

"There's been no such thing Mr. Albertson. I've now informed you of our decision so we can end this conversation if you have no further questions. Do you have any?"

"No, I have none," replied Randy in his agitated state.

"Fine, good day sir," replied Jack.

The phone went dead and Randy sat back in his chair. At least now he wouldn't have to worry about any other jobs being turned down due to potential abuse charges. But it didn't soothe his feelings. Instead, it only made him angrier.

Randy checked his watch. There was a job fair going on and he saw that he still had time to go check it out. He printed out some resumes and headed for the fairgrounds where it was being held. As he drove, he felt newfound hope. Surely there would be something available and he didn't have to worry about being turned down because of the potential charges that could be filed against him.

He arrived and paid five dollars for the parking. He jumped out of the car and ran toward the building where the fair was taking place. As he came up on the building, he saw that the line was long. For the first time he realized that he wasn't alone with his employment problems. Everyone in the line looked like him, tired but trying to be hopeful. Ready to put on his best face to get an employer interested.

Once inside he made his way around the booths. He looked at the different companies and made a mental note of the ones he was interested in. After walking around the fair and getting a feel for what was there, he returned to the booths that had piqued his interest.

At the first booth he started talking to the man behind the table and soon he was invited to another area for a quick interview. Randy and the man sat down. The company was looking for a recruiter, someone who could go to job fairs at the colleges and universities in the west and find potential employees from graduating seniors. Randy told him about his experience and bragged he had been involved in the college setting for over twenty years. The man listened with interest but then suddenly stopped Randy as he looked at his resume.

"Are you Randy Albertson, the former hockey coach?" he asked.

"I am."

"I'm sorry, but I'm afraid we won't be interested in you," he replied.

Randy was stunned as the man rose and walked back to his booth. He nervously looked around to see if anyone had noticed the snub and then stood and tried to blend into the crowd. He was devastated, absolutely crushed, but remained resolute. He would not slink away and he walked to another booth that he had been interested in.

He talked to the representative who asked him some quick questions about his qualifications. When Randy told him the representative quickly dismissed him, telling him that he wasn't quite what they were looking for.

Randy went through this experience four more times and then decided that he had been rejected enough for one day. He quietly walked out into the day and headed for his car; his mind was numb. He was not qualified for anything. He had a master's degree and he wasn't qualified for anything. He was trapped with no escape.

Homelessness was getting closer and the quiet panic in his gut continued to grow. Job searches had become hopeless. He was destitute and though he knew he had no charges pending it made no difference because even the hint of it made him unemployable. He thought about ending it. No, that would be too easy he decided. Somehow, he would find a way.

But he had no idea how.

∞

With the high school hockey season completed openings became available for coaching positions and Randy started monitoring them.

Everyday he took twenty minutes to check out the internet for positions that were available and he prepared his resume to make himself as attractive as possible.

As jobs became advertised Randy sent in his resume and filled out the school district's applications. He forced himself to avoid being optimistic for though there would be no abuse charges it didn't seem to matter. He was a man who had been marked, a potential time bomb to any employer and it did not matter that the charges were false and he had been cleared.

His spirits rose as two schools called him with some interest and set up meetings. He may be a risk but he was an accomplished coach and had a history of success which made him a risk worth considering. At both meetings he was asked if he was certified to teach any subjects. Though Randy had taught at Saint Paul University he did not have high school certification. He thought of the absurdity of this since his job had been to teach college students how to become high school teachers. Still, he was at a point where he could not walk away from any possibility so he promised both potential employers that he would contact the state's Department of Education and get his certification in place. Both schools were now extremely interested in him assuming he received certification and Randy became reasonably sure that he would soon have a new job.

He went directly to the Utah's Department of Education and was given the paperwork needed to get his certification. He called an old friend at Saint Paul and had them mail his official transcripts and within three days was turning in the paperwork. Randy hoped that his woes were coming to an end as he waited for his certification to come through.

Two weeks later a letter from the DOE came to Randy and he eagerly opened it but his heart sank immediately as soon as he started reading. It was another denial because of the department's determination that the applicant had a history of abuse accusations. He picked up the phone and immediately called the DA's office, and as he waited on hold his anger grew.

"Mr. Taylor, I can't do anything because of this damn abuse accusation," he roared after the assistant DA in charge of his case answered. "I thought I was cleared by your office!"

"You were, sir," Jack Taylor answered.

"Apparently the accusations are still up on the internet but your clearing of my name isn't."

"Bureaucracies take time sir. I'm sure it won't be long before your clearance is posted," replied the assistant DA.

"You need to speed it up," an agitated Randy barked.

"I don't need to do anything sir," Jack calmly replied.

"This is bullshit," Randy growled.

The man at the DA's office laughed into the phone. He was enjoying this banter because he was convinced that sooner or later the caller would make a mistake and he would have him.

"Sorry, have a good day," Jack said, still laughing, and he hung up the phone.

Randy immediately called Brenda. He had reached his breaking point and as soon as she answered he broke down. He was trapped with nowhere to go. He told her of his latest folly through his sobs and as he tried to regain his composure more tears fell as his body shook with each sob. She tried to calm him and worried about his state of mind. She thought of calling the police to have them check on him, make sure he wasn't doing anything rash, but he begged her to stay on the phone with him.

"Let me come back to Saint Paul, please," he cried, tears streaming down his face. "I've been cleared. The kids aren't in danger of being taken away."

"Randy, I'm just not ready yet," she replied as she began choking up. "The kids don't need anymore upheaval. I just think it's best for you to be in Salt Lake and us here."

His body shook as she spoke and he wailed in an emotional pain that he had never felt before.

"Please Brenda, I love you, please take me back," he begged.

"I love you too," she said, tears also streaming down her face. "But I need to decide if I'm still in love with you. You've got to give me some time and space."

"Please."

"Stop Randy, I've told you no. I'm still afraid that what happened before could happen again. I can't lose the children again. I won't risk it!"

"Brenda," he cried into the phone. "I've been cleared."

"I don't care," she replied softly. "I've learned that anything is possible. I won't risk it again."

"Brenda…"

"Good bye Randy," she said and she hung up the phone.

She grabbed her purse and ran to the restroom and into a stall, closing the door behind her. She slumped forward and her tears fell freely. She loved him but she loved her new life more. She didn't want to hurt him for he was now so vulnerable but she had to think of her and the kids and the more she thought the more she was coming to the realization that he no longer fit into the family picture.

He looked around his office as he dried his eyes and tried to regain his composure. He was trapped, in checkmate, but panic no longer set in, only resignation.

The two men lay on their cots staring at the garage ceiling. Randy told Adam of his latest failure and Adam talked about spending the last of his money. They had reached the bottom and both realized that soon everything would be lost. All they could do now was to watch it unfold.

"This sucks," Randy complained.

"Agreed," replied Adam bitterly.

"We have to do something, but I don't know what."

"I do have a little good news," replied Adam, "though it may be too late, Candace told me she is optimistic that my case could be dismissed."

"That doesn't really help us right now," replied Randy. "We need some sort of a plan. Still, congratulations bud, for what it's worth.

"Shit Randy, this isn't some game, this is life. You can't draw up some play to fix everything. There's no plan bud, only survival."

Randy sat up and put his feet on the floor and glared at Adam.

"We're not doing so well at that, my friend. You're bankrupted and I can't get another job to save my life," he barked. "We can continue doing what we're doing, which hasn't been working or we can do something else."

"Fine," a weary Adam replied. "What do you suggest?"

"You're the businessman," retorted Randy.

"I was, but I'm not so sure I still am anymore," replied Adam.

"Quit feeling sorry for yourself," said Randy, now standing and pacing.

"Look, you're right. Let's get some sleep so we have clear heads," suggested Adam. "If we're going to make a plan it might as well be a good one."

"Now you're talking," replied a pumped-up Randy. "We're two smart guys. We can come up with something."

"You're right," replied Adam, but not really believing it to be true.

"So, any ideas?" asked Randy.

"Yeah," responded Adam. "Let's get some sleep."

"I'm serious," an irritated Randy replied.

"So am I. Look, we're tired and frustrated right now. Too emotional, let's make sure we have some clear heads, do it right."

"You're right," Randy realized.

"Good night buddy."

"Tomorrow, OK?"

"I promise," replied Adam with his eyes closed. "You're right. It is time to fight back."

"We can do this," said Randy.

"I hope so," replied Adam. "You know something? We are truly alone now."

Both men were silent as Randy sat back down on his cot. His mind was racing, trying to come up with an angle.

"No, we're not," he responded finally. "We have each other."

"Really?" asked Adam hopefully. "I mean do you really mean that?"

"Really, I'm done looking. We're turning this bullshit around. I'm ready to fight," responded Randy intensely.

"I am too, thanks bud."

"For what?" asked Randy and he lied back down on his cot.

"For giving me hope."

"I love you bud," Randy said.

"I love you too, but I still prefer women."

Both men laughed at Adam's attempt at humor. As they lay in the dark, they realized it was the first time in ages that they had laughed about anything.

In the morning, a ray of sunshine found its way through a crack in the garage.

Chapter 12

CHINOOK

Candace leaned over and quietly whispered into Adam's ear and he nodded. She looked down at the file that was opened in front of her on the stained mahogany table they sat at. Beside them at another table sat the prosecution, also studying the files in front of them, though they seemed to show more animation in their quiet conversations with each other.

In front of them sat a large man with gray hair and beard. He wore wire-framed glasses and had the pained look of a man suffering from indigestion. He glanced at his watch that was peaking out from under the sleeve of his left arm of the large black robe that he wore, signifying his importance in the judicial dance that was taking place in front of him.

"Ma'am," he said politely to Candace. "I'm waiting."

"Yes, your honor," she answered as she stood.

Adam looked at the woman as she walked to the lectern and placed the file on it. She was wearing a red, tight-fitting blouse and her skirt, which fell just beyond her knees, tightly outlined her petite figure. He sat back to get a better view of it and was careful not to gawk, but still able to enjoy the full view of her bounty.

"The prosecution has not met the burden of even showing that a crime was considered, much less committed. For whatever reason they have chosen to conduct a witch hunt against my client, causing him much hardship and consternation," she said solemnly.

She stopped and took a long, disapproving glance at the prosecution as they continued to pore over the files in front of them.

"I would ask your honor to put an end to this charade and grave injustice and dismiss these so-called charges against my client, who I might add has been a long and successful business person here in Salt Lake City and prior to this incident had an honorable reputation with the public."

The prosecutor finally looked up from his files and rolled his eyes. She was as damn crooked as her sleazy client he thought to himself. Surely the judge could see this but deep down he knew that she was playing the best cards of this judicial poker game. He hadn't been able to show anything other than possibilities and he wished that he hadn't rushed it to court so quickly.

"Prosecution," the judge said as Candace sat back down beside Adam.

Adam looked at her and she gave him a slight smile. Every indication was pointing toward a dismissal. It would come down to the prosecution pulling out a smoking gun and she knew none existed, at least she hoped that was so.

The prosecutor finally stood and walked to the lectern. He had no notes before him as he began his argument to save his case.

"We stand by our case your honor," he said with false pride. "It is a complex circumstantial case of deceit and fraud carried out against the consumer for a long period of time."

The judge sat back in his chair and looked over his glasses, giving no indication of his thoughts or feelings of this case.

"We believe this case has a right to be heard and a seated jury to render a decision. Most importantly, we feel we have shown a crime has occurred and was most likely committed by the defendant."

The prosecutor walked back to his seat and sat down.

"I will render my decision after reviewing the facts presented," the judge said simply before rising and walking out of the courtroom.

Forty-six minutes later Adam's legal woes were behind him. Not only had the judge agreed with Candace, but he had taken it a step further by admonishing the prosecution and threatening to file contempt charges against them. He had ripped the chief prosecutor on the shoddiness of the supposed evidence. He had then looked at Adam and apologized that he had been forced to go through this ordeal.

Adam had nodded and when the judge left to enter his chamber, he had grabbed Candace and hugged her tightly, secretly delighting having her body tightly held against his own and having her return the hug with the same tight squeeze he was giving her. They had walked out of the courtroom and out into the daylight hand in hand and his heart pattered quickly. He did not know if this was because of the thrill of finally being cleared or by how turned on this woman made him feel.

A day later, across town from the sight of Adam's victory, Randy was sitting in a seedy office of Robert Taylor, Esq. who had agreed to look at the case because, frankly, it wasn't as if he had any other cases to work on at this particular time. Robert had once been a promising attorney, but his love for booze and floozies had been his undoing. Still, he found just enough business to keep a bottle nearby and on good weeks a cheap prostitute, which he also found to be good clients.

"I have good news and bad news," he said to Randy. "Which do you want first?"

Randy shook his head. This lawyer was just another tangible piece of evidence of how his life had fallen apart in the past year.

"You're the lawyer. How about you just give it to me straight," replied Randy, clearly irritated with the man in front of him with a cheap whisky smell emanating from his pores.

"Alright Mac, the prosecution is pretty sure you've been abusing your loved ones. To them, the fact your wife and kids left you and went back to Saint Paul confirms it," he replied, not caring that his client couldn't stand him. "But, outside of a few pictures your daughter drew of a sad family, they got nothing. Plus, we got those affidavits saying you did nothing by the supposed victims. So, as they told you, no case."

"That must be the good then," replied Randy softly.

"Right," replied Robert Taylor, Esq., "but they don't like you or your business partner. They think your friend is a sleaze who got by them and they're mad."

"What's that have to do with me?"

"You being his right-hand man taints the hell out of you," replied the lawyer. "So, while they can't file charges they can continue to 'investigate'."

"What's left to investigate?"

"That just it, Mac, there's not going to be any investigation, but because they are leaving it open, they can continue to irritate the shit out of you and make you and your buddy's life miserable."

"So, they're smearing us?"

"You could say that," he replied.

Randy sat back in the rickety rocking chair that showed the wornness of thousands of sittings. He stared at a spot on the ceiling where water had once leaked from and tried to digest this latest nugget of news.

"We have to have some recourse, something we can do to stop them, I mean, for Christ sakes we've both been found innocent."

"You haven't been found innocent on nothing," replied Robert. "They just can't make a case against either one of you. They're not doing anything overt, just keeping an investigation open. My guess is that sooner or later one of two things will happen…"

"What?" he asked apprehensively.

"They'll come up with something or you'll leave town. Either way they win. That's how it works, Mac."

"Shit," replied Randy. "Do me a favor, quit calling me Mac."

"Cheer up Mac," replied Robert, ignoring Randy's request. "Least you got some choices."

"Not really," replied Randy as he stood and laid a crisp 50-dollar bill on the desk.

As Randy walked out of the dank office, Robert Taylor, Esq. grabbed the bill and put it into his whore account. One more meeting and he'd have enough for a full hour.

❧

"He says there is nothing we can do?"

Adam had been enjoying his first full day being back at the dealership but Randy had given him disturbing news and he felt a slight feeling of panic building up.

"That's what he said, but then again I wouldn't consider him the top legal mind here in Salt Lake," replied Randy.

"There's got to be something we can do, someway we can fight this…"

"I don't know what it would be," replied a weary Randy. "Pour me a whisky, will you?"

Adam opened his bottom drawer and pulled out the bottle and poured the liquid into two paper cups that Randy had handed him. Randy walked to the window and looked out at the lot that was devoid of people but filled with shiny cars while Adam fingered the top of his cup.

"Let me call Candace," Adam finally said. "She's hungry and loves a good fight."

"We have no way to pay her," Randy said softly. "Lawyers don't like to work for free, as you well know."

"She might do it anyway, besides, a call can't hurt."

"Alright," Randy sighed.

That night Adam received a call from Candace telling him to watch the late news. Adam and Randy turned on the news at 10:00 pm and there was Candace holding an impromptu press conference talking about the injustices that were happening to her client. She also proudly pointed out that she had just accepted another client who was going through the same hell from this corrupt District Attorney's office.

Randy's phone immediately rang and the familiar voice of Robert Taylor, Esq. demanded to know when a change in lawyer had taken place.

"Just now," replied Randy. "You're fired."

The next two weeks more stories came out about the vindictiveness of the current office of the District Attorney and threats of lawsuits began to circulate. Candace instructed Adam and Randy to be seen but not heard. They were to look pathetic, beaten down by the monster DA's office that had been created by a hungry lawyer and local media that loved a good controversy.

Candace called Adam late in the evening after three solid weeks pushing the envelope and informed him that she had been contacted by the DA's office. The meeting was earlier that evening and the DA wanted to make a deal. She told him that they would be receiving a public apology and that all legal expenses incurred by both of them would be picked up.

Adam asked her what she thought of the deal and she told him that she was sure that they could win a lawsuit. Adam promised to call back but wanted to talk to Randy about it first. Adam and Randy both realized that if they filed a lawsuit there was a chance they would lose and besides, they needed money now. With a return of the legal expenses, they would have enough to survive for at least four more months.

"Take the deal," Adam told Candace twenty minutes later.

The next morning Adam watched the District Attorney's office press conference on the local news. At last Randy and Adam felt free. They were broke and homeless but the business was still alive and now they were getting positive coverage. Adam walked out of his office to give Randy the news. Randy was outside shining the cars and watching potential customers zoom by.

Adam walked up to him and spoke softly into his ear. Randy stopped shining and grinned. He looked thankfully up to the sky. Above the clouds were breaking up.

Adam decided it was time to go on the offensive while they were still news. He called Candace and had her schedule interviews with the local media and soon he and Randy were telling the sympathetic journalists about the hell they had experienced and all they had lost. The media ate it up and set up second interviews. These two guys were producing ratings and made excellent copy.

Adam and Randy used the second round of interviews to push for some business. Both men knew how to get out the story they wanted told and spin it around so that each interview turned into a short but free infomercial.

The strategy started to pay off as foot traffic finally returned to the dealership. Customers showed up for the curiosity and after Adam had worked them returned home with a new car. Randy on the other hand still couldn't complete the sale. His biggest problem was the fear of the turndown. Instead of pushing the sale he would back down if the customer showed any hesitancy.

Adam watched his friend and could feel his frustration growing. He knew it was a confidence problem but since his own belief in himself was only now starting to come back he was in no position to really help his friend. He could see money slipping away when Randy walked over to a customer. He knew he had to do something but didn't know what.

After a strong day in which Adam had moved eight cars Randy came into his office with some papers in his hand.

"Adam, I have something I want to show you," Randy said hesitantly.

"Sure, what is it?"

"Look, I'm a shitty salesman. You know it and I know it. There's just no other way to look at it. But I do have some talents."

"You still thinking of leaving," asked Adam, ashamed that he was hoping that this was the case.

"No, I want to stay but something needs to change," replied Randy.

"What do you have in mind," again ashamed that he was disappointed in Randy's answer.

"A little change to our business plan," replied Randy

"I've been pretty successful with mine," replied Adam.

"Times have changed," replied Randy. "Both Chrysler and GM have to restructure. Chrysler might not even survive. Word on the streets is that they'll be shutting down dealerships. I would say you are someone they are taking a hard look at."

"I doubt that. I've always been really profitable for them."

"Not this year," replied Randy. "Plus, it's just you and me."

"Let me look at it," Adam said as he took the papers from Randy's hand.

"All right, but no decisions right now, take a look at it and write down your thoughts. We can tweak it until we're both satisfied, that is if you still want me here."

"Of course I do," replied Adam, but he wasn't sure if he did anymore. He hoped that Randy couldn't see his true feeling.

Randy walked out of Adam's office and back to his. He sat down in front of his computer and looked at the plan he had made. He believed it was good but it didn't make him feel confident. Fact was, he knew that he was no longer wanted by his friend.

Adam walked into the garage of the dealership. It was just past midnight and Randy was lying asleep on his cot. Adam sat down on it and nudged him until Randy turned with his sleep-filled eyes and saw the Cheshire grin of his friend. Adam had just had his first official date with Candace that had started with dinner and ended twenty minutes before with both of them putting their clothes back on in her office.

"She something else," bragged Adam. "I mean she is a wild one."

"She might not be that wild," replied Randy. "She's at least 15 years younger than you. Your best days might be a thing of the past."

"Never, I'm like a fine wine, better with age," he teased.

Adam told Randy about the date and they started talking about how she made him feel. She had given him hope again, made him feel like the hunter. He had always prided himself on his fearlessness but it had slipped away with all he had gone through.

"I think I love her," he told Randy.

Randy moaned and rolled over. Adam had loved three women but had left them all. He wasn't a bad guy and he had treated them all well, giving them plenty of adulation and gifts, but business had always come first and the women of this life had not accepted this. Instead of living in a bad marriage he had given them a deal and then traded up to the newer model.

Adam went to bed, realizing his friend was no longer listening but he couldn't sleep. His thoughts were of Candace, the curves of her body, the sexy huskiness of her voice and the challenge of winning her. She was different from the rest. She would be the one to leave him, not vice versa. She was the first woman he had wanted that didn't need him.

The challenge invigorated him and he was determined to get her. He fell asleep dreaming of the catch.

Adam and Randy tweaked the new business plan until both were satisfied with it and began putting it in place. Randy would take care of all the marketing and promotions and Adam would handle the sales side of the business. They would split the take with Adam getting eighty percent for closing the deal and Randy twenty percent for bringing the customer in. Randy had hoped for a 60-40 split but had known that it was a longshot. Still, he realized this was a better deal than he had. If Adam was successful, he had money in his pocket. When he was relying on himself for sales that had meant his pockets remained empty. Twenty percent was far better than nothing and he knew that Adam no longer needed him so he was thankful the deal had been accepted.

As the business picked up Adam went to work on getting a mechanic. With the sales came the warranties and Adam knew that soon cars would be coming in. He contacted his old mechanic and soon George was back in the garage. The economy had changed the landscape. He had left with the expectation of a new job but had returned with an empty bank account and a foreclosed home. He knew Adam could identify and he gratefully accepted what was offered which was now 25 percent less than before.

Adam saw that the business plan had been smart. Randy was a genius at marketing and promoting without spending a lot of money to do so. The foot traffic increased substantially and soon two new salesmen working at the dealership. The books were finally turning black.

Though the business was picking up it was still nowhere near where it had been just a year and a half before. Randy began tracking sales of all the dealerships in the Salt Lake area. Chatworth Chrysler and Dodge was inching up the standings and eventually moved into the top three and virtually assuring itself survival from being eliminated as one of the dealerships that Chrysler was being forced to terminate.

Adam and Randy now had enough money to find a place to live. They looked at rentals around the town and settled on a house that had four bedrooms and two full baths for $1500 a month. The house showed some age but both men were just happy to have something besides a garage to call home.

Adam and Candace spent more and more time together and Adam began spending nights at her apartment. He felt young and energetic around her while Randy reminded him of how old he really was and how tired that age made him feel. Though Randy was showing promise with the promotional work, Adam was becoming more frustrated with his friend, the continual moping and general sense of sorrow, his fighting spirit seemingly gone. Adam was beginning to feel that Randy invited the pain in his life for it gave him his excuse to become a victim.

Late one evening not long after both men had moved into the house, Adam came home after spending time with Candace. He found Randy sprawled out on the couch they had brought from his office watching an old movie. Randy barely acknowledged his friend as he walked in and Adam went into the kitchen and grabbed a beer out of the refrigerator and came back and sat down on the couch.

"I think I'm going to ask Candace to move in," Adam said.

Randy's eyes never left the large screen in front of him, but he sighed heavily.

"Why?" he asked irritably.

"Because I like her, dumb ass," replied Adam in a short tone.

"What am I going to do," asked Randy, finally looking over at Adam. "I don't want to be your third wheel."

"It'll be fine," replied Adam unconvincingly. "You're not a third wheel. I want you to live with us."

Randy shook his head and looked back at the screen and neither man spoke for a moment. Adam took a swig of his beer and stretched out his legs, trying to hide his frustration with his friend.

"I don't like it. If you really like her, you don't need me here."

"Randy, shut up damnit. I'm sick of you feeling sorry for yourself," snapped Adam. "It'll be fine. I want you here. When you get back on your feet, I'm figuring you'll move. Really, it'll be fine."

Randy sat quietly and thought about walking out, but where could he go. He had little money and fewer options. He realized he was trapped with his friend and apparently his girl.

"All right," he said softly. "I guess you're right. I don't have a lot of choices."

"Good," replied Adam as he got up from the couch and headed to his bedroom. "It's settled then."

Randy continued to stare at the screen as he heard the door close to Adam's bedroom.

"I guess," he murmured.

❧

"Hello?"

"Hi baby, its daddy."

"Daddy, I miss you! Don't you like us anymore? How come you haven't come home?"

"Of course I like you baby. In fact, I love you very much and miss you really, really bad."

"Why won't you come home?"

"Daddy just can't right now, baby, but I think about you all the time. How is your new school?"

"I like it daddy. The teacher is really nice and funny, but she's hard too."

"Well, you're very smart sweetie. I'm sure you're doing fine."

The little girl giggled and it caused her father to smile, yet behind the smile was the ache of being away.

"I am smart, daddy. Are you still mad at me because of the pictures I drew? Is that why you and mommy don't like each other anymore?"

"Oh no my sweet baby, and your mom and I love each other very much. But right now we have to live in different towns. Listen sweetie, soon I'll come and visit. Soon we'll be together."

"You really promise daddy?"

"I promise. Now, you better let me talk to mommy. I love you very much and I was never mad at you sweetie. I love you forever, no matter what, OK?"

"I love you too, daddy."

He heard his daughter's voice yell to another room where he knew his wife must be. Her sweet youthful voice caused him to smile.

"Mommy, daddy's on the phone. He's promised to come see us..."

Still in the background he could hear Brenda's voice and his smile disappeared.

"That's wonderful Tisha. Now go play, I have to talk to daddy privately."

There was silence for a moment as the child ran off to play and Randy knew that the upcoming conversation would not be good.

"Randy," came her voice tersely, "don't do that again."

"What," he asked, but he knew.

"Make promises you can't keep. Don't do that to her or Sean. I mean it."

"What are you talking about?" he asked with an edge in his voice.

"So how are your finances?"

He didn't speak and knew exactly what she was saying. He couldn't come over, didn't have the funds to get there and she knew it. He was a failure as both a husband and father and they both knew it.

"That's what I though," she replied with controlled emotion in her voice. "Now she's expecting to see you. Haven't you done enough?"

"You know I've been cleared of the charges and Child Services has released me."

"Yes, I know, but I also know that you're in Salt Lake and I'm here in Saint Paul."

"They're my kids too, and you're still my wife," he retorted.

"Have you been drinking again?" she asked.

"I don't drink," he lied.

"Stop it Randy," she scolded him.

"Let me come back, Brenda. We can start over."

"No," she said simply.

"Brenda, please..."

"Randy, promise me you won't get the kids hopes up anymore," she implored.

"Brenda..."

"Promise me Randy."

"Alright, I won't," he said beaten.

"Good. I have to go now," she replied.

"But Brenda…"

"I have to go Randy," she said and she could feel tears beginning to form. She loved him but he was broken and as long as he was, he was a threat to her and the kids. She had to think of them first, not him. He had made his choice.

She hung up the phone.

"I'm losing them," he said to himself softly.

Randy stared at the ceiling. He was lying on his cot that he had moved from the garage to his otherwise empty bedroom in the house that he would soon be sharing with the new lovers. He felt numb, uncaring about anything. He had completely screwed up everything but at least he finally had a little cash. Unfortunately, he wasn't spending it well and now he was making promises that he and his wife knew he couldn't keep.

Suddenly, his phone rang in the darkness of his room. He grabbed it and saw it was Brenda. Maybe there was some hope, maybe she had reconsidered and was springing a ticket for him. Maybe…

"Brenda?"

"It's Sean, dad."

"Sean," he said in a stunned voice. He hadn't spoken to his son since the day at the dealership. "Hey buddy, how are you?"

They spoke for the next hour. Sean told him about his new school and sports and how SPU was doing in hockey. Randy lied to his son about how well things were going for him and how he was sure that soon they would see each other again.

Sean tried to apologize but his father stopped him and told him how proud he was of him. He broke down and told his son that he wasn't doing as well as he had said earlier but he told him he had a reason to try now. At last, the father and son ran out of things to talk about and the boy said good-bye to the father. The father wanted to say he loved him but was afraid and instead simply said good bye and the line went dead.

Randy turned and buried his head in his pillow and cried bitter tears. He tried to muffle the sound but Adam heard them as he walked by the room on his way to the bathroom. He leaned toward the door to be sure. Yes, it was crying. He walked in and sat down on the cot. Randy kept his head in the pillow, ashamed of his tears and ashamed of the man he had become.

"I want to do something for you," said Adam quietly.

Randy turned his head away from his friend, his shame continuing to grow.

"You don't need to do anything," he said sadly.

"Yes I do," countered Adam. "You kept me alive. You stayed with me when everybody left. You stayed with me even though it cost you everything you have and your family. I want to help you now."

"You can't help me," replied Randy. "She's slowly breaking away and there's nothing I can do to stop it."

"I can help you in another way," replied Adam.

"How?" asked Randy.

"I'm going to give you a piece of the company. I've talked to Candace and she's getting an associate to put it in writing."

Randy turned onto his back and looked up at his friend in disbelief.

"But Adam…"

"No buts, it's done."

Randy sat up, stunned.

"Adam, I don't know what to say," he stammered.

"Just say yes," replied Adam.

Randy didn't speak but instead grabbed Adam tightly and hugged him. For once the tears running down his face were not of pain.

Chapter 13

A WARM FRONT ON THE HORIZON

Adam walked through the front door of the rental he shared with Randy. It was nearly midnight and he was exhausted but still felt remnants of the wine he had drank at dinner with Candace. He smiled as he headed toward his bedroom, remembering how she had looked in the dimly lit restaurant with a solitary candle on the table.

They were becoming more serious in their burgeoning relationship and though she had turned him down tonight at dinner he knew it was only a matter of time before she would agree to move in with him. He thought of waking up in the morning with her beside him and how she made him feel like he had when he was a younger man. He loved her feistiness and how she could be alluring at the same time and he found himself thinking of her often.

Randy heard Adam and rolled his eyes. He was in his bedroom and had been debating all night whether to call Brenda and beg her to let him come back again. His pride had won out or maybe it had just gotten too late to call her, he wasn't sure which. He heard the creak of his door and knew Adam wanted to talk about Candace again.

"Come in," he said with a tired voice.

"You're still awake?"

"Who can sleep? You've been with Candace, I take it."

Adam happily told him about his night and how he had asked her to move in. Randy cracked a smile when he heard that Candace had turned him down but it turned to a grimace when his friend told him it was just a temporary setback.

Adam was in a happy mood. It had been a good month for the business and for him. All the monthly bills had been paid without him having to dip into his own pocket. He and Candace were spending a lot of time together. Life was returning to normal.

Randy wished he felt his friend's optimism but right now he had nothing but worries. He had blown what little his cut had been on booze and now he needed to tell his buddy that he couldn't pay his share of the rent next month. He knew Adam would take it alright but if Candace moved in, she probably wouldn't be nearly so understanding. He tried to hide his irritation as Adam continued to happily recreate the evening.

Randy realized he was jealous.

Adam stood at the door of the dealership watching another customer drive from the lot with a new car that he had just sold them. He smiled and waved good-bye to them but inside he was frustrated.

For the past month Randy had done absolutely nothing. He came to work late and always left early. He was half-hearted when he was with a customer and Adam would seethe when he would see them drive away in their same car. Randy was always coming up with excuses, prices too high, fees too high, wrong color, wrong this, wrong that. Adam was sick of watching his best friend give up. He knew that it was time to deal with it.

"Randy, let's talk," he said as he walked back to his office.

Randy looked up. He was pouring himself his sixth cup of coffee of the day. He looked back down and put cream and sugar in it and slowly stirred. Then he nonchalantly walked into Adam's office and plunked down on the sofa.

"You've been really quiet lately," said Adam. What's going on?"

"What do you think?" Randy replied irritably. "I'm broke."

"What about the money you made last month?"

"I didn't make shit last month. I don't even have enough for rent."

Adam shook his head disgustedly. After all the bills had been taken care of and the crew paid there hadn't been a lot left, but there had been a profit and he had given his new minority partner his share. It hadn't been a large amount but it was enough to cover the rent. Obviously, Randy had blown it somehow.

"We have to change the pay structure," Randy said bitterly.

"Randy, this is the business. Look, I know there wasn't much left after the bills were paid, but we're not having to feed the place. That's a step forward," replied Adam.

"It doesn't help me Adam," he replied sharply. "I need some money. I feel like you're screwing me which pisses me off. I kept this place alive for you. Nothing you promised has happened. This is all just bullshit."

"Come on Randy, calm down," but Adam wasn't sure if he was maybe saying that to himself also. "You've done a lot for me and your marketing has been great, but if you insist on not selling, you're not going to make any real money. The money comes from commission buddy. You've got to do some sales also, and you have to stop just going through the motions and spending what you do make on booze."

"I just think you're fucking me," Randy barked, his anger getting the best of him. "I say you brought me here under false pretenses and I'm sick of not having any money."

"Randy, you called me," replied Adam in a frustrated tone. "Things happen…welcome to real life! You can do something to improve your plight but I'm sick of your negativity. Either get in or get out. You have a good deal that can net you a good chunk of change with a high potential of return. But you have to make it happen."

"Whatever…"

"Right…well, I'm going to make some money. You can join me if you want or keep feeling sorry for yourself. It's your choice."

"I'm going for a ride," Randy said, standing up and walking to the door.

"Fine, go get another drink, that'll fix everything," replied Adam as he walked past his friend and headed to a customer.

Randy walked out of the showroom and hopped into his car. He roared the engine and squealed the tires out of the lot and headed for the freeway. He had to get away, had to find someplace where he could think, contemplate. He drove for twenty minutes and was soon outside of the city limits driving to some unknown destination.

Finally, he found a secluded rest area and he pulled in. He sat in his car and stared out of the windshield into nothing. He did not notice the trees or the buildings. He just stared as his mind raced. He grabbed his phone and pushed Brenda's number.

He breathed a sigh of relief when she answered. He hated it when it went to message and he needed to talk to her now.

"I can't take it much longer," he said forlornly to her.

"What's wrong Randy," she answered with alarm.

"I'm sick of having no money," he stammered.

"Randy, this is getting old," she said disgustedly.

"That's easy for you to say. You have a job, the kids. I've got nothing."

"You made your choices, Randy, now live with them," she scolded.

"So I screwed up, I don't deserve this and you know it!"

"I know, I know," she replied faintly.

"Adam should have given me more facts. Everything was rosy he said. Well, so much for that."

"Randy, Adam went through a lot. He lost his house, his business nearly failed and he was unjustly charged and lived with the thought of spending many years in prison. I don't think he had any idea any of this was going to happen," she admonished him. "Now, he's given you a piece of his business and a place to live. Quit laying all this at his feet. You're a big boy who made some choices that haven't worked out. So do something about it!"

"But what can I do?" he whined.

"Get better at your current job, find a new job, or go back to what you were successful at," she replied.

"Go back to coaching?"

"Do something."

"If I went back to coaching, would you come back?"

"I don't know," she replied wearily, "but you need to do something."

"Yes, I do," he agreed.

"I have to go now," she said and then she hung up.

"Thanks," he said softly.

Randy thought about what she had said. She was so wise, so perfect for him. He wondered how it was that he could have taken her for granted. She was worth fighting for and she had opened the door a little. It was time to quit being childish. It was time to put his pride away and become an adult again. It was time to become what he had always been. It was time to become a coach again.

He turned the car around and headed back to the city. He couldn't wait to get started on the search. He didn't know where he was going to end up only that it was time to be what he was. He pulled into the lot and walked into the dealership.

Damn, he thought. Adam was with a customer and couldn't talk. He walked to his office and got on the internet. He wanted to see what jobs were available and what might be opening up soon. He could see a clear path now and he was excited to start moving forward.

On the dealership floor Adam continued to work with customers. He glanced at his friend's office and saw him working, or maybe playing on the computer again. He knew nothing had changed.

❦

The customer was a well-dressed man but not flamboyant. He had a solid blue tie and a white shirt and his shoes were brown leather. He seemed to know what he was looking for and did not bother to wait for a salesman to come up to him, but rather made his way directly to Adam and politely asked him if Randy Albertson worked here.

Adam nodded and sent one of his employees for him, but Adam was a little nervous because he didn't know if Randy was here or not. Soon Randy walked through the door that led from the garage. The customer looked somewhat familiar to Randy but he wasn't sure where.

Adam excused himself when Randy arrived and the man put his hand out to shake Randy's.

"Hi Randy, I'm Alan Shankey. I had heard you were here now. I'm a college hockey fan," said the customer.

"How do you do," replied Randy as he grabbed the younger man's hand. "Alan Shankey, that's a familiar name but I can't think of where."

The younger man smiled.

"I played D3 hockey back in the day at Concordia-Saint Paul. We played you guys and you gave us some pretty good beatings," he replied, hopeful that maybe it would jar Randy's memory.

"That's right," smiled Randy, now remembering the man in front of him. "How are you doing, Alan? You were a pretty salty defenseman I believe, or so my players told me."

"I'm not sure I was really salty," smiled Alan as he nodded in embarrassment, "but yes, I played defense."

"Come in to my office," said Randy, leading the old acquaintance. "Let's talk some hockey."

Alan looked at the life-size picture on the wall of Randy during his playing days and gave a low whistle.

"Nice picture," he said evenly. "What position were you anyway?"

"I was a center. It's kind of embarrassing to have that in here but it was a gift from a friend. So tell me about yourself and what you're up to."

Alan sat down in the chair facing Randy's desk and the men started talking about hockey games and teammates and great moments. They laughed and lied to each other, enjoying the company of another who had similar experiences from another time and place.

"What do you do now, Alan?" asked Randy after their stories died down.

"I work over at Reynolds Corporation and I'm actually here for a business reason."

"Well let's see if I can help you," replied Randy.

"We need a new fleet of cars for our salesmen. I know that you and Mr. Chatworth have had some problems and I'm sorry you had to go through that. I followed all the stuff that happened to you."

"Yeah, well, the paper and television stations like a good story," replied Randy bitterly. "Fortunately, it appears to be behind us now,"

"Well, what do you say you show me what you have here," replied Alan. "I'd like to do business with another hockey guy if I can."

"You bet," Randy responded with a smile. "So what are you looking for?"

Alan told Randy about his needs and the two men walked out to the large lot. Randy espoused the positives of each make that they looked at and Alan took four different models out for test drives. After 50 minutes of looking and comparing they walked back into the showroom.

Alan asked Randy if he could make a phone call and Randy took him into his office and set him behind his large mahogany desk.

"Take as long as you want," he told Alan. "I'll just wait out here in the showroom.

Alan nodded and Randy walked out of the office and closed the door. His heart was beating hard and felt as though it would jump out of his chest. He felt the butterflies in his stomach and suddenly he realized that he had felt the same right before big games when he was still coaching. He took this as a good sign.

"What's going on," asked Adam who had been quietly monitoring the situation for the past hour.

"He's making a call. Hopefully…hopefully…" murmured Randy. "Here he comes."

Alan walked out of the office and came to Randy and Adam.

"Hey Alan, this is Adam Chatworth," said Randy, putting his hand on the customer's shoulder and gently guiding him toward his partner. "We were teammates back in the day. Alan here played defense at Concordia-Saint Paul."

"Oh yes, hey, great to meet you," smiled Adam and he shook hands with the customer. "Say, I have to excuse myself, got a customer waiting. Randy will take great care of you."

"So what can I do for you Alan?" asked Randy who was quietly cursing himself. He knew that he had been too quick. He should have waited for Alan to speak first.

"Well, you could sell me seven cars," replied Alan with a toothy grin. "Want to talk price?"

"Love to! Let's go to my office."

Twenty-five minutes later Randy and Alan shook hands. The deal was done and seven Sebring Sedans were now the property of Reynolds Corporation. As they were walking out Alan turned to Adam, who was standing at the door of his office and grinned, then he walked out of the showroom. Randy looked at Adam and wondered if this had been a set-up but he didn't care. He knew he was going to have a big commission check soon and it didn't matter how he had gotten it or who had help him.

He walked back toward his office but Adam motioned him to come into his so Randy did an about face and stood at the doorway.

"You set that up?" asked Randy.

"Why do you ask?"

"The way he looked at you when he walked out."

"Nope, it was all you. I've tried to sell to them numerous times but they have always bought Fords or Buicks."

"You're not lying to me?"

"I swear to God, buddy. I had nothing whatsoever to do with that. It was all you."

Randy smiled. He believed his friend and suggested they put out a news release welcoming Reynolds Corporation. Randy went into his office and sat down at his computer and began writing out a release which he would email and fax to all the local media outlets. He was just finishing up when the shop closed for the day and Adam walked in with a couple of cans of beer. He threw one to Randy and took a drink of his.

Randy opened his can and took a drink, then smiled at Adam.

"We still mad at each other?"

"Nah, you finally made a sale," joked Adam.

"I damn sure did," smiled Randy. "I was going to quit and go back into coaching, but maybe I'll stick around a little longer."

"Great," replied Adam. "I still believe in you buddy; you believe in you too."

Randy nodded. For the first time in a long time, he did.

Randy was finally getting it and it was intoxicating. Customers were coming in with the old and leaving with the new. Each one left with a couple of his business cards and pretty soon new customers were showing up asking for him. He now understood what Adam loved about this business. It was the thrill of the sale.

The money wasn't great, but it was better. Sales were steady, traffic was constant and his confidence was increasing. The lenders were finally opening up their wallets and letting the consumer have some though it was still a battle. But the rates were great and the government seemed intent to help in any way they could.

Randy started to call some of his creditors and negotiating away some of his debt. The settlements took most of his money but he still had a little left over and he was now able to pay his own way with Adam. It made him feel good about himself for the first time since he had arrived in Salt Lake. Maybe now Brenda would be ready to come back to him, or at least let him come home to her in Saint Paul.

After another busy day which culminated in strong sales at the end Randy sat in his office and dialed up his wife's number. He was beginning to feel like a man again and he wanted to share it with his wife.

Her voice came through his earpiece that he now wore and he smiled.

"Hey, how are you doing?" he asked her, confidence in his voice again.

"I'm fine," she replied, but she sounded weary and he knew that her defenses may be down.

"I'm having some good luck at last," he bragged.

"I'm glad," she replied and she sounded as though she meant it.

"I guess I owe you a thank you for the little kick in the ass," he said with sincerity.

"Well, you're still worth it I guess," she replied jokingly, letting her guard down.

"I like hearing that."

They laughed softly for a bit and then there was an awkward silence, the silence that comes when one has so much to say but no words can come out.

"So how are you doing," he finally stammered, ending the silence.

"I'm a little frustrated," she confided.

"What about?"

"My job," and that caused him to smile.

"What's wrong?" he asked.

Brenda started to whimper slightly. She told Randy how she felt trapped in her current position. She didn't feel that her talents were being utilized and it bothered her that people that had worked under her before moving to Salt Lake were now above her and making more money.

He listened to her and sympathized. He understood her frustration and fears and, in a strange way, he relished her vulnerability. As she talked, he debated about bringing up the subject of getting back together. What if she said no? Then again there was the possibility she would say yes. What should he do he wondered?

"I have a few bucks and I'm willing to change jobs," he said, but he only heard breathing on the other end. He decided to push it and see where it led.

"What do you think about getting back together, being a family again?"

She was silent and he closed his eyes tightly, afraid to hear her answer but at the same time wanting her to say something, anything.

"I don't know," she said finally. "I know I miss you and I love you."

She loved him, she still loved him. He knew she had but it felt so good to hear her actually say it.

"The kids miss you too."

"I have money to get there now," he said hopefully.

"I just don't know," she replied softly, but he knew she was breaking down.

"Look honey, I love you and miss you and it sounds like you feel the same. Let me come back, even if it's only for a trial period."

"I just don't know," she replied stubbornly but with an openness that hadn't been there since she and the kids had left him. "I guess I'm not ruling it out."

He smiled. The walls were coming down at last and he knew that soon there was a chance to be a husband and father again.

"Well, I'll take that. How about you sleep on it and we talk some more tomorrow?"

"Are you selling me?" she asked jokingly.

"Well, I am getting better at it," he laughed.

"Yes, you are," she said in an alluring voice. "I'll think on it, I promise, but not tomorrow, it's going to be a busy and crazy day. Why don't you call me in a couple of days instead?"

"Alright," he smiled. "I love you."

The phone went dead, but not before the words he had been yearning to hear came through the receiver.

"I love you too."

Randy called again in two days and they spoke some more about the possibilities. Her defenses had nearly been eroded but she still wasn't ready to say yes. Still, he could sense that it was just a matter of time. They promised to talk again tomorrow.

The next morning Brenda arose and got the kids off to school. As she drove to the office building where she worked, she received a text message instructing her to meet Robert Cantwell, the CEO of the company in one hour at his club's restaurant. She headed toward the club, wondering what this meant, but instead of feeling uneasy she had a sense of calm, that something good was about to happen.

She sat in the lobby of the club and Robert came out to greet her and led her into the fancy parlor where the leaders of the Saint Paul business world unwound. She took a seat in a leather and mahogany chair and after some small talk he made her an offer she couldn't refuse. He needed a Vice President of Marketing and she was the one for him. He offered her a raise plus a bonus which put her into six figures. She felt her breathing increase and tried to maintain her composure.

"Robert, I'm so thankful for this chance. I won't let you down," she promised.

He smiled at her, perhaps remembering his big break so many years earlier and offered her a drink at the bar.

"We're really glad you came back Brenda. When this position opened, I knew you'd be perfect for it," he replied as he slowly sipped on his Bloody Mary.

The alcohol loosened their lips and removed their shyness and soon they were talking about the privacies of their lives.

"How is your family," he wanted to know.

Brenda filled him in on her current situation but soon began talking about all she had gone through the past year and her feelings of betrayal towards her husband that she wanted to get past, but couldn't.

"You know Brenda, I'm recently divorced. Rebecca and I were married for 31 years," he said with a trace of sadness in his voice.

"I'm sorry," replied Brenda, feeling guilty for burdening him with her plight.

"Don't be," he smiled. "It was best for the both of us I believe."

"How so?" she inquired.

"Well, I love my job and I love my ex-wife. When I first started in the business world, I set a goal to someday hold the position I have now. I put in the hours and the extra things to get noticed…anything to get an edge. At the time Rebecca wanted it too and understood what had to be done."

He took a drink of his Bloody Mary and sat back in his chair, thinking back into another time, a time where the future brought nothing but excitement, not the stress he now felt.

"As the years went by and I continued to climb our goals as man and wife seemed to change without me noticing. Rebecca became pregnant and we had a beautiful daughter, but things began to change, subtly at first. Our daughter became her life while the climbing of the ladder remained mine. Rebecca remained understanding but I could tell that we were slipping away from each other and I knew that the day would come where I would have to make a very difficult choice."

He finished his drink and raised his hand to get the attention of the barmaid who came and took his empty glass away and put a new one in front of him on a clean napkin. He nodded his appreciation to her and stirred the drink as Brenda sat mesmerized.

"Well, our daughter grew up and went off to college just about the time that I got this position. I had my passion, this job, but Rebecca's had grown up and moved out. She was now alone. I couldn't give what I needed to the job and to her so the choice I knew was coming for so long was finally here."

"So, what happened?" asked Brenda, completely entranced.

"Well, one night my wife and I had a long talk. I thought of retirement but we both realized that wasn't the crux of the problem. We had become different people…time changes people."

He took another sip of his drink and carefully wiped his mouth.

"We still loved each other but we hadn't been lovers for a very long time. We talked and came to the conclusion that she deserved her freedom. She had been the dutiful wife and nurturing mother for my daughter and me. It was time for Rebecca to find that same passion I had so we decided to divorce."

"Was it worth it?" asked Brenda, now thinking of her own situation.

"I think it was. We communicate better now than ever before and believe it or not I actually see her more but now and it's because we both want to. I think it was the right decision…she's happy again. But God, it was so very hard to come to it."

They sat silently and Brenda knew that her situation was not so much different from Robert's.

"You know Brenda, that day may come for you also and if it does, I want you to know that my door is open. I'll help in any way I can. No one should go through it alone,"

She blushed, how had he known what she was thinking?

"Thank you, Robert," she replied softly as she put the martini to her lips.

"To the future," he said, putting up his glass to her for a toast.

"The future," she replied, but her smile was weak.

She didn't go to the office that day. She and Robert spent the day together talking about marketing ideas for the company. He showed her around the club and then had called the office to have her car picked up and taken home. He had his own driver and they were taken to an elegant restaurant where they continued to talk ideas while enjoying a quiet dinner in the corner.

She arrived home and her thoughts were everywhere. Her excitement of the new job could not be held back as she told the children. Tish danced with glee and Sean immediately began calling his friends to tell them that his mom was now a rich businesswoman.

She went into her bedroom and pondered everything with deep satisfaction. It was time to tell Randy the good news. She picked up the phone and started to dial his number. She had put the first six numbers in, but then she stopped. She couldn't explain what had stopped her and she felt guilty. She dialed two more numbers and again stopped. She walked to the window and looked out into the night. She stared at nothing, she felt nothing. The guilt was no longer there.

She walked back to her bed and closed her phone. There would be no call.

He got up the next morning, showered and headed to the dealership. Already customers were showing up and he made his first sale of the day by 10 am. He walked back to his office and picked up the phone, dialing her number. There was no answer so he called her office phone and a new voice answered with a new title. No, Ms. Albertson was in a meeting right now and couldn't be disturbed.

He wondered what was happening in Saint Paul, but shrugged it off because another customer walked in. He worked the customer and an hour later the man was driving off in a new SUV. He called her office again and the new voice told him that she couldn't take any calls at this time, but she would get the message to her that he had called. He called her cell phone but it was now turned off and he went straight to her voice mail. He thought of leaving a message, but decided against it.

The rest of the day was a steady stream of customers and by the end Randy had sold nine. He did a quick calculation of what his commission for the day would be so that he could brag to her tonight. He rushed home and called her cell again. There was still no answer so he left a short message, hoping that his apprehensiveness did not come through. After an hour he called again, still no answer so he left a second message.

He called twice more before going to bed. He had a sinking feeling. Something wasn't right. He tried one more time. In Saint Paul, Brenda was lying in her bed and her phone began to vibrate. She picked it up and saw Randy's name on it. She held it and stared up at the ceiling. After four vibrations it stopped and dinged, informing her that she had another message.

She lay for a moment and thought of calling him back, but instead the light of the phone went off. She had turned it off.

She realized that her difficult choice had arrived.

Chapter 14

A SPRING RAIN

Brenda sat in the conference room with the other vice presidents as Robert droned on about sales and stocks and bottom lines. She wanted to be interested but other thoughts kept invading her mind though she did her best to try to stay focused. The clock on the wall caught her attention and she watched the second hand slowly make its way to the 12 at the top of it. She tried again to focus on Robert but the monotone voice he was using quickly had her slipping back into thoughts of her marriage.

She finally gave up on following what Robert was saying and began thinking of the past year. It had been such a calamitous time for her and the children. They had been uprooted and moved to Salt Lake on a whim. Once there she had seen her dream house in Saint Paul snatched from them through foreclosure and loans turned down in Salt Lake because of job changes. They had found lost all of their savings and good retirement plans had disappeared with Randy's inability to make a sale. The ultimate nightmare had been when children's services had for a time taken the children away.

As she thought of this, she could feel her anger rising with her husband. He had been the cause of all of it. She didn't know why, perhaps it was some form of a mid-life crisis. Whatever the reason, it was clear that his arrogance and pride had nearly destroyed them. Moving back had been the best possible thing she could have done and now it was paying dividends with her promotion to Vice President. Now he was begging to come back which she knew would endanger them all over.

The meeting finally came to a close and she walked back to her office and instructed her secretary that she wouldn't be taking any calls for the next hour. She walked into her office and sat down and pulled out a piece of paper and wrote PROS on the right-hand side and CONS on the left. She started listing all the aspects of her marriage and placing them under one of the two headings. She worked for 45 minutes on the list and then crumpled it up and threw it in the garbage. All it had done was make her angrier at her husband. After 45 minutes of thinking and writing she had only been able to put one thing about him in the PRO side and then she had scratched it out and moved it to the CON side. He wasn't a good father she had thought to herself. Otherwise, the kids would have never been taken from them.

She picked up the phone and her secretary answered. She instructed her that under no circumstances was she to patch Randy through to her anymore. She then asked her to connect to Robert. When Robert came on the line she asked if they could have a lunch meeting. She was thinking about her marriage and she needed advice. He agreed immediately and told her he'd be ready in 15 minutes. She gathered her purse and grabbed her coat and walked out of her office, stopping only to inform her secretary she would be back in two hours. Then she walked to the agreed upon restaurant to wait for Robert.

He arrived shortly and sat down, ordering quickly as she sipped on her water. She had no appetite and they chatted briefly about the earlier meeting. She confided in him that she hadn't been paying attention as she should and told him why and then told him about the list she had made. He listened to her and nodded and she felt comfort in talking to him.

"Robert, do you really think getting your divorce was the right thing to do?" she asked.

"Whoa…well, I…"

"I'm sorry Robert. I know that this is private and none of my business and I don't mean to pry," she said with reluctance in her voice. "I just need some advice and I don't know who else to turn to."

"I see, so you and Randy have some very serious issues then."

"I think so," she answered while averting his eyes.

"Listen Brenda, divorce is a big decision. I tried to make that decision the same way I make any important decision. I would have to say that for me it was the right one, but it is painful, especially for the children. You have two at home still, don't you?"

"Yes," she replied as she thought of Tish and Sean.

"Ours was out of the house, and it was still terribly difficult for her."

"I know," she replied softly.

They sat silently for a few moments and Robert took a bite of his lunch. She looked at him and for a moment felt something that she knew was forbidden.

"I think for me and I hope my former wife it was liberating once we got through the pain of the decision. I have a sense of freedom I didn't have before and I like seeing her happy. We are actually closer now than we've been in many years."

"I still love him," she replied, "but I don't trust him anymore."

"Did he cheat on you?" he asked, and Brenda wondered if there was a small sense of hopefulness in his voice. "What happened?"

"Oh no, nothing like that," she replied. "It's just that, well, we've gone through a lot this past year and I've finally realized that he was responsible for all of it. Not on purpose, mind you, but still…"

She looked up at him and smiled in embarrassment but she didn't know if it was because of what she had just said or if she was attracted to him.

"I'm afraid to be with him because it could happen all over again."

"Do you still love him?" asked Robert.

"Yes, I think so," she replied, her cheeks turning crimson under the blush.

"Then you need to really think about this decision you have to make. You still have your kids at home and deep feelings for him."

She nodded.

"If you do get a divorce you want to make sure it's the right decision made for the right reasons," he advised.

"Yes, I suppose you are right."

"Sleep on it," he told her. "Take your time, don't rush into it. If you need a friend, you know you can always talk to me."

"Thank you, Robert," she said, feeling her attraction to him increase. "You've already done so much for me. I don't want to be a burden…"

"Not at all, but Brenda, remember, I'm still your superior. It is very important you don't let this affect your work," he admonished her and inside she felt shame for the feeling that were developing inside of her.

"Of course, I won't," she replied, though not convincingly.

"Brenda, I'm not trying to threaten you so I hope you don't take it that way. It's just advice. I found the work to be my escape when I was going through my divorce. Your work can be very positive for you while you are going through this," he said.

"I understand, really. I do appreciate this, Robert. You have become a wonderful friend and mentor and you always have been a great boss to work for. I won't let you down."

"Of course you won't. Now since you just recently got a big raise, I'll let you take care of the tab," he joked.

Late that evening, after taking care of the kids and doing work that she had brought home she went into her bedroom and prepared to go to bed. She pulled the covers back and felt the fatigue of the day hit her all at once, yet her mind continued to race. She lay down and plugged in her phone and saw that there were some messages. She looked and saw seven messages and went to missed calls. As she thought they were all from Randy. She went back to the messages and deleted them without listening to them.

She had made up her mind and as she closed her eyes to fall asleep, she saw a man, but it was no longer Randy.

⚬✖⚬

"She's a beaut, she's perfect for you," Randy told the customer he was working as he led him into the 'money pit' which was the nickname of the room the salesmen used for the small office they negotiated price.

He felt his phone vibrate in his pocket and took a quick glance. It was a text from Brenda and his heart skipped a bit. It told him to call as soon as possible on her cell phone. He put it back into his pocket and worked price with the customers. They were easy and had obviously not done any homework. They left feeling they had a great deal but he knew that this commission check was going to be a big one.

He walked into his office and closed the door. He was feeling good and as he was dialing, he decided to put her on the defensive for not calling him back like she had said she would. He was feeling like a man again and he thought of her and the kids coming back here. He could see that Adam had been right and there was money to be made. He could see his plans falling in place, though it would still take awhile.

"Well, nice to finally talk to you." he said as she answered the phone.

"Randy, I…"

"I called and called. I called your office, the house phone, your cell…" he barked.

"Randy…"

"I thought we were going to…"

"Randy, shut up!" she ordered. "I have something important to tell you."

"Fine Brenda, what is it?"

"Randy, I…I," she stammered.

"Just say it, what is it?" he demanded.

"Fine, Randy, I want a divorce."

It was like he had been hit in the stomach without expecting the punch. He couldn't breathe, he felt himself perspiring immediately and a thousand pins suddenly pricked his skin.

"But…" he stammered.

"I'm sorry, but I'm ready to move on with my life," she said as she took the upper hand in the conversation.

"But, the other night…you said…" he choked out.

"I know, I'm sorry, things have changed."

"I don't know what to say," he said as his eyes began to water and a bead of sweat rolled down the side of his cheek.

"I just don't think we're the same people anymore," she said quietly.

"Is there another man? Is that what has changed?" he asked her defiantly.

"No, stop that, Randy. Of course there isn't," but she thought of Robert as she spoke.

"Then what is it?"

"I still love you, I always will, but it's not the same anymore. We're no longer lovers, just former room-mates. You use to be my life but you're not anymore. I've learned that I can do things for myself. I have self-worth and abilities. Simply put, you've become a hindrance in mine and the children's life. I'm sorry, I know this hurts but this is how I feel. It's best to move on."

He was stunned. He had no retort, no snappy comeback. His strength was dissipated and his head spun. He had never dreamed that she would want this, even when she hadn't let him come to Saint Paul. He always believed that sooner or later they would be together. But it had been a pipe dream. It would never happen.

"Uh, I need to go Brenda," he stammered.

"Randy," she said but the line went dead and he was gone.

He sat at his desk and wondered if what had just happened really had. He knew she loved him but something had changed in the last 72 hours and she no longer wanted nor needed him.

◈

Adam looked towards Randy's office door. It was still shut, had been for the past hour and he wondered what was going on. He wandered over to it and saw Randy, his back turn staring up at the large picture of him in his college days. He turned the knob but the door was locked. He knocked on the window but Randy merely raised his hand and waved him away. Adam shrugged but decided that it was best to leave his friend alone.

For the rest of the day Adam periodically looked at the door that never opened. Finally, around closing time the door open and Randy walked out and went into the garage area. Two minutes later Adam saw his friend driving out of the lot and onto the street. Something has happened, he realized, something obviously bad. He closed the shop down and headed to their rental.

Randy wasn't home and now Adam started to become concerned. He called Randy's cell but there was no answer. He went into the house and poured himself a drink and sat down in front of the television. He listened for the car drive up but hours passed before he finally heard the familiar sound of the engine. A short time later Randy staggered in; he had been drinking again.

Randy wobbled his way to the couch. He was loaded and he farted as he sat down, laughing at the sound of it and the uncomfortable face that Adam made.

"Where you been?" asked Adam.

"Out," the drunk replied.

"Had a few, huh?"

"Maybe a couple," he replied.

"So, what's the occasion?"

That was all the invitation Randy needed. He recounted the conversation he had earlier in the day with Brenda and pretty soon the liquor loosened up his tear ducts and he began to sob. Adam was very uncomfortable and he didn't know what to say. His friend was a train-wreck right now and it wasn't something he wanted to witness. He finally rose to his feet and gently patted Randy on the shoulder as he walked by him and went to his bedroom.

Randy continued to cry silently. How could she do this? He loved her. There had to be a way to win her back. Hell, he was a salesman now and he could work her. He loved her and the kids too much to lose them. He slowly pulled himself up and walked toward his room, nearly tripping on the stairs but catching himself before he went down. He collapsed on his bed and opened his phone and found Brenda's name. It was late, but so what, he had to win her over.

"Brenda, you can't leave me..." he slobbered into the phone after she answered.

"Randy, you're drunk," she replied crossly.

"Maybe a little, but you can't leave me. I know you still love me and you need the money I'm making now," he said, but his words came out slowly and were slurred.

"No, I don't," she replied tersely. "I'm a vice president now and I got a big raise. I don't need you and money isn't a reason to stay together anyway."

"Damnit you bitch, you need me," he roared into the phone.

"Just stop it Randy, its over."

"No, please," he said as he started to cry again. "I'm sorry, you're not a bitch. It's the liquor talking. I love you and the kids more than anything."

"Look Randy," she replied in a tired and irritated voice. "My mind is made up. I don't want you to call me anymore. It's time to move on."

"But we can get help," he whimpered. "Counseling, something, I just can't lose you."

"Stop…and don't call me anymore."

"But Brenda, please…"

She clicked the phone shut and then opened it again and turned it off. She didn't want to hear from him anymore. She had moved on, made her decision. It was best…best for both of them. She turned off the light and rolled to her side. She felt liberated but incredibly sad. In some way she felt she had failed, but so had he. She felt her eyes watering and she turned back onto her back.

She let it out, let the tears cleanse her. She felt some guilt because she knew how bad he was hurt but there were also tears of joy for now she felt truly free. The hard part was over, difficult times would come, but the hard part was over.

Though she was crying she was also smiling and her heart no longer hurt.

❧

Randy lay on the couch in Adam's office and stared at the ceiling. It was early afternoon and his head still ached from the alcohol he had consumed the night before. Adam was going through the books and telling Randy that they had just hired two more mechanics. The dealership was continuing to grow and the checks were getting bigger at the end of each month.

All the bills were now caught up and Adam was feeling good, but the sight of his friend lying on the couch told him that Randy was still in a precarious state. Fortunately, here at the dealership Randy had been all business so far and hadn't let the hangover he was feeling or the sting of the impending divorce slow down his sales. Adam finished up the books and told Randy what his take for the month would be and both men smiled. They decided to go out and celebrate but Randy made it clear that he preferred dinner to drinks.

At the restaurant they ordered sirloins medium and Randy added sautéed mushrooms to his. Their meals came and they enjoyed the ambiance of the meal and aroma that came from it. After the meal Randy, much more coherent than the evening before, updated Adam on his marriage situation. Again, Adam was uncomfortable hearing this. He wasn't big on marriage in the first place and knew there was little he could offer his friend but support.

"Look buddy," Adam said to his friend, "maybe she's right. Maybe it is time to move on."

"Don't say that," snapped Randy.

"Look, it's something you have to face. It's out there now, you know where she stands."

"I don't want to face it," he retorted. "Besides, are you really the one who should be giving me marriage advice?"

Adam snickered. "No, but I'm probably a good guy to get divorce advice from."

Randy couldn't help it and laughed but he was still irritated with his friend and they didn't talk much the rest of the meal. The gorilla was out and now it was sitting on both of their backs.

They paid their bill and walked to Adam's car. He turned the ignition and they headed to the movie theater and took in the latest hit from Hollywood. After the movie they still didn't know what to say but both were feeling better. They drove home and walked into the rental they shared and Adam grabbed a couple of beers out of the refrigerator. They sipped on them quietly and sat down in front of the television, looking at the figures on the screen with the volume down as beads of condensation formed on the bottles.

"We need a vacation, bud," Adam said suddenly. "We haven't had one since you moved here."

"Yeah," agreed Randy. "A vacation would be nice, where to?"

"Let's go to Vegas. Do some gambling, take in some shows. As you know, what happens in Vegas stays in Vegas."

"That sounds like a really good idea," agreed Randy, perking up.

"We leave on a Friday after work and come back Sunday night."

"Alright, I'm in. If we're going to do it let's get some airline tickets now before we change our minds," suggested Randy.

"Let's go!"

They went to the computer and pushed the internet icon. Soon they were checking out airline prices and found the cheapest flights that fit their schedule. Twenty minutes later they had their tickets paid for and in less than a week would be on their way. They checked hotels and decided on the MGM Grand. Everything was set, there was no turning back and both men felt a strange sense of accomplishment.

Adam smiled as Randy headed to bed. He had gone through three divorces, each painful in its own way. No, he couldn't give marriage advise, but at least he could help his friend navigate through the hell he was about to go through.

❧

The two friends stepped off the plane and made their way to luggage. For a few days they could leave the past year behind them and just have some fun. They had some money and the warm Las Vegas air felt so good after enduring the cold winter and winds that shot off the Great Salt Lake in the spring.

They quickly grabbed a cab and headed to the MGM Grand Hotel and Casino where they checked in and headed to their rooms. Both men quickly showered and changed into some casual wear and they met at the entrance of the casino 40 minutes later. They warmed up on the slots and then moved to the tables. Adam got a hot streak going for awhile and found himself $700 up, but Randy struggled but managed to stay even up. After gambling and taking in some drinks they headed for the show they had bought tickets for that night.

The show featured beautiful women in feathers and men on high wires. It was almost a circus, but the clientele was well to do. After the show the men headed to the lounge and started enjoying the view of young women in slinky dresses and high heels. By now they were exhausted and headed back up to their rooms for some rest.

The next day was a repeat of the previous, only this time they checked out the casinos at other hotels. The beauty of Vegas is that everything is on the same block and if your luck is down at one place, simply pick up and walk to the next. They each enjoyed a steak dinner at the Venetian and made their way back to the Bellagio for the evening's show.

It was another spectacle of women dancing, men flying and music blaring. After it was over it was straight to the nightclub, but this time they had the energy to stay and soon they were on the dance floor feeling 20 years younger.

Adam soon spotted a couple of women in their early 30's who had been eyeing them and sent them some drinks with an invitation to join them. Randy protested half-heartedly but Adam reminded him that his wife had just asked for a divorce, ending the brief protestations. The two women received their drinks and looked at the two men who had just bought them and they gathered their things and made their way over.

The brunette with the sharp nose and big breasts sat next to Adam and the blonde with the shapely ass took the seat next to Randy and told them their names while thanking them for the drinks. The brunette's name was Sandra and the blonde was Wendy. They talked and drank for the next hour, only interrupting this ritual with a couple of slow dances in between. Before they knew it the clock read 1:30 in the morning and they decided to go out for a walk.

The walk led to the MGM Grand and Sandra and Adam soon disappeared into his room. Randy, not accustomed to this, was shy and not sure what the rules were. He was slightly drunk and his heart told him it was best to go to his room alone but his head convinced him to bring Wendy with him and soon they were at the door of his room, passionately kissing as he struggled to get the card into the door to unlock it. At last, the green light came on and they moved to the other side, still locked together.

They moved toward the bed and she nibbled on his ear and soon he felt a swelling below his beltline. Again, his heart told him to stop and this time his head agreed and he gently pushed her away.

"I'm sorry," he said. "I can't do this. I'm married."

"I am too," she replied as she dropped her eyes.

"You are?" he said in surprise.

"Yes, but obviously it's not much of a marriage," she said and she looked as though she were going to cry. "I guess he's grown tired of me. Look, I'll go. You're a nice guy. You have a lucky wife…"

She stood up with as much dignity as she could muster and tried to fix her hair as she headed toward the door.

"Wait," he said.

"Yes?"

"I don't know, I just don't want to be alone," he stammered, but he meant it also. "What do you say we order a nightcap and just talk? Conversation is good, isn't it?"

"Yes," she smiled. "Conversation would be nice."

"Do you like wine?" he asked as he picked up the phone and dialed room service.

"I do."

"I'll order a bottle and two glasses," he told her and then he made the order over the phone.

"This sounds very enchanting," she said as he hung up the phone.

The man and the woman smiled at each other and waited for the knock on the door.

The next morning Randy sat at his table enjoying the breakfast buffet and waved over Adam as he entered. Adam immediately told him he wanted all the details and Randy grinned and began telling his friend a whopper, ashamed to be doing so but not wanting to let his friend know that nothing had happened. At the conclusion of the story Adam gave a low whistle and the two men laughed. Adam then began to recount his sexual experience from the night before, but suddenly Randy interrupted him.

"Wait Adam," he said. "I have to be honest. I couldn't do anything last night. She's a nice lady so we drank a bottle of wine and talked, then fell asleep, fully clothed I might add."

"There's nothing wrong with that," said Adam encouragingly.

"I feel like I cheated," replied Randy.

"Maybe you did a little, but you stopped yourself for a reason…why?"

"I love Brenda," replied Randy sadly.

"I can see you do buddy," Adam said soothingly. "So, what are you going to do about it?"

"There's nothing I can do."

"Oh bullshit," said Adam disgustedly.

"What?"

"You heard me. You can fight for her," replied Adam, leaning forward toward his friend. "If you love her enough to fight off that cougar from last night, fight for her and the kids. Damn, do I have to give you some balls? Fight for your family, you dumb ass."

"All right, I hear you," replied Randy with a smile. "Thanks Adam."

"Your family's worth it."

"You're a good friend, better than I deserve," replied Randy.

They ate their breakfast and then headed to the airport. It was time for Randy to fight for his family.

Chapter 15

PLANTING SEEDS

Adam was thumbing through the paper, looking at the latest adds from the various dealerships in the city when Randy joined him in the kitchen, pouring himself a cup of coffee, dumping some sugar and a splash of milk and turning the brew to a brown hue. Adam always made it too strong for him so he needed to lessen the impact that he knew would be coming. He sat across from Adam and took a sip of the bitter tasting liquid and squinted. It was both hot and strong.

"Adam, I think I'm going to find a place for myself," he said nonchalantly as he took another sip

"But we save on the rent," replied Adam, looking up for the first time since Randy had walked into the kitchen.

"Yeah, I know. The thing is I don't want to live in a rental anymore," he replied.

Adam looked up from the paper. When they had left Las Vegas, he had thought that Randy was going to fight to get Brenda back, but what he was proposing now didn't sound like a guy ready to fight, it sounded more like surrender, and worse, Randy had to know that buying was practically out of the question.

"Look Randy, we're doing better, but your credit won't be high enough for a loan and you know that. Especially since your house in Minnesota is in foreclosure and you were evicted from the rental here. Plus, do you really think Brenda will drop everything and move back?"

"I know, but I was thinking that maybe I could find a rent-to-own deal or something along those lines," replied Randy defensively.

Adam shook his head and wondered what had gotten into Randy. He was a smart guy but right now he just wasn't making a lot of sense. Still, he was his best friend and had to be supportive.

"I doubt it," Adam said solemnly, "but I tell you what, I know this lady, Jen Tagmire. She's a realtor who helped me a number of times. If anyone can help you, she can. You want me to call her?"

"That'd be great, but what about that one gal, Barbara something," smiled Randy.

"She's out of the business. Another victim of the recession I guess," replied Adam.

Randy knew the odds were stacked against him but he finally had a few bucks in his pocket and his bills were all up to date except for the foreclosure in Saint Paul. He hoped that by getting into a rent-to-own he could pay for a couple of years and then take over the payments. He knew it was his only shot given his circumstances.

"I figure I got nothing to lose," he told Adam. "Worse case scenario I find another rental."

"I still say you stay with me," replied Adam, looking back at the newspaper and spotting the dealership ad in the corner.

"Look Adam," replied Randy. "If I move out, I bet Candace moves in. No woman wants to move into a house with a third wheel in the basement."

"You think so?" asked Adam, suddenly very interested in seeing his friend move out.

"And you're the so-called ladies' man," laughed Randy.

"All right, all right," smiled Adam. "Maybe you're right. In that case you have 24 hours to get out."

"With friends like you…"

"I'm joking."

The two men laughed and Randy took another sip of the bitter coffee and then got up and grabbed the sugar. It was still way too strong for him.

"Hey Adam," he said from the counter.

"Yes?"

"Thanks," replied Randy.

Adam smiled and nodded and then got up and walked to the coffee pot and poured himself another cup.

"Hey, what about Brenda and the kids, though. This puts you here for a while."

"Yeah, it does," replied Randy.

"I thought you had decided to fight for her."

"She doesn't want me anymore," Randy replied softly.

"Have you got papers?"

"Not yet, but I'm sure they're coming."

"I really think you should fight for her," Adam said intently. "I know that means I'll probably lose you, but that's what I think you should do."

"Maybe," agreed Adam, "but she seems pretty intent on moving on with her life without me in it."

"But…"

"Look Adam, I don't want to stand still anymore. I want to start living again instead of going through the motions. Remember, I didn't say I wanted a divorce, she did…well, then so be it. I can stand still or start living. Being in Las Vegas reminded me that I want to live my life, not just get through it."

"Alright bud, I'll call Jen for you then."

"Thanks," replied Adam as the two men grabbed their coats and headed out to their cars to race to the dealership. Thirty years before they had always raced to school from their apartment, now, in their new cars from the dealership they were those youngsters dragging again.

For the next week Randy split his time at the dealership and with Jen looking at various houses. Jen was amazing and soon Randy had two houses that were possibilities. One was a rancher and the other was an old colonial just outside of town. As soon as he saw the colonial, he fell in love with it but refused to get his hopes up. He had gone through too much in the past year and he was sure that something bad lurked around the next corner.

Incredibly to him a deal was made. He would pay rent for two years and then, depending upon his credit score he would be given the option of buying. He knew that because of the foreclosure this was the best he could hope for and he quickly agreed to the terms and signed a two-year lease.

After the deal was made Randy went to the empty house and quietly walked around it, picturing how he hoped the rooms would look in the near future but realizing it would probably take longer since he no longer had furniture to speak of. In the living room at the back of the house was a large picture window and Randy sat down against the wall adjacent to it and stared out into the decent size backyard.

The sun was starting to go down for the day and the trees partially blocked the light from coming into the room. He stared out and thought of Brenda and the kids. He wasn't sure if this was the type of house she would have wanted, but he knew that the kids would have loved it. He could picture Tish playing on a swing set and laughing gleefully. As he thought of them, he felt more sadness creeping in. He knew that he was now on the hook for the next two years and that this would probably end any chance of getting back with her and being a family again.

He thought back to their days when they were dating. He had first seen her at SPU as a freshman and had worked up the courage to ask her out. She was the most beautiful woman on campus in his eyes and for a simple farm kid like himself she was more than he could ever have hoped for. They dated through college and had married upon his graduation. Those first ten years of marriage had been blissful but as the years piled up his attraction to her had waned into a middle age comfort.

Now that he was losing her, he realized what a wonderful gift she had been and he was ashamed for taking her for granted. He prided himself in being an optimistic man and he chose to remember the good and dream of a return to the bliss but he knew that their separate paths were taking them further away from each other, never to return.

Brenda came home tired but invigorated from the new responsibilities of being a vice president. She liked what she was doing but there was so much to learn so quickly. Sometimes during the day, she felt completely overwhelmed yet inside was a hunger to conquer all obstacles. She liked the fact that Randy was becoming more of a distant memory during the day, replaced by the thrill of the new job.

She sat at her desk in the condo her and the kids were now living in and worked on some papers that needed her attention before tomorrow's meeting when her cell phone buzzed. She looked and saw that it was Randy and she debated for a few moments on whether to answer it or not. After a short deliberation in which she was unable to come up with an adequate excuse she flipped the phone open.

"Randy, I'm busy…" she said, immediately regretting her decision to answer.

"You answered," he replied, somewhat surprised that she had.

"What do you want?"

"Look, I'm not the enemy Brenda, I just called to talk for a few minutes, that's all," he said with irritation.

"You're not going to change my mind," she said, referring to the divorce.

"I'm not going to try," he replied.

"You're not?" she said, unable to disguise the hurt.

"Do you want me to?"

"Of course not," and she hoped she sounded convincing.

"I just called to tell you about the little house I just got."

"You bought a house?" she said incredulously.

"I wish," he replied. "You know my credit's shot. No, I got a nice rent-to-own. I signed the lease for two years and then depending on my credit I will have an option to begin payments to buy."

"I see," she said, her curiosity piqued. "What did you get?"

"It's a colonial. It's two stories high and has a basement. It has three bedrooms and two baths. It's also got a decent size yard and is just outside of town."

She didn't reply. She didn't know how she felt about this. She wanted the divorce but she never dreamed he would give up this easily. She realized she had never ruled out getting back together but now there was no way.

"Brenda? Are you still there?"

Now she could feel herself feeling hurt and betrayed. He didn't believe her. He figured he would get this house and she and the kids would come running back. He was such a controlling asshole, she thought to herself. It always had to be about him.

"Brenda?"

Now she was furious, furious at him and at herself. No, she would not be made the fool. She was done being the dutiful wife. She and the kids were not part of his trophy case, not anymore anyway.

The line went dead and Randy wondered what he had done wrong this time.

Adam looked at the books again and didn't like what he was seeing. After three consecutive months of growth the sales had slid slightly. Normally this wouldn't be a major cause of concern, but after everything that he had gone through any shift now brought fear to him and the panic that the bottom was going to fall out again. This was compounded because he knew that soon Chrysler would be making another round of dealership cuts and if he was included it would result in a bankruptcy he knew he would not be able to come out of.

Sales are stagnant," he said as he walked into Randy's office. "We're down from last month."

"Yeah, I need some commission money," replied Randy. "I have rent now."

"You and me both," replied Adam as he sat down in the leather seat across from Randy's desk.

"You think this is a repeat?"

"God, I hope not," replied Adam apprehensively.

"Think we should change our marketing?" asked Randy.

"I don't want to spend a lot," Adam said.

"Gotta spend money to make money…isn't that the old saying?"

"Gotta have money to spend money," responded Adam.

"Yeah, well, let's do some thinking. We obviously have some time."

Adam looked out and saw that the showroom was empty except for some antsy salesmen with time on their hands. He nodded and Randy followed him out the door and the two men walked through the showroom and out the front door. The lot was filled with hundreds of cars, but no people were looking at them.

"This looks eerily familiar," said Randy. "Let's go for a ride."

The two men got in Randy's car and they drove around the city, looking at the lots of the competition as well as the used cars sellers. Everywhere they looked they saw a sea of cars without any customers looking at them. As they drove, they both felt the panic of going through it all over again what they had just come out of.

"What about a sale?"

"I don't want a one-shot deal," replied Adam. "We need to come up with something that's going to keep people walking in."

"It's pretty obvious sales are down everywhere," replied Randy.

"Then it better be a good plan," said Adam tersely.

They drove back to the dealership and Randy followed Adam into his office. Adam handed Randy a piece of paper and a pen.

"What's this for?" asked Randy.

"We're going to come up with that marketing plan," replied Adam.

Randy smiled and nodded. It was time to brainstorm.

He reached for his phone as his car maneuvered through the traffic and made its way toward the outskirts of the city. He had been excited about telling her about his new house, hopeful that it might spark something, even a visit from her and the kids, but instead, as had been the case since leaving Minnesota, it backfired and had only increased the distance that was now between them.

He pressed the button that automatically dialed her number. He listened to the first ring and wondered if she was there. He heard the second ring and hoped that he would soon hear her voice. The third ring brought the realization that she wasn't going to answer and the fourth ring immediately took him to her messages.

"Hi…I'm sorry if I upset you about the house," he said into the phone. "I just want you to know that I love and miss you and the kids. I also understand why you left and are afraid to let me back in but I do love you and I was once a good husband and I just pray you'll give me another chance to be a better one. I love you Brenda, I love you."

He snapped his phone shut and immediately wished he hadn't left the message but it no longer mattered and so he hoped that maybe it would give her cause to call him. He tried not to think about her anymore but as he drove toward his house, she was all that was in his mind. It felt as though the game was slipping away from him but he knew it was much more than that. He was stuck…unable to go back and eliminate the mistakes that had brought him here and not able to go forward for it meant being alone.

Brenda looked at the old photo album and the pictures of the life she had once had with a man she had vowed to be with until death departed. There were pictures of the two of them at a lake, a party, and at a baseball game. She admired her wedding dress as she looked at the photos of their reception. She remembered the vacation to Florida with the kids and him. There were pictures of him in the swimming pool holding up little Tisha while Sean climbed on his back. Where had these times gone? How had they lost their way, she wondered?

There was a message on her phone and she saw it was from him. She debated whether to delete it immediately or listen to it and finally decided to hear him out. She continued to thumb through the album as his words poured into her ear and she realized that she not only still loved him, but she was still in love with him also.

As the message ended, she sat and debated whether to call him or not. What could it hurt, she thought to herself? He has done more good than bad and he obviously still wanted to make the marriage work. She put her finger on the green send key and prepared to push it but then suddenly remembered the awful moments when child services came in and took the children.

She had been unable to move, to speak, to defend her kids from them. She had been paralyzed by the panic that had overtaken her physically and he had let them walk out with the kids. He had stood there and watched as the police had led them out of the house, and she knew that this was something she could never forgive him for. No matter how much she loved him, if she was with him there was always the chance it could happen again. No, it would do no good to call him. She realized it was time to move on. It was no longer about her happiness but the safety of the Sean and Tisha. She closed the phone and put it down.

She heard sniffling outside of her door and she called the child into her room. The child climbed onto her bed and snuggled close to her mother. She tried to remain strong but soon broke down in a mournful sob as Brenda pulled her closer.

"Baby, what's wrong?" she asked the child.

"It's my fault, momma," Tisha spoke through her tears.

"What's your fault?"

"I did something bad," she replied and her crying made her hold her mother tighter.

"What did you do? You can tell me honey, I'm sure it's not that bad."

"It's my fault daddy doesn't live with us anymore," said the child as she broke down completely.

Brenda pulled her on top of her and squeezed her reassuringly and rocked her back and forth as the childish sobs filled the room.

"No, it's not honey, your daddy and I…"

"It's my fault," moaned the heartbroken girl. "I made him feel bad about missing my birthdays and then I drew terrible pictures of him. Now he thinks I don't like him anymore so he won't come home."

"Honey, your daddy has never felt that way about you," she admonished the child. "He loves you very much, probably more than he ever has. It's just that sometimes mommies and daddies have to be apart."

She pulled Tisha closer and used all her strength not to cry herself.

"Sometimes things happen that make it better if they aren't with each other anymore," she said softly as she continued to rock her back and forth.

"Don't you like daddy anymore?" Tisha asked her.

"Of course I do, I love him just like you do but your daddy and I just can't be together anymore."

"But why mommy?"

"We just can't Tisha, but that doesn't mean you won't see him or that he doesn't love you anymore. I know it's hard to understand but someday you will. Until then, just always remember that he loves you so much, just like I do."

They hugged tightly and neither wanted to be the first to let go. Time stood still for a brief period for the two of them and they were safe in each other's arm, both feeling the loss of one that had been the center of their lives. Finally, Tisha loosened her grip around her mother and Brenda knew that it was time to let her go. The child kissed her on the cheek and rubbed her eyes, then sadly made her way out of the bedroom. Brenda followed her and lovingly tucked her into bed and kissed her on the forehead. The child's energy had been drained by the tears and she was quickly asleep.

Brenda walked back into her bedroom and closed the door. She put on her nightgown and climbed into her bed. She rolled onto her side and into the fetal position and then buried her head in the pillows.

She could finally let her own tears escape.

Randy wandered around the empty house. It was past midnight and he couldn't sleep, or maybe it was that he didn't want to. When he slept, he would dream that he and Brenda and the kids were back together and everything was normal. They were doing the mundane things that families do. Eating dinner together, watching television, out for a walk around the neighborhood. It wasn't exciting, merely wonderful and it always seemed so real until the alarm would go off in the morning and bring him back to the reality of his lonely existence.

As he walked from room to room, he thought about what furniture he should put there and tried to picture it in different settings. He had known that he needed to get something soon because he wanted the children to come and visit and he needed a home for them to come to. All he had now was a cot and a sleeping bag, but the roof over his head was his or at least he hoped at some point it would be.

He went into the kitchen and made some coffee. He poured a cup and walked out onto the front porch and sat down on the step, sipping and staring out into the peaceful evening. He looked up to the sky, another starless night, the little bulbs covered by the thickening clouds that never seemed to leave. He looked at his watch, almost one in the morning, and though he knew better he pulled out his phone and called Brenda.

To his surprise he heard her sleepy voice on the other end and he was heartened because she didn't hang up. They spoke quietly for a minute about the kids and then Randy decided to push the envelope.

"I know you still love me Brenda, I know it," he said to her.

"Yes Randy, but there are other things to consider," she replied, the sleepiness slowly dissipating.

"Brenda, I'm cleared, exonerated. You don't have to worry about anybody taking the children from us."

"It's more than that Randy," she tried to explain to him. "I never dreamed that what happened to us could actually happen, but it did, it did and you let them take our children away."

"Brenda, I didn't know what to do then, I admit it, but you know that there was no way I could stop them from taking them, no way," he pleaded. "But I've changed, I have. I'm a different man now, more cautious, not impulsive."

He was silent for a moment and he listened to her breathing and he tried to imagine those breaths against his own skin.

"It affected me too, Brenda. I swear it won't happen again, and we still love each other. That's a good place to start, isn't it?"

"I don't know Randy," she replied, but she felt her defenses weakening. She did love him and she wanted him, but the thought of having him back terrified her.

"I only know that anything is possible now."

"That could be a good thing," he replied soothingly.

"So far it's been bad," she said quietly.

"I'm doing well now financially," he said, but he knew it was a lie. Yes, he was doing better but he had a long way still to go. "I'm paid up on everything and have paid down the credit cards. I have money put away for rainy days. I swear, you can trust me..."

"I've heard that before," she said and he knew she was right.

"It's true, I swear it is," he said desperately.

"But don't you see Randy? If I come back to you in Salt Lake than I lose my salary, if you come here to Saint Paul, we lose yours and we're right back in the same quagmire."

"Brenda..." he pleaded.

"No Randy, this is no longer about you and me, it's about the children, their well-being."

"And don't you think part of that is having a mother and father together, under the same roof, guiding them?" he asked.

"Not anymore."

His heart sank when she spoke those words and they were quiet. He felt a knowing pain in his stomach and he wanted to cry but he had to be strong, not give her another reason to consider him weak. She felt guilty for having to tell him the things she was saying but she knew that sooner or later he needed to accept that she and the children had moved onto safer ground.

"Well," he finally said, groping for a life line. "How about just letting me come back for a trial period, see how it works."

"Randy, stop," she admonished him.

"But Brenda..."

"No, stop it Randy, just stop it. This is so difficult, please don't make it harder."

They were silent again and though Randy tried to remain stoic, he could feel tears filling his eyes and rolling down his cheeks.

"Can I at least see the children?" he asked meekly.

"Yes, we can set something up. I know they want to see you and they miss you. Tish is afraid you don't love her anymore but I told her that you do," she said, and she wondered why she felt a little satisfaction about the pain she knew this would cause him.

"You've done good with them Brenda," he finally managed to say after feeling the blow of Tisha's thoughts.

"Thank you," she replied. "Randy, it's late and I'm really tired. I'll talk to you soon and we'll set up a time for them to visit you."

"I could come to Saint Paul," he said, knowing that the house wouldn't be ready for them soon enough.

"No, I don't think that would be good," she replied.

"Please Brenda, I'm begging you," he said as another tear dropped from his eye.

"Randy, I'm tired. I'm not going to change my mind," she replied firmly. "It's time for us to move on. I'll be happy to discuss the children with you but we both need to face the fact that our marriage is dead."

She had said it and it hit him across the face like a two by four. He felt woozy, unbalanced and suddenly very afraid.

"Damn it," he stammered. "It's not dead."

"It is to me," she replied.

Again, all the energy was sapped from his body. His hand that held the phone shook and his neck constricted, air was not getting to him and his chest tightened. He feared he was having a heart attack.

"Brenda," he cried. "Please…"

"Good night Randy," she said as she closed her phone and set it down on the nightstand next to her bed.

He was weak, exhausted, beaten. She had said the words he had feared. The marriage was dead to her, it was dead. She had taken everything to a new threshold; one that he knew would in all likelihood be out of his reach. It couldn't be, he thought to himself, God, please. It just couldn't be.

His fell backwards and he felt the tremors shoot up and down his body. He tried to think but he couldn't. All he could do is feel the pain of loss. Tears streamed down his face and he sobbed uncontrollably. In his worst nightmare he never believed that it would come to this but it had and he had been the one responsible for it.

His family was rapidly falling away from him and it was too late to pull them back.

Chapter 16

FLOWERS

Robert sat at his large desk studying reports detailing the latest deal the company was attempting to close. Everything seemed to be in place but the clients still harbored reservations and he did not want to lose this deal. There had to be a way to quell the clients, loosen them up, so he had decided to bring in the latest member of his executive staff.

"Hi Brenda," he said as she entered his office. "Have a seat."

Though he was professional he couldn't help noticing the tightness of her blouse against her bosom. It had been a while since he had been with a woman and at night, in his bed he harbored fantasies of making love with her.

"What is it, Robert?" she asked as she sat and crossed her legs.

Robert filled her in on the nuances of the deal. While he spoke, he struggled not to let his eyes wander from hers. He noticed that small wrinkles had developed around her eye sockets and he wondered if the stress of her impending divorce or her new job were the cause. She had a sweet aroma about her and he thought of her putting the perfume that caused it on her sweet neck and behind her ears.

As he talked, he realized that the thrill of the deal often led to heat between co-workers and wondered if she harbored the same thoughts about him. She was always very friendly with him, but professional also.

Yet she had opened herself up to him, telling him intimate details of what she was going through in her marriage.

"So, if we want to be ready for them, we're going to have to work late for the next couple of weeks," he heard himself saying to her.

"But Robert, my kids…" and he was immediately taken from the fantasy he was developing in his mind.

"Look Brenda, I made you Vice-President specifically for a deal just like this. Late nights sometimes come with the territory," he said sternly.

"I realize that Robert, it's just…" she tried to protest.

"Brenda, this is non-negotiable. If you can't do it, I'll have to find someone that can."

"Meaning?"

"I think you know exactly what I mean. Look Brenda, I'm not trying to be threatening but this is the job and as you're superior I expect you to fulfill the functions of it. This deal nets us millions of dollars. This is the business we are in," he replied intently.

"You're right Robert, I'm sorry," she said, realizing that he was indeed correct. "Of course you can count on me. When do you want to get started?"

"Tonight," he replied. "We don't have anytime to lose."

She nodded and stood and walked toward the door. He stared at her ass as she walked away and again his thoughts returned of being with her. He wanted her, but he also feared that maybe he had picked the wrong person for the position and business always came before pleasure.

Brenda stared out of her window at the skyline of Saint Paul. Another cloudy day, she thought, seems like it is always this way. She thought of Sean and Tisha and realized that she seemed to be seeing less and less of them. She comforted herself in that she was providing for them and that the financial problems that had plagued them for the past year had been eliminated. Yet she wondered if the price of not seeing them was worth it.

Maybe it would be good to let Randy come back, move in and become a family again. At least then the kids would have someone at home when they arrived from school. They would have the life that they had lived before the nightmare had begun. But she realized that Randy would go back into coaching and so nothing would be different. Then she shuddered and realized that it could be worse and Randy would not be able to get a job and would begin to resent her. That resentment would have a horrible effect on the kids who were just now starting to feel safe again.

No, it was best that he stay out of the picture. They were doing fine. Sure, this new position caused her to be away from home more than she liked but it provided them with financial stability and, for her, freedom from the insanity that her husband had driven her too in Salt Lake. Suddenly, Robert entered her mind and she felt her cheeks redden. He was older than her by a decade but was still a very handsome man and maintained a wonderful physique. She wondered if he noticed her looking his way and how he would feel about the attraction she was experiencing.

Sean was waiting for her when she arrived at the condo and his look of excitement made her smile. He had grown so much in the past year, truly a young man now.

"Mom, I got the part I tried out for," he exclaimed excitedly.

"Part? What part?"

"The school play, we're doing 'Oklahoma' and I'm playing Curly in it."

She was taken aback. She had no idea he was interested in drama.

"That's wonderful Sean. When did you try out?" she asked. "When did this all come about?"

"Mom, I told you," he said, hurt that she didn't remember. "I joined drama when we moved back. I had to take a drama class in Salt Lake and loved it so I joined the drama club here."

"You didn't tell me that," she said but knew that he probably had.

"Yes, I did. You're just like dad was when he was coaching," he said crossly. "You don't listen or care about me and Tish anymore. All you care about is your work."

"That's not true," she said defensively.

"Yes, it is," he replied.

"Sean, look honey, regardless, I'm so pleased and excited for you," she said as she grabbed and hugged him. "When is the play?"

"One month from now," he told her, again excited. "Opening night is on the 17th. Will you go? You have to be there for my debut."

"Absolutely. I can't wait," she exclaimed. "In fact, I'm going to brag to everybody I see that my son is now a great thespian."

"Mom…"

"No, mothers get to do that," she said half-jokingly.

"Thanks mom," he laughed. "I knew you wouldn't be like dad. I knew you wouldn't let work get in the way."

He hugged her and she held him tightly and gave him a kiss on the cheek. They broke their hold on each other and he went into his room to memorize his lines while she walked into her home office and clicked on the internet. She went to her e-mail account and entered her password and began checking the messages.

As expected, there was a message from Robert. She quickly scanned it and then stopped. The message was a schedule of things that had to be done and meetings that she was needed at. Her heart sank as she reached the end of the message. She had forgotten it but there it was. There was a dinner meeting scheduled a month from now, though a date had not yet been picked. "Please don't let it be the 17th" she thought to herself.

It was true what Sean had said she realized. Work was becoming more important than the kids. She had to be at the meeting but she didn't want to disappoint Sean again. He had gone through enough the past year. The least she could do would be there for him on his opening night. She had to find a way, even if the meeting ended up being the same night.

She was immediately tired, another crisis coming up. How could she get out of this meeting though she knew she really wanted to be at it? She wanted to because she wanted to be with Robert she realized. She was too tired to deal with it tonight but knew that soon she would have to. But it would another day's problem. Tonight, she would relax because she knew the next month would be truly a test.

Three weeks had passed and Randy was getting tired of playing phone tag with Brenda. It had been months since he had last seen the kids and he was desperately missing them. Brenda had promised they would talk and schedule a time but every time he got a hold of her she was busy and would promise that they would talk about it later. Now he was afraid that she was stalling and had no intention of letting the visit happen.

It was near midnight and he picked up his phone and tried again and was relieved to hear her answer it. Hopefully tonight they could figure out a time. Since she had made it clear that she didn't want him in Minnesota he had bought some second-hand furniture, nothing fancy but at least the house was no longer empty and he had enough to provide comfort for his kids visit.

"I'm hoping we can schedule a time for me to see the kids," he said to her. As he spoke, he realized how tired he had become. Must be the stress he figured.

"Do you have any dates in mind?" she asked resigned.

"I don't know your schedule so not really," he replied, "how about during their spring break?"

She thought about this for a moment, looking at a calendar she had in front of her.

"That could work," she said softly, almost to herself.

Suddenly she heard her phone beep and she took it away from her ear. It was Robert calling, undoubtedly from the office. He had been spending more and more time there working to complete the deal.

"Randy, could I call you back? I have to take this call," she said.

"It's always something Brenda. Christ, its damn near midnight!" he said harshly. He was sick of being put on the backburner. "Can't we get through this first? It's important."

"I realize that Randy but this is my work."

"Fine, what the hell, should I schedule an appointment to talk to you so we can get this done?" he replied irritatingly.

"Randy." She was sick of him acting like a child.

"Whatever," he huffed and hung up.

He was so frustrated with her. He wanted to kick something but reason quickly prevailed. He knew his frustration with her was not because of some scheduling difficulties but because he missed her so badly. Everyday increased the likelihood that the marriage was over and it stung him. He wanted her back so badly, wanted everything to be normal again. Deep down he knew that a normal life had left him long ago and the chances of it coming back were remote.

Then remorse overcame him. She was doing the best she could, and truth be told she was doing better than him. She had pulled herself back from the abyss and had succeeded in building a new life for her and the kids. In truth he was jealous of her. She was supposed to rely on him but since he had failed her, she had found she had strengths that had been hidden by years of his neglect. God he was so proud of her, yet he knew that her success had guaranteed the demise of their union, and that pride quickly turned to pain.

He realized that he had been stupid. She didn't need a fight right now, she needed him to work with her and he had even screwed that up. What had he been thinking? Stupid pride had caused him to hang up on her. He was going to teach her lesson, well, that had gone well, he thought to himself. You are a stupid son of a bitch and every time you let your pride get in the way you push her away a little bit farther than before. He vowed to pull himself together. He had to because she was damn near gone now.

Brenda looked at the phone and felt irritation toward her soon to be ex-husband. He just wasn't going to make anything easy. He didn't seem to understand that he was no longer the only person in the family who had responsibilities that had to be met. Sure, all those years when he had been coaching it had been perfectly fine for him to cut off conversations because his work was so important. Now she was the awful person because she was doing the same thing. Well, he could go to hell. She pushed the receive button and heard Robert's voice.

"Brenda, I need you to work your magic one more time," he said. She had earned the clients trust since coming into the deal and had smoothed the rough waters, but they still had doubts.

"I thought the signing was all set up," she replied.

"It is, but they're still having second thoughts," he replied pensively.

"What's the problem," she asked, alarmed that the deal could fall through in the last minute.

Robert told her of his conversation with the negotiator. The clients were afraid that mass layoffs were going to occur and they wanted to know that their loyal work force was going to be taken care of. Of course, this last roadblock was tricky and couldn't be promised, but how could they overcome it? They were savvy business people. They had to know this was a promise that could not be made so obviously there was something deeper that was troubling them. Robert knew that the rapport Brenda had built up with them was the only chance of salvaging all the hard work that had been put into this deal. He was desperate.

"They trust you Brenda, I know you can find out what the real problem is so that we can address it and smooth it over," he said.

"That's fine," replied Brenda. "When's the meeting?"

"The 17th," he replied.

"What?"

"The 17th," he said again.

"Robert, I can't do it then. Isn't there another time? That's Sean's opening night for his play and I've promised him I'd be there and besides; I already have that other meeting scheduled also."

"Brenda, I'm sorry but no, this deal has to be completed. You'll just have to re-schedule your other meeting. I have your plane ticket and reservations at the Hilton," he replied forcefully.

"But my son is in a play that night. Its opening night and I promised…"

"Brenda, I sympathize with you," but she could tell by the tone of his voice that wasn't true. "This is your job though. You're going."

She was silent for a moment. She was tired and frustrated with both Robert and Randy but she knew that she could not let her emotions overtake her right now. She surrendered to the facts; she had no choice. Hopefully she would be able to make Sean understand but she knew that probably wasn't going to happen either.

"All right Robert, I'll go. When do I leave?"

All day she dreaded going home. She had put off telling Sean that she wasn't going to be able to be there. She had tried to tell him, but then he would talk about it and the excitement in his voice would not allow her to let him know of the unplanned interruption she was facing.

Tomorrow morning, she would be on the plane and she knew that time had run out. At home she would have to face him and let him know and his hurt would be deep. I'm such a bad mother she lamented to herself.

The workday ended and she was readied up herself for the confrontation she knew was coming, but as she drove toward the condo her fear built up. How could she tell him she wouldn't be there? Why hadn't she let him know earlier? The knot in her stomach grew as the distance closed and soon, she arrived. There was no turning back now.

Inside the condo Sean excitedly told his mother about their preparations. He couldn't wait and he was so happy she was going to be there. He told her how thankful he was that he could count on her, how she followed through. She wasn't like his dad. He had always missed everything, but not her.

Finally, she couldn't take anymore. She knew she had to be honest and get it out.

"Sean, I can't be there opening night," she blurted out, "but I'll be there on the 18th. I promise."

Sean was stunned. She was no different than his dad.

"But mom, you promised you'd be there opening night!"

"I know son, I'm sorry. I have to go out of town. It just came up. Some clients…"

"You sound just like dad," he exploded. "I can't believe you two. It's always something. Everybody else is more important to you than Tish and I!"

"That's not true," she pleaded. "Nothing is more important than you two."

"Then you'll be there opening night," he said angrily.

"I can't," she replied, her heart breaking because of the disappointment she was causing him. She should have told him earlier she thought to herself angrily.

"That's what I thought," he said sarcastically.

"Now listen, young man," she said intently. He would not speak to her in that tone. "I would give anything to be there, but I can't."

She glared at him for effect. He had stepped over the line and she was now angry.

"I work so that you and Tish have the opportunity to do these types of things. Your father did too. We're not perfect people but we do the best we can."

"You and dad always have time for work," he protested, "just not us."

"Stop it Sean! In a perfect world I would have all the time for you and Tisha, but that's not real life. You have it pretty good mister, a mother and father that love you and provide for you."

She was sick of him acting this way. He had been doing this for over a year now and she knew that it was time to stop him from being this way. It was time for him to grow up and quit being a spoiled brat.

"I'll be there the 18th. You'll just have to figure out a way to make through the 17th without me!"

"Don't bother!" he screamed. "Maybe I'll start living on my own. I don't need you or dad. I haven't had you anyway."

He ran from the kitchen to his room and slammed his door. Brenda leaned back against the counter and closed her eyes. She had known it was going to be hard, but this was brutal. She realized she had given him far too much latitude since moving here. He didn't respect her anymore. He didn't respect anyone.

She walked back to her bedroom and began packing for tomorrow's trip. She laid out her clothes that she would take and began putting them carefully into the suitcase. As she was working the phone rang. She knew it was Randy but she decided not to answer. One fight with an Albertson man was enough for one night. She completed her packing and put on her nightgown and prepared for bed. Tomorrow would be a whirlwind and she knew she had to get rest.

She lay on the bed and thought about all the things she would have to do tomorrow before taking off for the airport. She grabbed her phone and called her answering machine at work to remind her of things that needed to be done. After she finished with the call, she saw that Randy had left a message. She was going to delete it but changed her mind and decided to hear what he had left.

"Hi, it's me," the voice in the phone began. "I'm sorry I hung up. I just miss you and the kids so much.

The voice stopped for a moment, and the came back on.

"I just wish I could have a mulligan for the last year. I would do everything differently, but… well, I don't know…"

Again, there was silence and Brenda felt a lump developing in her throat. He sounded so beat, so down and out. He really did love her. His broken voice was telling her how much.

"I'm sorry honey," he finally said, sounding almost like a child. "Maybe you're right, you probably are better off without me."

Again, it was silent except for a slight sniff. She realized that he had probably been crying.

"I gotta go," the voice said softly. "I love you."

She felt a tear beginning to fall down her cheek. He was so broken, but it was too late. The marriage had come and gone and she knew that it was for the best. The pain of losing him felt like a death but it was worse because what had once been was no longer though the person she had once vowed to spend her life with, for better or worse still remained.

The company sent a car over to the condo to pick Brenda up and she had the driver stop by the office before going to the airport. There were a couple of items that she needed to do and some papers that she needed to take with her. As the car made its way to the office, she looked out the window. It was a gray day with a misty rain that caused everything to feel damp. Yet that grayness had a certain beauty in its darkness as she watched the people in their overcoats make their way on the sidewalk.

The car stopped in front of the large building that housed the corporate headquarters and the driver climbed out and went around the car, opening her door. She told him she would be down in twenty minutes and he nodded. She walked into the building and showed her ID and made her way to the elevator.

The elevator quickly filled with people but no one spoke. All eyes stared at the numbers above the door as it rose and they slowly disembarked as they came to their floors. Brenda stood in the corner and at each floor had more room to move as the car emptied until there was just her and another passenger.

At her floor she politely nodded to the other person and stepped out, walking to the glass doors that led to the corporate office. She waved to the receptionist and made her way to her office. Her secretary was waiting for her and handed her some messages and papers she would need.

"Do you have my tickets," she asked.

"Yes, I'll give them to you when you leave."

"Thanks Darla, I don't know what I'd do without you."

Darla smiled and Brenda walked into her office, looking at the messages in her hand and mentally making a note of who to call first. Out of the corner of her eye something caught her attention and she looked up. She stared at her desk, stunned at the sight and slowly walked toward it.

A vase of a dozen red roses adorned it. She walked slowly to it and saw a small card. She was almost afraid to open the little envelope that held it, but she did and slowly read it.

Have a safe trip. I probably shouldn't say this but I love you.

R

She smiled and grabbed one, pulling it out and gently sniffing it as she looked at the card one more time.

She loved him too.

Chapter 17

ACCEPTANCE

He wrote the last check for the last bill of the month and looked at what he had left. It was such a pretty sight, he thought to himself. His account had been slowly building up and now he actually had a little bit of savings.

He walked out of his house, his checkbook in his back pocket. He was still old school and used the checkbook instead of the ATM card the bank had given him. He learned early that it was too easy to spend his way into trouble with the card but with the checkbook he always knew exactly where he stood with his finances. He hopped into his car and drove into the city.

Three hours later he was back home setting up his new flat screen television and waiting for the couch to be delivered. He had a satisfaction that he hadn't felt in years. He had new furniture. No, it wasn't the expensive stuff, but it was new, smelled new, looked new and it signified that he was on his way back from the abyss he had put himself into.

The next day he bragged to Adam about the new items in the house. He couldn't stop smiling and Adam enjoyed seeing him this way. Randy told him about his great negotiating skills in obtaining the two items and Adam laughed as the story unfolded. After the story was completed, the men turned more serious. It was time to talk a little business.

"You remember Alan Shankey?" asked Adam.

"Shankey…Shankey, oh yeah, yeah I do. He's the guy who worked for that company that bought seven of our cars," remembered Randy. "He's a big hockey fan. That sale probably saved me in this business."

"Yeah, that's right. He gave me a call earlier."

"You, why you?" replied Randy, a little hurt. "He's my client,"

"Now Randy, don't get excited. I'm not stealing your client," Adam assured him.

"I know," replied Randy, but the way he was shifting in his chair showed that he was clearly agitated. "It just bothers me he called you and not me."

"Maybe he lost your phone number. I don't know…would you just listen to what I have to say? It's important," Adam shot back, a little irritated.

"All right, what'd he want?"

"He called me about you. He wants to meet with you and me about some kind of deal," said Adam as he sat back and put his feet up on the desk.

Randy smiled and thought about the possible commission.

"More cars I presume?"

"I don't know. He didn't say, but you'd have to figure that would be what it's about. Anyway, he just said he wanted to meet tonight. Is seven good for you?"

"Well, let me check my calendar," laughed Randy. "Of course it's good for me. It's got to be about getting more cars, don't you think?"

"I don't know Randy, as I said he didn't say."

Randy sat back in his chair and started thinking. Surely this was a good thing. In fact, maybe it was a gold mine. Shankey was a good guy. He wants to give all of his business to us or maybe he wants to refer some people to us, he thought.

"It's got to be a good thing, right?" he asked. "Wait, you don't think they're unhappy with the cars, do you?"

"No, I don't think so," said Adam. "Christ Randy, you're driving yourself crazy. We'll find out tonight, meanwhile let's sell some cars."

"You're right," smiled Randy.

"We'll get some dinner and go tonight after we close shop," instructed Adam.

"Candace fine with that?" joked Randy.

"Of course," laughed Adam. "Besides, no chickadilla's going to tell me what I can and can't do."

"Remember bud," cautioned Randy. "She's a lawyer and a woman you love going to bed with, sounds to me like she owns you. Hey, maybe you're her trophy boyfriend."

Adam laughed as the two men rose and walked out into the showroom. There were customers waiting and they headed toward them. As Adam listened to his customer, he glanced toward Randy who was busy schmoozing a family and smiled. It was good to see him like this. He was a man again.

That evening they drove into the parking lot in front of Alan's office and parked. They walked toward the office building where Reynolds Corporation resided and were quiet as they entered the elevator. The car stopped at the 18th floor and the two men stepped out. Randy looked at Adam, who had a Cheshire cat's grin.

"What's going on?" asked Randy.

"We'll find out soon enough."

"Why you smiling like that? Something's going on."

"Nothing's going on," protested Adam. "I just love these kinds of meetings. It like Christmas when you see a gift you want to open but you have to wait until after dinner. Well, it's after dinner."

Randy nodded and the two men walked into the reception area of the company. The lights were off but it was still light. There was activity going on in the back so they made their way around the empty receptionist desk. Alan saw them walking back toward him and quickly came up to greet them.

"Hey Adam, Randy, come on in. Have a seat. It's good to see you," he said cheerfully.

"How you doing Alan?" said Randy with his hand outstretched. Alan grabbed it and they shook.

"Good," replied Alan and then he looked at Adam. "You fill him in?"

"No, I thought since you came up with it maybe you should."

Randy looked at the two men and wondered what was going on. Alan smiled and led the men into his office. As they walked Randy gave a quizzical look to Adam but he merely shrugged but still had that same grin. Alan led them to a mahogany table with four chairs around it and each man sat.

"What's going on guys?" asked Randy.

"Well, our company is in negotiations with a good size outfit in the Midwest to merge together," explained Alan. "Basically, they would be acquiring us but we would be a subsidiary of theirs with freedom to do certain things and run our own shop."

Come on Alan, I'm a simple car salesman," replied Randy, leaning forward and putting his elbows on the table. "You lost me."

"Well, I don't know if you realize this, but you own a small bit of our operations," replied Alan.

Randy sat straight up, shocked. "I do, how's that?"

Chatworth Chrysler and Dodge, LLC owns a small percentage. In fact, for only the last month has that been true. If I'm not mistaken, and correct me Adam if I am misinformed, you now own a piece of Chadwick. Thus, though your share is tiny, you also own a piece of us."

Randy let this information sink in. Obviously, Adam had been doing some business behind the scenes.

"I see," he said finally before looking at his partner. "Thanks for telling me."

"Consider it an early birthday present," replied Adam.

Randy smirked but now was intrigued.

"Well, go on," he instructed Alan.

"If the sale goes through, and at this point we have every reason to believe it will, there are going to be some changes to our company and a new business plan."

"What's that got to do with me?"

Alan got up and walked to his desk and then came back with a binder and placed it in front of Randy.

"Here," he said. "Why don't you take a look at the new plan we will have."

"All right," replied Randy and he began thumbing through the binder. The three men sat silently for a few minutes as Randy looked at what was before him. After thumbing through it he looked up at Alan, and then slowly glanced at Adam. Adam was still grinning and Alan now had the same grin. Randy looked back down at the binder, not believing his eyes and then looked up again. He was stunned as Adam patted him on the back.

∞

Brenda sat frustrated at her desk. Sean was still very upset with her for missing the opening night of the play and now Tish was acting up. She felt alone, isolated and friendless. Work wasn't going any better. At times, she hated coming to work and that caused her to feel guilty. Somehow, she had to find some semblance of balance in her life and she knew she had to do it soon or she would be unemployed.

Robert knocked on the door and came in. She looked up and smiled at him, but he did not return it and she immediately became very concerned. Was she about to lose her job? She had done so well helping to close the last deal. But she had also bickered with Robert and other members of the management team on the deal and then had protested about going to visit the clients. He sat down in front of her and she noticed that his face was stony.

"Brenda, you have some time?" he asked, but she knew it wasn't a question.

"Sure Robert, what can I do for you?"

"I have some concerns that have been building and I think we need to address them."

Brenda was now paralyzed with fear. She knew that if she lost this job finding a new one would be extremely difficult. The economy was a mess, thanks to a stimulus that wasn't stimulating anything, and she was now in management. There were a lot of managers looking for work right now and the chances of her finding even something like she had before being promoted was unlikely for now she would be over-qualified. Most companies did not want to hire that type of person because they would leave for a better job as soon as they could. She had learned that the hard way in Utah.

"I see," she said quietly, trying to remain calm.

"Look, on this last deal we did you made it happen but it was difficult at times getting you to do it," he said sternly.

"How do you mean?"

"Two things come to mind right away. You always seemed to want to re-schedule appointments. You weren't willing to work after hours. Brenda, there are people here who would have killed to have a shot at that deal. You seemed to fight it. Why?"

She was desperately trying to keep her composure. Right now, she had to be the consummate professional. She had to eliminate his doubts and calm his concerns.

"I understand what you're saying, and yes, I suppose I was difficult. I have no doubt others would have loved to have been in my shoes. But I want to point out that I got the job done. I developed a relationship with the clients, cultivated it and played a major role in closing the deal. Robert, the deal closed because of me. Because of that I'm not sure what the problem is."

Robert was silent for a moment and looked down at his hands. Brenda was not sure whether he was angry or contemplating. Still, she knew that she had delivered a strong rebuttal and her nerves began to calm a little.

"The problem," Robert finally replied, "is what if it hadn't gotten done."

"That's not a problem," she said, now a little angry but still being professional. "That's a supposition that didn't happen."

"Please Brenda," he told her in a measured tone but now knowing that his bluff had been called, "don't be angry. I'm only letting you know that I have concerns."

"Robert, I'm never going to be like the others. I'm a working mother who is going through a divorce and trying to give my kids as normal a life as possible," she explained. "I can promise you that I get my work done right and timely, but my work will never override the needs of my children. I lost them once, had them taken away and I will never let that happen again. Can you understand that?"

He nodded

"I like my job, love it even, but it's a profession. My children are a part of me and they are non-negotiable. I can do this job and I do it well for you as I showed with the last deal."

"Brenda, I have a board of directors I have to report to," he replied. "They want to know that we are going to find a way to make money despite today's economic perils. I have to know that I can rely on you. If I can't I have to get somebody else."

Brenda sat forward and stared intensely into his eyes.

"Only you can decide that Robert but I have already shown you I can get the job done. Maybe not exactly as you want me to do it, but closed all the same."

He stared at her in silence. She was such a strong woman and so very beautiful. Randy had been stupid to lose her, he thought to himself. She deserves a man who can match her intellectually yet provide the passion in her life that is obviously missing. I can do that, he though, not that stupid weak jock strap she was married to.

"I believe you," he said finally. "I just wanted to make sure you have the fire for this, but to be honest I was sure that you did."

"Do you do this with the men also?" she asked angrily, feeling as though he were being condescending toward her.

"That was uncalled for," he replied, his face turning to stone. "Your predecessor was a man; you'll notice he is no longer here."

"You're right," she said meekly. "I apologize."

"Listen Brenda, I know what you're going through is difficult. Just hang in there. We have something in the works that I think is perfect for you. When we get further down the road with it, I'll bring you in," he replied, his tone softening.

"What is it?" she asked curiously.

"I can't go into it right now, but it should be soon enough. I'll let you know then."

They both stood and she walked him to the door. She wanted to reach out and grab his hand and pull him back. She wanted to make love to him. The heat was growing, and the fear and anger only increased her desire for him. He began to open the door and then turned to her.

"So, are you going through with the divorce?" he asked, praying silently that she was.

"Are you talking to me as a friend or my boss?" she asked back.

"Brenda…"

She silently beat herself up. Of course, he was talking as a friend, but she wanted him to be more than that.

"I'm sorry. Yes, I'm going through with it."

"Brenda, maybe your marriage was different than mine," he said softly. "Remember, I loved my job more than my wife and family. Can you say the same?"

He reached out and gingerly rubbed her cheek and then opened the door and walked out. She stared at him and thought about what he had just said. Then she blushed, for it was his buttocks she was watching and she began to feel whorish, wanton. She quickly closed the door and walked back to her desk.

Brenda looked out of the window from her room at the condo. The kids were both in bed and she thought about what Robert had told her earlier in the day. Maybe he was right and she needed to see if Randy and she could reconcile. She knew that he would agree to about anything right now and she did still love him. She knew he was probably right that it was unlikely that the children would ever be taken again.

She grabbed her phone and called Randy. It rang once, then twice and she hung up. Why was she fighting her feelings? It was Robert that she wanted, that she trusted now. She began to dial his number and then stopped. What if he didn't feel the same about her? She opened the phone again and dialed the first three numbers but then stopped. She snapped the phone back shut and lay back on the bed. She had to pull herself together and that meant she had to change the way things were. She decided that tomorrow she would go to his office but she had to get some kind of balance in her life. Things had to change with her home life and the only way it would happen was if things changed at work. She decided she had to talk to Robert tomorrow, face to face.

When she arrived to work, she dropped her things off at her office and went straight to his. It was still early and the secretaries were not there yet. She knocked on his door and heard his baritone voice telling her to come in.

"Robert?" she said pensively.

"Yes, what is it, Brenda?"

"I want you to know that I am going through with the divorce. I thought about what you said yesterday and I appreciate that you made me think about it one last time."

He nodded and tried not to smile. He wanted this woman. She had been all he had been thinking about since their meeting yesterday.

"But like I said yesterday, my family is still first," she said nervously. She was not sure how he was going to take it. "I have to be there for my kids."

"So, what do we do?" he asked as he admired the outline of her breasts against the silky blouse she was wearing.

"I just have to believe there is a way I can balance my home life and work. I believe we can do something that is innovative and gets some positive press, which as you know relates directly to marketing."

He laughed. She was a persistent woman and that was a major part of his attraction to her. He waved her over to his desk and admired her as she walked toward him.

"Alright Brenda, let's figure something out," he said.

She smiled and looked into his eyes. He wasn't sure but he thought he saw love in those eyes.

Randy was standing at the window of Alan's office and looking out into the skyline of the city. It was late afternoon and he and Alan had gone over and tweaked some of the business plan that had stunned him the day before. They had worked on it all morning and then had gone out to lunch. After eating fish and chips the men had returned to the office and finished their work, agreeing upon the plan that would go into effect if the sale went through. Alan had left his office to get copies of the agreement and Randy decided to call Brenda with the good news. Surely this would at least give her pause to think about whether or not to proceed with the impending divorce.

The phone rang four times and then went to the message and Randy thought of hanging up. No, he had to tell her and a message was better than nothing.

"Brenda, you have to call me, please. Something amazing happened today that may change your mind about leaving me. Please, I can't believe the news I have for you. Please call," he said into the phone as his excitement grew. "I know you love me and I love you so much. Don't give up on us sweetheart. I promise you that the news I have is worth it. Please call, I love you."

He hung up the phone just as Alan walked back into the office. He handed Randy a copy of the plan they had just put together and a memorandum of agreement. Randy quickly read it and then grabbed a pin out of his shirt pocket and signed his name at the bottom. Alan, who was standing just behind patted him on the back and the two men smiled.

At his house after a late dinner of Chinese and two bottles of Guinness, Randy lounged on his new couch watching the late news on his big screen television he had just bought. The volume was low and Randy wasn't really paying attention to what was on the screen in front of him. Instead, he wondered why Brenda had not called. Yet he wasn't surprised for she had made it clear to him that she was intent on following through on the divorce. If only he could talk to her, tell her about what was happening.

He grabbed his phone out of his pocket and pushed her name under contacts and soon the familiar ring came over the earpiece, but no answer. The message came on and he contemplated whether or not to leave another message. He was about to hang up but realized that if he did, she would probably never call back.

"Brenda, please, I'm begging you to call me," he said into the receiver. "I know you think that a divorce is what you should do but I swear the news I have could change that. I love you so much…you and the kids. The news I have could make us a family again. Please call honey, please..."

He tried to think of something more to say. Nothing was working at all. She was nearly gone and he was helpless to stop it. He put the phone down. All he could do now was wait and hope.

It was morning now and still no return call. She was giving him her answer but he didn't want to face it as he drove to the dealership. Inside he made a few phone calls and worked a couple of customers, making a sale with the last one and then retired to his office. It was lunch time now and he grabbed some peanut butter he had brought with him and rice cakes. He spread it on and quickly ate two of them and then downed it with a bottle of water.

Finally, he could take it no longer and he called her office. The secretary answered but told him that Brenda had told her that she can't talk to him. Randy demanded to know why just as Adam walked into his office. Randy saw that Adam had a serious look on his face and finished his conversation with the secretary.

"What is it?" asked Randy.

Adam didn't say a word, but instead walked to his desk and set a manila envelope that had just come down in front of him. Randy looked at him, not comprehending, while Adam averted his friend's eyes. Randy grabbed the envelope and looked at it. It was from some law firm in Minneapolis and Randy began to open it. Suddenly he stopped when he realized what it was.

The papers had arrived. She would not be talking to him anytime soon.

Randy sat at his kitchen table and stared at the envelope. If he didn't open it maybe it would all just go away, but he knew that was just a fantasy. He continued to stare at it as he got up and poured himself a cup of coffee. He sat back down and fingered the envelope until finally he scolded himself and ripped it open. He pulled out the papers and began reading them page by page. After each page he carefully put the paper down on the table and soon he had a small pile built up.

As he read it, he realized that she had been most fair. She wasn't asking for anything nor was she expecting anything. She was being very liberal with the children's visitation but was asking for custody. He debated whether or not to fight her for the custody, but in reality, he knew that it would be best if they were with their mother. He was beaten and he knew it. She wanted it to be quick and painless and he loved her too much to challenge her. Besides if he did, he would lose her forever and he wasn't prepared to even consider that, much less accept it.

He went into his bedroom and lay down on his bed. He thought of the years they had been together. He remembered the first time he had seen her and the last. In between had been a good, strong marriage. They hadn't been perfect and of course had their share of fights, but what married couple hadn't? He hated child services and the prosecutor and the judge right now, for they had made this not only possible, but likely by the injustice they had put him through.

Then he remembered the night he and Brenda had gone on their date here in Salt Lake. There had been tremendous hope then, a belief that everything was going to be fine. They had found the house they were looking for and had celebrated with a romantic dinner and then making love at the hotel. It had been perfect and now everything was lost.

As he thought about her, he realized that he was crying. He hadn't noticed at first, so engrossed in his thoughts of her. But now he felt the horrible hurt of a love lost and he was unable to control his emotions. The tears poured out of his eyes and his chest heaved as he sobbed. She was gone, he had lost her. It had been one thing when she talked about getting the divorce, but the reality of the papers for the first time made it real.

She didn't want him anymore and he couldn't blame her. The man he was two years before had died and left a sniveling child in its wake. He hated himself and thought of dying. Without the chance to spend the rest of his life with her what reason was there to continue?

She drove from the office to the condo and listened to the radio. The messages from Randy were breaking her heart but she knew that sending the papers had been the right thing to do. It was time and their marriage was dead. It had been for a long time but she had refused to recognize it. In a sense she felt liberation, but also the deep feeling of failure. She had failed at the most sacred commitment between two people. No, she hadn't, she thought to herself defiantly. He had and she had moved on.

She now loved Robert and she was hopeful he loved her too. After all, hadn't he given her the beautiful vase of red roses? She was ready to become a new woman, a free woman and go after the things she loved. She would no longer be one of Randy's many trophies.

As she thought of this, she suddenly heard a song from the past. It had once been hers and Randy while they had been dating all those years ago. The melody drifted through the car and suddenly she felt a familiar lump in her throat. So, this is how it is going to be for a while, she thought, the marriage may be over but the good memories will continue to linger.

A tear clinged to her eye but finally fought its way loose and fell down her cheek. She felt so many different things right now. Fear, excitement, loss, and hope were all of hitting her at once. She knew that she would survive it because to stay with him would be a mistake that could cost her the kids.

Above her the dark skies shed the precipitation that had clung to the clouds and drops began to fall on the windshield.

He wanted one more chance to talk to her, to convince her that he was worth it so he picked up his phone. It was early morning and he hoped that calling her at this time of the day would produce a different outcome. He listened to the ring and each one made him more apprehensive than the one before. Her message came on after the fourth ring and he closed his phone. There was no reason to leave another one.

He tried again as he drove to the dealership but again it ended with her voice telling the caller she was unable to answer. He again hung up and but immediately called her office. Her secretary came on the line and he felt a faint sense of hope.

"I'm sorry Mr. Albertson," she said to him. "Ms. Albertson is out of the office."

Brenda stood over her secretary and nodded.

"Could you please have her call me when she gets back in?" he pleaded.

"I will give her the message, Mr. Albertson," she said as Brenda wrote her a quick note of instruction. "Could you please hold?"

Then Darla quickly read the note and looked up to her boss. Brenda nodded yes and the she brought Randy back from hold.

"Mr. Albertson, Ms. Albertson has returned."

His heart leapt. Maybe now she would talk to him so he could give her his news. He just knew that if she was aware of what was happening here she wouldn't be in such a hurry to end their union.

"Please patch me through, would you?"

"I'm sorry Mr. Albertson but Ms. Albertson has instructed me to inform you that all further communications with her must go through her attorney. His name is Leonard Goldstein."

"Please let me talk to her," he begged.

"I'm sorry sir. As I said all further communication must go through Mr. Goldstein."

"Do you have his number?" he asked, now resigned to the fact that she was not interested in hearing from him.

"Just a moment," Darla replied.

She quickly read the number to Randy and then hung up. Randy kept the phone to his ear and hoped that this was just a bad dream but he knew that it wasn't. The dial tone changed to a busy signal after a few moments but Randy didn't notice. He stared into nothing, seeing only his wife in his mind and missing her immensely.

Adam stood out in the showroom and watched as his friend finally hung up the phone. He murmured some instructions to his salesmen and then made his way to Randy's office. He knocked quietly but Randy did not look up so he walked in.

"You all right?" he asked quietly. He had been through this himself and he knew the pain his best friend was feeling.

"I feel dead. She's lost," Randy replied quietly.

He got up and walked past Adam and out into the day. The sun had been shining earlier but now a thunderstorm was coming in. He didn't hear the roar from the sky. He didn't hear anything.

Chapter 18

SPRING SHOWERS

Alan threw the business plan into the garbage and sat back in his chair. The acquisition had taken a significant turn and the other deal he had been working on, the one he really wanted to close was now within his grasp. He picked up his phone and pressed the numbers and shortly his silent partner's voice came on the line.

"Alan here, I have some news," he said. "Can we meet this afternoon?"

"What time?"

"How about two p.m.? It's probably going to last a while so I'll order dinner."

"Sounds serious," replied the silent partner. "Can I expect good news?"

"Sure looks that way," replied Alan.

"I'll be there then. Should I bring in our candidate?"

"Yes, it's time to make an offer he can't refuse."

"I doubt if that will be a problem."

"Good. Are you sure you're all right with the plan as we talked about?"

"It's a very good plan. I think we'll end up making some nice money with this," the silent partner said.

"Alright, I'll see you at two o'clock sharp then," Alan said.

"We'll be there," replied the partner and then he hung up.

Alan went to the safe in his office and quickly spun the dial to the numbers that unlocked it. He opened the iron door and pulled out papers that had been in there for the last month. At the top was a contract and he quickly scanned it to make sure it was in order. This afternoon everything should be in place he thought to himself. I'll finally reach that goal I wrote down all those years ago at Concordia-Saint Paul.

⌒∞⌒

Brenda answered the phone while she was pouring another cup of coffee. She was working from home today and enjoying the quiet. The silence of the condo was in stark contrast to the office environment and she had made good progress on the assignment that Robert had given her. There were rumors of a merger but no one knew if they were being acquired or buying and the office had become tense. Everyone knew that if they were being acquired there would be downsizing and the fear of the unknown had put everyone on edge.

On the phone was Robert and he told her that she needed to get to the office quickly. As usual Robert gave no indication of what this meeting would be about and she didn't know whether to be fearful or excited. She decided not to think about it as she walked to the parking garage and climbed into her car. She played the radio as she made the short trek to the office building that housed corporate and tried to stay relaxed.

When she arrived Robert's secretary ushered her into the conference room. She sat down at the large table and wondered what it meant that she was the only one there. Robert walked through the door and again gave no indication of his mood or what was about to be discussed but Brenda had a foreboding feeling in the pit of her stomach. She had heard the stories of management members walking into the conference room and coming out unemployed and she feared that she was about to meet that same fate. Obviously, they were being gobbled up by a larger corporation who would want to bring their own management team in.

"We're expanding," he said simply.

She let out her breath and he saw her visibly relax. It was obvious that she had feared the worst and he gave her a smile as he sat down beside her.

"That's a relief," she finally stammered.

"I'm working out the details but you're going to be a major player in what we are planning to do with our new acquisition," he said.

She nodded and he admired her features. He wondered to himself if he was capable of being with one woman for the rest of his life. If he could, it was her that would tame him but he liked his lifestyle. No strings, no attachments. Money afforded him the opportunity to attract beautiful women for short bursts of pleasure and then he could drop them off in the morning. But Brenda was different and he wanted more from her than just the pleasure of invading her body.

"What do you want from me now?" she asked him.

He smiled and touched her cheek and she put her hand on his. They both knew that the moment had arrived and they moved toward each other and lightly touched their lips to each other.

"How about an early lunch?" he said.

"Meet me at the Hilton in twenty minutes," responded Brenda and she again kissed him. "I'll be in the corporate suite."

The food remained untouched on the tray and Brenda cuddled tightly to Robert, her breasts softly lying against his chest. The moment had been as both had fantasized and now they tried to catch their breaths. It had been so long since she had last made love, given herself completely to a man other than Randy. For Robert this had not been just another conquest. He had made love to this woman, become one with her as they had entwined in a desperateness that neither had known existed within them.

Yet he knew that he could never have her for she was not a woman who could be the second love of any man. As much as he wanted her, business would always be his first love. But that was a problem for a later time, a later date. For now, he lay with his arm around her, fiercely holding her tight to him, not wanting this moment to end.

At last, the lovers sat up in the bed and nibbled on the food that awaited them on the tray. As they ate, they spoke of the lovemaking and heaped compliments to each other of their abilities. All too soon it was time to return to the reality of their life and that was the business. As they showered and prepared to go back to the corporate office the talk turned from the things lovers speak of to the business and acquisitions. As they walked to the door Robert stopped for just a moment and pulled her close to him again. He passionately met her lips and she returned the love he was showing. Then they walked out, ready to move forward on the tasks that lay before them.

As they waited for their car Brenda turned to him.

"I never thanked you for the roses and the beautiful vase," she said quietly but lovingly.

He looked at her with a quizzical face.

"I never sent you any my darling," he replied.

She looked at him and immediately felt her heart sink.

"Before my last trip?" she said. "Those weren't from you?"

"No," he replied. "Brenda, I can never be the type of man that you want. I want you to know that I believe I love you, but the love of my life is the business and you are too wonderful of a woman to be second."

She stared at him, stunned that everything she had just thought was not to be.

"Of course," she stammered. "I'm so embarrassed Robert, I didn't want to make you feel that…"

He pressed his finger to her lips to stop her from speaking.

"He loves you very much," he said to her. "He obviously always has. I'm not sure he deserves you but he does love you."

"Yes," she said quietly.

"Maybe you should reconsider," he said. "Maybe I'm wrong and he's who you are supposed to be with."

"No, I've made up my mind and he has the papers. It is too late, too much has happened. I'm glad this happened, it only reinforces my notion that it is time for me to become my own woman."

She looked at the man she loved right now, realizing that she would never have him but thankful that she had at least experienced him, felt him, became one with him.

"Thank you, Robert," she said. "But it is time we move forward. We have a deal to complete and a meeting coming up."

The car pulled up and both jumped in. As she looked out the window a light rain began to fall.

Adam and Randy pulled into Reynolds Corporation and went to Alan's office. Things were moving quickly and Randy felt the excitement of being a part of the changes that were soon to happen. Alan was offering him stability in a business that would continue to grow with the resources available from the merger. They were ushered into Alan's office and both took a seat at the large table as Alan walked in.

"Guys," Alan said. "This morning at 9:00 a.m. negotiations concluded and the company was acquired as anticipated."

"Congratulations," smiled Adam and Randy nodded and smiled.

"And to you also," replied Alan. "That ten percent is going to be worth tremendously more now."

"I like that," replied Adam.

"So, to put it simply," continued Alan. "I was very well off at the start of the day but now I am a very rich man and Adam, I would say your goal of eliminating your financial problems are now met and exceeded.

Adam smiled and clapped his hands.

"Randy, this also obviously helps you, but not to the same extent financially."

"Every little bit helps," smiled Randy.

Alan then walked around the table and sat down next to Randy.

"Now, as you know I had you look at the new business plan which included you in our new endeavors under the new management structure, it included a nice salary and bonuses, etcetera."

Randy smiled and nodded. He was ready to get started.

"Unfortunately, I had to agree to some things with the buyer to complete the deal which eliminates our plans for you."

Randy's smile disappeared.

"That's all right. I enjoy the car business and we're doing fine," he replied, trying to put on a brave front but he was bitterly disappointed. "This little income from the sell will help too so I'll be fine.

He scooted his chair back and prepared to rise.

"Alan, I do appreciate you thinking of and including me earlier, though."

Alan put his hand on Randy's shoulder.

"Hold on a minute Randy. You're getting ahead of yourself."

"How's that," asked Randy.

"Listen to what he has to say Randy…" Adam said. Randy looked at him and then Alan again, confused as to what was going on.

"After the sale I also concluded another deal I have been working on that was contingent on the completion of this one. This second deal was finalized at noon and had been in the works for a while," Alan explained.

"Alan, what exactly were you here at Reynolds?" asked Randy. "I knew you were up in management, but what were you?"

Andy sat back and looked at Adam and both men started laughing. Randy wondered what the joke was and if it was on him.

"I guess I wasn't really honest with you. I am the majority stockholder and President here. I started this company after I graduated out of my garage. I'm from Park City, where I grew up. As the company became bigger, I moved it here to Salt Lake."

"You knew this?" asked Randy to Adam.

"I've known Alan for a long time," Adam answered and Randy felt his cheeks getting warm. He hated being deceived and to have Adam do this made him want to storm out and leave. "Calm down buddy, just hear us out."

"So, you've known him for a long time, huh? What about that day at the dealership?"

"I had to do something to get you going," replied Adam, "so I called Alan."

Randy stood up and began pacing around the room. He wanted to hit both of them. They had played him as the fool and Alan hadn't been a client, just charity for the dumb-ass hockey coach who couldn't get it done.

"You asshole," Randy stammered, he felt so foolish.

"You told me to coach you so I coached you. It worked," replied Adam with a more serious look.

Randy stopped pacing and looked at Adam. He couldn't argue that point. Since the sale of the seven cars Randy had consistently been the second-best salesman, only behind Adam.

"I suppose you're right," he said finally and he sat back down at the table. He would hear them out.

"Don't be mad Randy; I've been a fan of yours since my college days. Adam and I met out here at a bar watching your team at nationals a few years ago," Alan said as he again placed his hand on Randy's shoulder.

"Son of a bitch," muttered Randy. "Became friends watching us play huh?"

Alan nodded and Adam smiled again and sat back in his chair.

"Randy, I can't use you for what we talked about, but to be honest I never intended to anyway because I felt if this second deal came through, I had a perfect position for you that I can now officially offer you," Alan told him.

"So, what's that?" asked Randy, now also sitting back in his seat.

"As you know I've always been a hockey fan. Always wanted to be involved in it professionally," Alan explained as Randy sat up and leaned toward him.

"At noon today I purchased the Cincinnati Cyclops and am relocating them here."

Randy glanced at Adam, completely taking by surprise. Adam continued to smile and he gave Randy a slight nod.

"As you know they are the top affiliate of Colorado of the NHL. At nine tomorrow morning I am announcing the acquisition of them and their new name, the Salt Lake Pioneers."

"Congratulations," Randy replied, "but what's that got to do with me?"

"You own a piece too," replied Alan.

"What?"

"Adam has agreed to put the original ten percent he paid for the company into the hockey franchise. You own two percent of that but you will have the option to buy up to fifteen which Adam already has. I would like you to join us and buy ten percent of the franchise. In addition, the buyers of my company have agreed to buy another ten percent of the Pioneers. I currently have 65 percent of the team and will agree to relinquish five percent to you, but will remain majority owner. If I decide to sell, you and Randy will have the right of first refusal."

"But I don't have enough money for ten points. As you said I have two points from the sale of the company. How do you figure I will be able to get up to ten?"

"From the sale of the company, you made a three percent profit. If you wish to put that in you will have five percent right away. In addition, Adam has another five percent that he is willing to deed over to you in exchange for the same amount of his dealership. You would still own 15 points of it."

Adam got up and sat down next to Randy.

"This is where you belong, buddy," he said.

"You trying to fire me or what?" joked Randy.

"Nah, I like having you around there but you have always been a hockey guy, I can use you for free advertisement though. That's where you'll earn your 15 percent…but you better win!"

Randy smiled and looked back toward Alan.

"I need a coach," he said.

"Guys, I appreciate all of this, really I do, and I'd love to be involved. It's a great deal, but my days of coaching are over. It's just not something I want to do anymore and besides; pro coaches are hired to be fired. It wouldn't look good on my resume if I had to fire myself, or worse, you guys did. Fact is, I really like you guys right now and I don't want to have to hate you one day."

Both Alan and Adam laughed.

"You don't understand," said Alan.

"You really are thick aren't you," chimed in Adam.

"I asked Adam if he thought you would be interested in coaching and he said you wouldn't, still I figured you at least deserved the offer, but all along we've had another place for you."

"Yeah, what's that?" asked Randy.

"I want you to be the Vice President for Hockey Operations. You'll also serve as the General Manager of the team," Alan told him.

"Are you serious? Look, I appreciate this, and I'm inclined to accept, but, and it is a very big but, if I do this it's my show on the hockey side."

"No meddling," replied Alan. "I promise."

"Someday you're going to want to, and if you do, I'm done. You understand that?"

"I do, that's why I gave you a piece of the franchise. I figure you'll be very careful about spending OUR money."

"So, you're really serious about this?" asked Randy.

"I am," replied Alan.

"Jesus, don't forget about me," chimed in Adam. "I own some of this too you know."

"Here," said Alan. He handed him a contract and Randy took a few minutes to look it over.

"You are really serious about this," he said finally after looking at it.

"I want the Cup," replied Alan.

"These financial terms are right?"

"That's the going rate," he replied. "Now go get me a coach."

"I thought I told you no meddling," laughed Randy.

"You haven't signed the contract yet," replied Alan.

"I accept," Randy said as Adam gave him a pen.

Alan went to his phone and gave instructions to his secretary and soon she wheeled in a cart with Dom Perignon on ice in a silver champagne bucket. He popped the cork and poured the bubbly into three glasses and handed one to Adam and the other to Randy. He made a quick toast and the three men drank from their crystal glasses. Randy's head was spinning and it wasn't from the champagne. This morning he had been a cars salesman and now he was back in the hockey business. Soon after the secretary let in the caterers and the men sat down to a prime rib dinner. They talked hockey and made plans for tomorrow's press conference. It felt good, really good.

After dinner Adam and Randy walked out of the office, stomachs full and thoughts racing. At the door Randy turned around and looked at Alan, who was standing at his desk, looking down at something that Randy could not see.

"Say, who bought the company?" asked Randy.

Randy's mouth dropped as Alan answered.

Brenda and Robert rode quietly in the elevator. They didn't know what to say to each other and stood awkwardly on either side of the elevator. Both of them wondered if what they had done earlier had been a mistake, yet at the time it had felt so right. As the doors opened on their floor, she waited for him to walk out first and then she followed him to his office. Inside they took off their coats and Brenda sat down across from him. It was again time to do business.

"Brenda, I have a new job for you," he said.

She nodded.

"We've just completed negotiations on the acquisition of two small companies, similar to ours in both the eastern and western part of the United States. With these companies joining us it increases our visibility west of the Mississippi River and gets us onto Madison Avenue. It will allow us to grow from a regional company here in the Midwest to a national corporation and should set us up long term to move into international markets once this downturn in the economy ends."

She was no longer thinking of earlier in the day, but was completely engulfed in what he was telling her.

"I see," she said. "What do you need from me, Robert?"

"Well, we need to send transition teams to each of these companies, bring them up to speed with what we do. We also need to change the marketing strategies of both and improve each company's technology. Both are rather rudimentary," he replied.

"And…"

"We want you to head our transition team in the west. You will become one of three executive vice presidents and will have a large increase in salary, bonuses and benefits, but there is also much more travel and responsibility involved. Because you will be stationed in the western United States you will have to come back here at least once a month. There will be no more working from your house and your time will be limited because you will be the CEO of the western office."

"I see," she said with a very serious look on her face.

"I know you want to spend more time with your kids and you're going through with the divorce and these things will tax your time, but if you accept this job, it will give you financial security for the rest of your life."

She nodded and for a moment wondered if this was his way of getting rid of his latest conquest, but then she put that out of her mind. Robert had been too good to her since moving back. He had shown kindness to her, given her advice, opened up about his own life. No, she was not one of his conquests. He was providing her safety in an unpredictable time. Still, the consequences of saying yes were large.

"It's a big decision," she said finally.

"I know Brenda, and I realize that this morning probably makes it more complicated for you, but I don't regret that, not for a moment. The fact is that this is your moment. You just have to make the decision of whether or not you're going to accept it. I think you should or I wouldn't be offering it to you."

She was relieved that he felt the way she did about this morning. She also knew that he and she would never be a couple. He was a businessman first and foremost. If he hadn't been he never would have made this offer.

"I know, thank you Robert. I have to talk to my family about it. It's an awfully exciting offer. How long do I have to decide?"

"No more than 24 hours," he replied. "Things are moving fast right now."

"Where would I be living?"

"We haven't made that decision yet, but it will be somewhere in the Rockies, either Colorado or Utah because of their tax codes. We'll be making that decision shortly."

"I'll have an answer for you tomorrow," she told him.

"Sooner, if possible, but all right," he replied.

She wondered how the kids would feel as she walked out, but she knew that soon they would be moving. She went to her office and gave Darla several instructions and then left.

For the first time since she and the kids had moved here, she never once thought of Randy.

❧

Brenda and the kids sat in the living room of the condo they owned and she told them of the offer she had received that day. She told them about the pay increase and the time she would have to put into her new position. After she had laid it all out for them, she told them that they would have to move to either Colorado or back to Utah.

"That's alright mom," Sean told her. "It's not the same here anymore."

"How do you mean," asked Brenda.

"Daddy's not here," replied Tish without thinking.

"Yeah, she's right," agreed Sean. "If we're in the west we are at least closer to him."

Brenda had not realized that they missed their father this much. She silently scolded herself for missing all the signs and wished that she had been better about getting back to him and scheduling a time for the kids to visit.

"So, you wouldn't mind moving?"

The kids nodded.

"Remember, with this new job I'll have to work more. I probably won't get to go to some of your things, maybe even a lot.

"We're getting use to that," said Sean.

"Yeah, it will be fine if we get to live in a house again," added Tish.

Brenda and the kids laughed.

"Are you going to take it?" asked Sean.

"You think I should?" she replied.

Both kids again nodded.

"Well, I'll think on it a little longer," she replied. "I don't have to let them know until tomorrow."

"Mom," Sean said. "If you do, can we see dad more?"

"I hope so," she replied.

"Then take it," he told her.

She smiled and they all stood and she watched them scatter, Sean to his room and Tish into the den to watch television. She walked into her room and sat down to think about it some more, but suddenly she realized she didn't need to. She knew what she was going to do and she knew why she was. There was no use prolonging it and besides she wanted to hear Robert's voice again.

"Hi Robert," she said when he answered. "I'll take it."

"That's wonderful," he said excitedly.

"Have you decided where I'll be?"

"Probably back in Utah," he told her.

"That'll be good for the kids. They'll be able to see their father more often." She no longer mentioned Randy's name.

"I'll let you know when it's finalized," he told her. "For now, you'll start here tomorrow and we'll be flying you out on the corporate jet in the next few days so you probably need to make arrangements for your children."

"All right," she said, "and Robert…"

"Yes?"

"Thanks," she said softly, "for everything."

"You know I love you, don't you," he said. "But you also know that I can't be with you."

"I know, and I love you too," she replied.

The next morning was a whirlwind. When she finally had a few minutes to herself she locked herself in the office with explicit instructions to her secretary not to be bothered. She then dialed the number of her lawyer and the receptionist at the firm patched her through.

"Has Randy sent in the papers yet?" she asked.

"No, we haven't received anything," Leonard replied.

"Do you anticipate any problems?"

"You were more than fair with him, but in a divorce, you never know," he replied matter-of-factly.

"Has he called you? All communication is supposed to go through you as you instructed," she said.

"He has," responded the lawyer. "He had some questions which we answered for him."

"How did he sound?" she wondered.

"Business like."

"Alright, thank you Leonard."

"Hang in there Ms. Albertson. It'll be over soon and you can move on with your life, by the way, congratulations on your new position. Once you've found out where you will be let me know and I'll recommend some firms for you."

"Thank you, but how did you know?"

"Ms. Albertson, I am a VERY good lawyer."

"Yes, you are," she agreed. "Thank you again."

"Good day ma'am," he said.

She smiled as she put the phone back on the hook. Her new life was here and the possibilities made her feel exhilarated.

Randy sat at his table, a pen in his hand. Before him were the papers that would end his marriage and he knew that there was nothing left but sign them. He thought back to the day she had left for Saint Paul. He never dreamed that it would be the last time he would see her, that she would eventually see her future without him in it. He had taken her for granted far too long, always assuming she would be there but now she was gone and the swoop of the pen would make it official.

He looked at the places he was supposed to sign and put the pen to the paper but he couldn't get himself to do it. He tried; he really did but he couldn't do it. He put the pen down and leaned back in the chair and rubbed his eyes. How had it come to this, how? Yet he knew the answer to that, he had blown it, he had failed at the single most important responsibility of his life; him and him only. He got up and looked for some paper. There had to be a piece somewhere around the house. He found a piece in an empty bedroom and walked back to the kitchen.

The phone to her office rang and she picked it up.

"Hi Brenda," Robert said to her. "I'm happy to say that everything is now finalized."

"Good," she replied. "When do I leave and where am I going?"

"You'll leave tomorrow. We have purchased corporate offices in West Valley, Utah."

"Just out of Salt Lake," she said softly and for a moment she finally thought of Randy.

"That's right…oh, of course, that's where you were living for awhile," he remembered.

"Yes," she replied.

"Anyway, we'll run our west coast operations from there."

She remained silent as she wrote down what he was telling her.

"You leave tomorrow to find a house…"

"But my credit, our house here is in foreclosure…"

"Don't worry. The company is underwriting your loan. Find what you want, believe me, you can afford it now. We want you starting as soon as possible."

"Sounds good," she told him.

"By the way, is your husband still coaching?"

"No, he's a car salesman now."

"Not a used one I hope."

She laughed at his joke and hoped the same thing. She didn't really know anymore.

Randy looked at the empty sheet of paper and then at the divorce agreement. He would sign them, but he would also send her one last message as a married man. He steadied the pen in his hand. He wanted to make sure his penmanship was good. He wanted to be proud of his last message to her.

Dear Brenda,

I don't know if you'll read this but I just wanted to make sure you know how I feel about you while we're still married. I haven't signed the papers yet, and yes, I will sign them.

You are and have been the love of my life since that day I saw you on campus. When I saw you, I knew that you were the woman I wanted to grow old with. You were (and are) so beautiful, so lovely and, yes, sexy. My eyes never strayed during all the time we were together, why would they, I had the perfect woman.

Then when I got to know you, I discovered this caring, smart loving person who made me a better man. The more time I spent around you the better I felt about me because if you could see something in me, I must not be that bad.

But then I forgot what I had. I took you for granted and didn't take the time to tell you what a special and wonderful woman you are to me. I just figured that you knew and I didn't need to tell you anymore. I was such an important man, a big coach who was more worried about others that I was about my own. I was wrong of course, and now I guess its time for me to pay the price.

Just know that I do love you and always will. Know that I thank you for loving me all those years and for the wonderful gift of being my wife. Now that I'm losing you, I finally realize that you were a gift, a privilege that I assumed to be a right. You do deserve better and I hope, no, pray that you find it.

I love you always and I'll always be here for you.

Your husband,
Randy

He read the letter and then re-read it. It wasn't perfect nor did it express what he completely wanted, but it was from the heart so he left it as it was. He put it down gently and then he grabbed the divorce papers. He took a deep breath and then he did it, he signed it.

He had thought that when he signed it, he would cry, but strangely he didn't. He felt a horrible pain, sadness deep in his gut, but it did not bring the tears he had expected. He realized that the time that had passed had been the grief, but the letter he had written had been the acceptance and a weight was lifted off of him.

He grabbed the manila envelope that had been sent with the papers. It was already postmarked and addressed to her lawyer's office. He carefully put the papers and the letter in and then sealed the envelope. Fifteen minutes later he was at the post office and he dropped it into the box that said OUT OF TOWN. Before he let go of the envelope, he said a silent prayer which he knew would probably never be answered, but it made him feel better.

As he walked out, he realized that he was just a middle-aged man who was now alone.

Chapter 19

JUNE

Randy walked into the showroom at the dealership. It was the first time he had been there in a month and he was happy to see each salesman with a customer. Adam sat in his office doing paperwork and as Randy walked to his door, he noticed that his old office had a new nameplate on it:

RANDY ALBERTSON
SALT LAKE PIONEERS HOCKEY

He laughed quietly and turned the knob of Adam's door. His friend looked up as the door opened and he grinned and stood and greeted his friend. They made some off-colored jokes to each other and Randy sat back on the couch and put one leg up.

"So, how's the new office?" Adam asked.

"Not as nice as the one you had for me. No life-sized posters hanging over my desk."

They laughed and Adam filled him in on the business. Randy still had 15% of the company and was happy when his friend gave him a check for the month's take. It had been a good one with the cash for clunkers help from the government. Adam ran some marketing ideas past Randy and Randy made some suggestions for each.

"I'm hungry," said Adam. "Let's go get a bite."

"Don't have to ask me twice," Randy responded. "Who's driving, me or you?"

"I'll drive," Adam said. "You're a shitty driver, way to slow. You're one of those troublesome guys that insist on following the speed limit."

They both laughed as they walked out of the dealership and climbed into Adams brand new pickup. Randy admired Adam's ride as they drove to an Irish restaurant. As they walked in the hostess welcomed them and took them to their table and a waitress soon followed. Both men placed their orders and flirted with the waitress and then sat back as they waited for their food to arrive.

"Well bud," Adam said. "We seemed to have survived."

"Barely," agreed Randy, "but we're still kicking."

"I miss having you around," Adam said.

"Adam, I own 15 percent. I'll be around, gotta make sure those checks keep coming."

"I suppose you're right. But seriously Randy, you're a hockey guy now. Remember that I have a piece of the Pioneers. We can do all the marketing in the world for them, but if we're not winning games seats will be empty. I want my checks too so make damn sure you're making good moves. Remember, it's about us, not the damn Avalanche."

Both men laughed. They were enjoying each other's company just like the old days when the whole world was in front of them.

"We'll be fine," said Randy. "We have some talent coming from the parent club and a nice mix of youth and vets. You'll make your 15 percent."

"So, what's up with your divorce? You a free man yet?"

"Yes, I guess it was ratified or whatever the courts do last week. I haven't heard from Brenda in a long time. It was hard signing the papers, really hard."

"I'm sorry buddy. I know how much you loved her."

Randy gave a weak smile and shrugged. It was what it was and now it was time to start over, but at least he had a few bucks in his pocket and some new furniture in his house.

"I did a doozy on a perfectly good marriage and family, that's for sure," Randy said. "Soon I'll get to see the kids though, or at least that's what her lawyer tells me."

"That's good," Adam replied. "What's Brenda doing now?"

"I don't know. Nobody will talk to me. I assume she's still up in Saint Paul with the company. How about you and Candace, I really like her and since I'm single now..."

"Slow down there big fella," warned Adam jokingly. "She's a great gal and fun to be with, especially at night if you know what I mean..."

"I have an idea, though it's been a long time," laughed Randy.

"But, well, neither one of us is the marrying type," continued Adam. "We'll ride the horse for as long as it takes us and then move on, hopefully with no hard feelings."

"Word of advice," warned Randy, "don't piss off a lawyer."

"Boy, ain't that the truth," agreed Adam.

Their food came and they started eating. Adam put some ketchup on the hash browns he had with his eggs and Randy peppered his Reuben sandwich. They ate and talked some more, but mostly they just enjoyed their time together. They had gone through more than they had ever dreamed they could handle and somehow, they had come out the other end in better shape. The economy was still dragging and millions were out of work, but, at least for now, they were survivors and they celebrated their victory.

"Well, I need to make some money," Adam finally said. "Don't have a salary like some people do."

"Yeah, I need to make you some money too," joked Randy. "You make more than me so you can buy."

"Bullshit," countered Adam. "I know what your salary is now so you can pay."

Randy laughed and reached into his pocket and pulled out his Gold Card.

"I guess this one's on the Pioneers," he said.

"So, we're both paying then, huh cheapskate?"

"So is Alan," smiled Randy. "In fact, he's picking up 65 percent of it."

They both laughed as they headed back to the dealership.

⚬❈⚬

The spring in Salt Lake brings in the rains from the Pacific Rim, or so the locals have said, and another storm had arrived as Randy drove back to the Pioneers offices in West Valley. The windshield wipers fought the drops as the car sped onto I-215. Randy's mind was now on hockey and the upcoming NHL draft that the parent club had asked him to help with. In all likelihood he would be getting most of their draft choices that came out so he had spent the past month learning all he could about the top possible picks.

He merged onto SH-215 and sped toward the office. The new company was moving in adjacent to them and he just hoped they would stay out of the way. Let hockey do our thing and they do what they do, he thought. Alan would keep them separated. He was like a kid in a candy store having his own team now. Everyday seemed to be press conference day as Alan worked to get season tickets sold and players signed. He was keeping his word and staying out of the way and Randy was thankful that the little defender from Concordia-Saint Paul had come into his life.

Ahead he saw the office and he slowed his car down. The rain continued to fall but seemed not to be as heavy as it had been but maybe that was because he was going slower now. He turned into the parking lot and pulled up to his personal parking spot when suddenly his cell phone rang. He looked at the number that popped up. It was a Utah number but he did not recognize it. For a moment he debated whether to answer it or let it go to messages but he realized that as the head of hockey operations he probably needed to answer.

"Randy Albertson here," he said.

"I miss you," she replied softly.

Above him a single ray of sunlight broke through the darkened clouds.

9 798889 762362